D1113730

Upon the Rock
A Novel

Patricia Mote

Patricia Mote

Quixote

Published by
Quixote Publications
490 Merrimak Drive
Berea, Ohio 44017

Printed in the United States of America.

0-9677583-5-1

This book is a work of fiction. Although certain historical characters, events, and locations are portrayed, they are used fictitiously to give the story a proper historical context.

Library of Congress Cataloging in Publication Data available upon request.

Cover design and author photo: Susan Lee
Cover photo: Courtesy of The Berea Historical Society
Sculpture at Coe Lake: Thomas Harmon

Dedicated in loving memory to my husband,

W. Newton Mote
1927-2001

He believed in this book from the beginning.

"Listen to me, you who pursue righteousness
and who seek the Lord:
Look to the rock from which you were cut
and to the quarry from which you were hewn;

Isaiah 51: 1

The wise man built his house upon the rock,
and the house on the rock stood firm.

Children's Praise Song

"Gaudeamus Igitur," used by Johannes Brahms to end his "Academic Festival Overture," 1881.
"Once to Every Man and Nation," James Russell Lowell, 1845.
Song from "Pippa Passes," *Robert Browning's Poems,*
    Thomas Y. Crowell & Co., 1896.
"Softly Now the Light of Day," George W. Doane, 1824.

Acknowledgments

A product of small towns myself, I often thought of writing a novel set in Berea. In 2000, the Berea Historical Society's oral history project—interviewing descendants of those who worked in Berea's sandstone quarries—caught my attention. Those members who recorded the memories of Violet Barnum, Jim Jaworski, Pat Livengood, John Siodla, and the late Syl Bobinsky gave me a setting. Transcribing and editing their reminiscences brought to life what Berea was like when it was the sandstone capital of the world and the home of two Methodist colleges. I am grateful to the officers, staff and volunteers at the Berea Historical Society not only for the use of the Society's materials in my research but also for their keen interest as the writing progressed.

Other groups of supportive friends kept up my spirits and drive: my First Congregational Church family, the Berea Fine Arts Club, the Tuesday A.M. book group, friends among Southwest General Health Center's staff and volunteers, and members of the Berea Bonnet Belles.

I had valuable editing and support from colleagues Lavern Hall, Writer's World Press; Sandra Warren, Arlie Enterprises; Carol Starre-Kmiecik, Famous American Women; Barbara Sherwood, *Berea News Sun;* Beverly Maxwell, Naturally Gifts; Diane Marcou, author and consultant, and Kathleen Mihalek, Kathy's Cookies.

Quixote Publications has published twenty books, and Tammy Sanderell has been a valued partner in each of them. Not only is she skilled at the technical and prepress processes, but she also lends insightful editing expertise. Chrissy Kadleck has virtually walked the streets of old Berea with me for the past two years. Her creative editing enlivens every chapter. Relieving me of many bookkeeping chores is Judy Strittmatter, dear friend and business associate for many years. Ron Strittmatter keeps the equipment humming, while Deborah Sherwood lends able assistance wherever needed. Jim Jaworski advised me on the business of quarrying and also introduced me to friends at the Polish Village, Theresa and Russ Hocevar, Carol Glowacki Cathcart, and to Sophie Golinski. All supplied colorful details about the Polish culture as did a delightful couple from Alaska I met in the Bahamas, Al and JoAnn Karcz. Father Gerald Keller provided insight into historic St. Adalbert's Catholic Church.

I drew inspiration and strength from my own family—Pam Weinantz, John and Mary Dietsch, and Susan Lee; Susan, Leslie and Ralph Mote and the delightful parade of grandchildren—Brian, Jessica, Emily, Jennifer, Benjamin, Leana, Latricia, and Hannah. They offered encouragement when I needed a boost, diversion for laughs, and pride and joy when the book finally became a reality. My brother Joe McDonald and his wife Nancy have always been among my favorite "balcony people"—those folks who sit high on your list and give you the ever-needed thumbs up. That phrase, as well as one of the themes of this novel, came from former pastor, longtime friend and fellow author, Joe Emerson. "Looking for the Rock" from his *Sermons from Stones* series recorded in 1993 was based on the Isaiah text I've quoted. It seems to have set the stage for *Upon the Rock.*

Enjoy old Berea, but don't expect to draw a map of the town from reading *Upon the Rock.* Although many actual places, names, and events appear, remember, there's always the fiction writer's prerogative.

Patricia Mote

People of Berea

Stephen Ballard, acting superintendent, Berea Quarries

Dr. Thomas Koeller, professor at German Wallace College

Leila Koeller, his wife

Jane Koeller, their daughter, a teacher at Union School

Martha Adams, neighbor of the Koellers

Mrs. M. B. Longwood, owner of the City Hotel

Franklin Pritchett, organizer for the Knights of Labor

Walter Maxson, sheriff of Berea

Amelia Pierce, president of Berea WCTU

Sarah Carman, friend of Jane Koeller's, also a teacher

Rufus Warner, foreman at the Berea Quarries

Fast Jack (Willem de Huis) hermit-like town character

Rose Wolinski, works at the City Hotel

Sophie Wolinski, mother of Rose and George

Anna Mikolak, Rose's cousin

Mary Stawicki, Rose's friend

Rebecca Morabovich, Rose's friend

Gretchen Janovick and Lucy Zielinski, Quarrymen's wives

Quarrymen	Water Boys
George Wolinski	Sam Mikolak, Chris Janovick,
James Janek	Jacob Zielinski
Viktor Mikolak	These actual persons are portrayed
Harold Damboski	in their various roles:
John Seidler	G.H. Worthington, president, Cleveland Stone Co.
Anthony Carabelli	E. Christian, mayor of Berea
Peter Serafine	Rev. Stanley Beard, Congregational Church
Lon Sobieski	Father A. Suplicki, St. Adalbert's Catholic Church
Pavel Prohaska	Elijah Peebles, editor, Berea *Advertiser*
	Billy Simpson, jeweler and inventor

Published Sources

And Then There Were None. Mickey Sego. King's Court Communications, 1996.

Of Grit and Greatness. Walter F. Holzworth. 1970, 1986.

Microfiche records of the *Berea Advertiser.*

Microfiche records of the *Cleveland Plain Dealer.*

The Catholic Encyclopedia. Christian Burial. CD-ROM © 1908. Robert Appleton Company. Online edition © 2003 by K. Knight

Berea, Ohio
1896

*N*early a decade before, the Cleveland Stone Company had absorbed all of the sandstone quarries around the small town of Berea and surrounding communities and become the giant of the burgeoning sandstone industry. The clear, light-colored stone called Berea Grit had been used for decades in manufacturing grindstones and whetstones, vital for sharpening tools in thousands of industries, and it had become in demand as a building stone. Canada's Parliament buildings in Ottawa were built from Berea sandstone as were the Palmer House Hotel in Chicago, and Boston's Hancock Building and many large buildings in Cleveland. Now that the effects of the Panic of 1893 had subsided and times were getting better, the Cleveland Stone Company saw no end to the demand for Berea sandstone. Even inferior quality stone was suitable for rough work such as bridges, curbing, culverts, and foundations.

"We have an inexhaustible supply of sandstone," George H. Worthington, president of the company, often asserted.

The eight Berea quarries employed 775 men, about one-fourth of the town's residents. The equipment consisted of 46 steam-operated derricks and 46 steam hoists, 19 boilers and 16 engines, 12 channeling machines, 18 steam drills, 11 steam-driven pumps, 6 grindstone-turning lathes, a saw-mill of 6 gangs of saws, one of 15 gangs and one of 17 gangs, and one 46-inch turbine water wheel. Near the quarries were a grindstone frame factory and three grindstone factories, and a large machine shop of lathes, planers and shapers with a complete line of blacksmith equipment.

To think that such a tremendous industry had developed since a farmer named John Baldwin had discovered sandstone on his two hundred-acre farm in 1842 seemed all but inconceivable. Now fifty-four years later, a number of smaller quarries that had been unable to compete success-fully against one another had been consolidated into the Cleveland Stone Company with its main office in down-town Cleveland. The quarry industry had made this the largest town for miles around, drawing settlers from older towns – Strongsville, Columbia, West View, Olmsted Township, and Rock Port.

A newcomer's first impression of Berea would be one of the perfection of sandstone as a building material. The town's Union Depot welcomed visitors with its Gothic grandeur. It resembled a church more than a place where smoking, panting locomotives arrived and departed, pulling strings of mud-spattered cars. A sandstone building that resembled a church, however, bespoke both Berea's industrial pride and its religious heritage. With two church-related colleges, Berea had earned the nickname, "The Cradle of Ministers," many who became missionaries to foreign lands. The buildings of Baldwin University and German Wallace College proudly testified to scholarship and theology.

Within shouting distance of Union Station lay the pulse of the Berea Quarries. Hundreds of Polish, German, Irish, and Italian immigrants had settled in Berea to work in the quarries. Some rented houses from the Stone Company, but most lived with their families at Berea's north end in neat homes they'd built that clustered around their Catholic churches — the Poles around St. Adalbert's, the other nationalities around St. Mary's. Though their work was extremely dangerous and toilsome, the quarrymen and their families were a proud lot who clung to their native traditions. Many of the older residents had not even learned English though they'd lived in Berea many years.

On the opposite, the South Side of town, stood two proud colleges bordered by well-kept, spacious homes of professors and merchants, well-established Congregational and Methodist churches, and an area of thriving businesses known as The Triangle. At the north end of town the atmosphere was one of Old World villages: the immigrants kept to themselves, for the most part, and they cared for one another like members of a family. The residents of the South Side recognized the value of the immigrant population to the financial well-being of the community, yet they were content for them to "keep their place."

One

Stocky, square-jawed George Wolinski followed close behind the dogged steps of James Janek as they left the quarry for the day. George was speaking in a low tone but rapid-fire. "He'll come and talk to the men whenever we say the word. Right here—at our lunch time."

James, always practical, asked, "Do we have to pay him any money?"

"Of course not—not until we're ready to join up with the union. Then each man pays his own dues." George kicked a stone out of his path. "I say we go with it—see how many men are for it."

"You can hope Ballard don't get wind of it beforehand." James half-turned, his words muffled by the bandana he'd worn all day to fight the quarry dust. "He'd run him off. Afterwards, it won't make no difference."

"Sure. Once the men start joining up, we'll find someplace to meet. He wants to come here first off to show he's not scared of the Cleveland Stone Company, I think." George's voice had an excited edge as if he couldn't wait for the action to begin.

Twelve-year-old water and pick boy Sam Mikolak was straining to hear the conversation between the two men walking just ahead of him. Because he had to keep shifting his load of picks, the noise blotted out some of their words. George was his cousin and they got along together fine. George never treated him like a little boy; sometimes they even went fishing together. Still, he didn't want George to know he was purposely listening. George was twenty-one and a full-fledged sandstone quarryman—a derrick tender—and Sam, like most quarry workers, was starting at the very bottom of the hierarchy. He worked the same ten-hour days as the men, keeping them supplied with water and fresh picks for fifty cents a day.

The flimsy walls had stopped shaking, and dense silence hung like an invisible curtain in Stephen Ballard's Berea office of the Cleveland Stone Company. Rubbing the back of his neck, the young quarry superintendent straightened up from his payroll records to glance out the single, sand-streaked window. The lingering sun's rays stenciled salmon-colored stripes across the pieces of horizon he could see between the trees around the top of the quarry. The last dinky engine had gone past for the day, whistling its way to the mill, puffing white curls of steam and straining under its burden of sandstone. Creaking derricks, shouting workers, goading bosses, periodic dynamite blasts causing showers of stone—all were silenced for the day.

Soon a curving, dust-crusted line of quarrymen would pass by single-file across the swinging footbridge. Some would walk as far as three miles to their modest dwellings. All would taste quarry dust along with their suppers. All would seize a few precious hours of family time and sleep, then return at six o'clock tomorrow morning.

His title was acting superintendent of the Berea Quarries, but Stephen Ballard's office furnishings consisted of only a scarred desk and a rumpsprung cushion in a spindly-legged chair that cramped his frame. On a battered table beside his record books stood the company's nods to 1890s office equipment—a telegraph that clattered and a telephone that crackled. The thin walls of the rough plank building trembled with explosions from the quarry, and the place exuded mildew in spring and fall and was stifling in summer.

Today the door stood open, letting in the freshness of a mild, blue-sky June day. Without warning, a reed-slim boy burst in. "Mr. Ballard, sir." Water boy Sam Mikolak's heavy-lidded eyes were wide with alarm. The narrow shoulders that carried a heavy yoke and two wooden buckets all day trembled noticeably.

"Sam, what's on your mind?" Stephen began piling up some ledgers to take home with him. "Janek and his boys giving you trouble again?" He grinned at Sam, trying to put the frightened boy at ease.

"I guess that goes with my job, sir. I just can't seem to get back and forth to that well quick enough for some of the men. But, sir," he gulped nervously and glanced at the doorway behind him, "there was a man over in McDermott's Quarry this afternoon when I took that load of picks over. He was talking to my cousin George, mostly. I couldn't get close enough to hear everything, but I heard 'wages cut,' 'three years,' He had on a fancy suit and was smoking a cigar." Sam drew a quick breath and plunged on. "He all the time kept looking around like he didn't want someone to see him. And that's not all, sir."

"What else?" Stephen's tone was patient.

"Coming out of the quarry, I was behind George and James Janek. They was talking—low, I couldn't hear everything, but I think they was talking about this same man, that he's gonna come here to the quarry—to talk to the men—"

As he put a steadying hand on Sam's shoulder, Stephen could feel the boy still trembling through his rough shirt. "Thank you, Sam. You're a good scout. He's another of these chaps trying to get our quarrymen to join the union. You've heard talk in your family, I'm sure, that the quarrymen want higher wages and safer working conditions, and some of them think the union is the way to get those." Sam was nodding, twisting his rumpled hat nervously. "You did the right thing, Sam. I need to know when strangers are in the quarries." Stephen dug in his pocket for some coins. "Here, Sam. Buy those little sisters of yours a treat on the way home."

Beaming, his panic forgotten, Sam headed pell-mell down the path toward Carman's Grocery on the Triangle.

The first of the line of dusty-white workers reached the Stone Company office just as Stephen was locking the door and starting for his own lodgings. "Evenin," Mr. Ballard," some called out as they passed. Stephen half-waved, half-saluted to his men. Their shoulders drooped with fatigue. Some still wore kerchiefs over their noses and mouths to keep out the deadly dust. They moved in nearly total silence as if they were relishing the quiet, glad to be away from the incessant, daylong noise of the quarry.

He caught sight of George Wolinski in the line. Head ducked down, intent upon his boots, George did not look in Stephen's direction. Was he feeling guilty about talking with a union organizer? Stephen wondered. Or was he still angry because he had heard about Stephen talking to his sister Rose several times when they'd happened to meet on the Triangle? Even though he knew dozens of disapproving eyes were boring through them, Stephen had sensed a weightless feeling of freedom when he was near the friendly Rose. Her morning-bright smile greeted him every day when he breakfasted at the City Hotel dining room; yet, Rose was lively and gracious to everyone and helped many Bereans start the workday in a cheerful mood.

As a newcomer to town, Stephen especially appreciated her friendliness. But one evening last week, as Stephen headed to his lodgings, George Wolinski's stout form emerged from the shadow of the bandstand on the Triangle. His daring but firm words lingered on Stephen's consciousness like a warning finger shaking at him: "You're not one of us, Mr. Ballard. You'd best leave Rose alone."

Stephen was having trouble adjusting to Berea's social strata. Because he represented the owners of the Cleveland Stone Company and because he was a third-generation American of Protestant and English heritage, the new quarry superintendent was regarded by people at the north end of town as an outsider.

"You'll want to live on the South Side," Mr. Worthington, the president of the Stone Company had told him. "That's what Bereans call 'God's side of town.'" He had laughed heartily, causing his pince-nez to wobble on his nose. His remark left Stephen somewhat puzzled. Now he was beginning to understand.

Stephen's mood lightened a bit as he headed to his lodgings and walked past the barn that housed

Billy Simpson's cluttered workshop. In the doorway, framed by saucer-sized hollyhocks taller than Stephen himself, Simpson, a jeweler and part-time inventor, was tinkering with a primitive-looking vehicle. With a single handcrafted mahogany seat and a tiller to steer by, the contraption stood poised on its Goodyear rubber tires as if waiting to hear a starting command.

"How's she behaving today, sir?" Stephen had been following the progress of this vehicle with interest. Yet, Simpson's thus-far futile efforts to power a gasoline-combustion autocar entertained many Bereans, old and young. He was the butt of jokes, sometimes good-natured but often cruel. Stephen admired the tenacious little man's courage and regretted the teasing he suffered. Besides, he really believed the crafty fellow would succeed , just as he had with a steam-powered vehicle several years before.

But this pleasant June evening a weary face, lined with discouragement, squinted up at Stephen. "This cussed fuel line. Engine keeps sputtering out. Can't get the dad-blamed fuel-line packing to stop leaking." Simpson wiped an oily hand across his forehead, unmindful of the black streak it left. "Maybe tomorrow will be better." He sighed wearily and began throwing his wrenches into a canvas bag.

"I hope so, Mr. Simpson. Don't give up. That's going to be a fine autocar one day."

Stephen strode on toward Dr. and Mrs. Thomas

Koeller's comfortable gabled home on East Bridge Street where he rented a spacious front bedroom. This was now his home, but since arriving in the bustling quarry town of Berea three months ago, Stephen had spent little time here. The only neighbor he knew well at all was pleasant Mrs. Adams, the widow next door. Sometimes he would chat with her when he came home in the evening if she was out tending the roses around her tidy home. He seldom saw Dr. Koeller, a professor of literature at German Wallace College, or their daughter Jane, who taught at the Union School. Mrs. Koeller, a laudable cook, kindly left succulent German dishes for him on the back of the range each evening since he never arrived home in time to join the Koellers at their five o'clock dinner hour.

Long daylight hours found Stephen out in the quarries—supervising the stripping of buried sandstone, as well as the channeling and blasting and the removal of enormous slabs of the building stone in demand throughout the nation and even in other countries. All of these skills Stephen had learned from the time he was a twelve-year-old water boy in the now-Cleveland Stone Company-owned quarries of his home city of Stone City, Michigan. He had expected someday to take over the quarries in that town when his father retired, but the company had sent him to Berea to replace Superintendent Benjamin Carstairs after his near-fatal fall from a prize mare had broken his back. Carstairs was nearly sixty, and the outlook for his ever returning to his job was bleak.

After scrubbing up at the backyard pump, Stephen attacked Mrs. Koeller's mouth-watering wienerschnitzel with sheer joy. The steady tick of the Regulator clock and the lingering, yeasty aroma of the kitchen wrapped him in soothing comfort after his long day. He noted with appreciation the checked table cover that set off the blue and white crockery and the small vase of tight-knit yellow roses Mrs. Koeller had set at his place. She was kind to think of these homelike touches.

As he relished his meal, Stephen read a letter from his mother that he'd found propped against the cut glass spoon holder. His mother's letters were always mirthful and filled with bits of news from Stone City. They helped Stephen feel less disconnected from all of his roots. Mopping up the last bit of rich gravy with a piece of sourdough, he pondered her last paragraph—a serious one.

> *Stephen, I know you feel that you might not be ready for the responsibility you've been given at age 29. But you have the needed skills and you work well with others. Remember to ask for God's help in all you do each day. Also, you must make new friends where you are. You will not forget Sally Westin for a long time, but eventually time heals or at least assuages all wounds. Sally's pretty head was turned by the idea of being*

*a banker's wife, I fear. I hope she will find
happiness in her marriage to Curtis
Thatcher, and that you will forgive her.*

Your loving Mother

Stephen creased the letter with care and wiped his
misted-over eyes with his sleeve. Sally . . . Sally. How
many times a day did he tell himself that he must forget her? But in the few quiet moments of his crowded
days and nightly in his dreams. . . there was Sally's
enchanting face with the deep, green-blue eyes and
china-doll skin . . . listening to concerts, picknicking
by the lake, their families sitting together in the Congregational church . . . he and Sally had even talked
of when they'd be married there. They had been practically engaged for two years. . . Now all of these
visions were replaced with a picture of her hostessing
in widower Curtis Thatcher's stately, white-columned
home . . .

The vision of Sally faded suddenly as gentle female
voices trailed along the hallway from the direction of
the front door. Then a shrill giggle pierced the evening
quiet. Startled, Stephen leaped up to put his dishes
on the wooden drainboard and dash up the back stairway. He had no wish to see Jane Koeller and meet her
friends when he was dusty and tired at the end of a
working day. That would not be a good way to make
new friends.

Two

Around the bandstand at the Triangle, Berea's hub of social and business activity, ladies in their next-to-Sunday best flitted back and forth like nesting, plumed birds. Their broad-brimmed hats dipped and bobbed as they arranged stacks of goody-filled baskets, preparing for the auction that would soon begin.

"Put this one out in front, Eulalie," puffed a buxom woman as she handed a large, ribbon-decked basket to her helper. "It's Mary Wallace's and bound to be packed to the hilt. Should fetch a mighty high bid."

"What a splendid turnout of baskets," said a woman in a navy-and-white polka-dotted dress. "The McLaughlin family should realize a lot of help from this auction." Last month Charles McLaughlin, a railroad engineer for the Cleveland Stone Company, had his leg crushed when a steam boiler exploded and fell on him in the quarry. He'd been horribly scalded as well. His burns were healing slowly, but he would never walk again without crutches.

A spirit of neighborliness swept over the town on this Saturday afternoon as Bereans streamed toward the Triangle to enjoy a Summerfest. The entire town was united in this desire to help the injured railroader and his family. Shop doors remained closed. Silence even lay over the quarries. From second-story windows of the Triangle's buildings onlookers leaned on windowsills in offices and rooms of friends where they could get a commanding view of the scene below. There'd be music, dancing, games, treats, and the auction of the goody baskets. From a brilliant, sapphire-blue sky the early summer sun lit up the scene. Arcs of gulls wheeled down, diving for stray peanut shells or anything else edible. At the whirling carousel set up at the broad junction of Bridge and Front Streets, a squirming queue of youngsters jockeyed for position. The carousel, the Cleveland Stone Company's unusual goodwill gesture (along with the closing of the quarries for a half-day), arrived by railroad flatcar two days ago, creating a stir among hordes of children who strained for a chance to mount the prancing ponies.

All about the Triangle little tableaus acted themselves out as the crowd continued to fill the streets. A brother and sister, neatly dressed but ready to scuffle, nevertheless, resolved their squabble over a new-fangled treat—store-bought chewing gum.

"It's mine."

"T'ain't neither."

"I'll tell Ma."

"Here, tattle-tale. Take half my piece and don't say I didn't never give you nothin.'"

A chorus of childish, treble voices chanted: "Hey, Silly Simpson, where's your auto? You *auto* know it'll never run." A knot of small boys in short pants exploded with peals of laughter and then ran quickly behind a building. Billy Simpson flushed and tried to look amused.

His wife patted his arm. "Never you mind, Billy. That's what they all said about your steam-powered car and that finally ran. And what about the street sprinkler you invented to keep down the dust? The town uses it every day. It makes a healthier town for everyone." She kept patting his arm as if she could drive away the resentment she knew he must feel. "Those silly boys don't know about things like that." Muriel Simpson truly believed her husband was a genius.

The town bandmaster Peter Eliot, in flame-red suspenders and a straw sailor hat, spaced chairs and music stands for his players who would soon be filing in. Although most folks had only recently finished their noon dinners, the pungent aroma from the frankfurter vendor's cart was luring many buyers who washed them down with the ever-popular root beer. From the north end of town, a train whistle pierced the carnival atmosphere, a reminder that business was going on as usual in most of the rest of the world.

On the steps of the bandstand, the Janowicz twins, Jean and Joan, in native Polish costumes, pumped forth a spirited twin accordion rendition of the "Put-in-Bay Polka." It seemed to Rose Wolinski that the little dears had played it at least six or seven times. Leaning against the City Hotel doorway, Rose put one hand behind the small of her back to ease the strain she felt. If she shaded her eyes from the beaming sun, she could make out Stephen Ballard's rangy form across the Triangle. Standing alongside him were his landlord and his wife, Dr. and Mrs. Koeller. That Adams woman, the one who got elected to the school board was with them, too.

Rose toyed with damp tendrils of her honey-blonde hair framing her face. She wished she dared go closer to the bandstand when the bidding on the baskets started, but she'd been at work at the hotel dining room since early morning. Blobs of flapjack batter spattered her full-length apron and her blue and white striped shirtwaist, and she felt as if she must smell like a yeast roll. Still, she'd like to know who bid on her basket of goodies. She'd packed it with great care—two apple dumplings, a special nut roll, and a fresh raspberry slump. It would be a week's worth of lunchtime treats for a quarryman or a delight for any growing family.

27

Without thinking, Rose found herself watching Stephen Ballard again. She wished she could stand behind him. When he left the dining room this morning, she had noticed how his dark hair lay, gently curling, just above his collar. What would it feel like, she wondered, to run her fingers through those curls?

She gave herself a silent scold for her silly thoughts. He's Stephen Ballard, superintendent for the Berea Quarries. Even if he stops to talk with her occasionally when they'd meet on the Triangle, as a Polish girl from the north end of town, she thought the nearest she'd ever get to him again would be when she'd fill his coffee cup. But he treated her with such courtesy each time they'd talked. She still couldn't understand why he talks with her instead of someone from his side of town. She forced herself to shrug off the thought and turned back inside to finish clearing the now-deserted tables in the dining room.

Abruptly, at the bandstand the wheezing accordion music stopped. The twins scuttled to either side of the steps, looking half-miffed, half-fearful. Through the crowd a murmur rippled as George Wolinski and James Janek, slicked up in their church clothes, leaped to the bandstand, their faces solemn and intent. They unrolled a boldly lettered banner that declared:

STOP STONE CO. GREED
JOIN THE UNION NOW
MORE MONEY—SAFER WORKPLACE

From an upstairs window over Machovina's Dry Goods store, young, freckle-faced Frederick Schultz leaned forward with his trumpet. Everyone knew Frederick would play that horn for anybody, anywhere. Through his entire blary rendition of "The Battle Hymn of the Republic," George and James held the banner aloft. They made no speeches. The crowd had no reaction, although some heads bobbed slightly as Frederick and his horn swung into the "Glory-glory-hallelujahs." Then it was over. The quarrymen rolled up their banner and jumped down, and a throng of their fellow workers, now cheering lustily, swept them out of sight. Townspeople stole glances at one another, trying to pay little heed to the demonstration.

Stephen knew he'd see that banner more often than he'd wish. But he'd be relieved if there were no outbursts any more unsettling than this one. Still, he'd have to report this incident to the president of the stone company even though the men were totally in their right. But their actions portended things to come that he would have to deal with . . .

"Stephen, is there a serious movement toward unionizing in the quarries?" Martha Adams' matter-of-fact tone cut through his thoughts. Recently elected to the school board and the first woman to hold public office in Berea, Martha thrived on a knowledge of business and political affairs.

Stephen chuckled and tried to give Martha's question a light touch yet an honest answer. "Well,

Martha, there are some who've joined, but I haven't seen any union organizers lurking around behind piles of sandstone." He grew more serious. "But judging from what we've just seen, that could happen any day."

Leila Koeller bobbed her chubby face around Martha to chirp, "This accident of Engineer McLaughlin's has them all stirred up. My Sonya talks of nothing else when she comes to clean. They all think the company should be forced to have the boilers inspected more often."

And they have a point, Stephen thought, yet not daring to utter the words.

But he didn't have to. Dr. Koeller spoke out in his mild but firm manner: "We might not be having this fundraiser for the McLaughlin family if there were such regulations." Dr. Koeller, a literature professor at German Wallace College, could speak his mind freely. He did not live in utter dependence upon the Cleveland Stone Company as did the hundreds of those in the north end of town who eked their livelihood from the quarries.

To Stephen's relief, a drum roll quieted the crowd—and Dr. Koeller. "La-dees and gents," Peter Eliot's stentorian tones rolled cross the crowd. He hardly needed his megaphone. "We're about ready to start the auction for these marvelous, delectable goody baskets—handmade treats from our own Berea belles. Remember, all the money we raise goes to

Charles and Pauline McLaughlin and their four children.

"But first, an important announcement from Amelia Pierce, worthy president of our town's chapter of the Women's Christian Temperance Union. You know 'em as the WCTUs." He gave a courtly bow toward a tall, angular lady at the edge of the bandstand.

Preening and nodding like a duchess, Amelia tilted her cabbage rose-decked hat slightly and gave her skirts a swish before sweeping across the bandstand.

"Dear friends and neighbors," she began in a slight falsetto, "since the WCTU was founded in Cleveland, the national organization is aware of our nearby chapter's fine work. Therefore, we have been singled out to be one of the first towns to organize the Loyal Temperance League for our children." Amelia warmed to her subject, gesturing grandly.

"Very soon, your children can become members of this marvelous group and learn the *horrible* physical effects of the *Devil Drink*." As Amelia punctuated the last two words with an emphatic nod, the cabbage roses on her hat appeared ready to take flight.

"Over in front of Carman's store," she gestured grandly in that direction, "Letitia Marks and Eliza Sterling are prepared to give you important *fr-ee* information about the *soo-perb* benefits your children can gain from joining the Loyal Temperance League.

"Remember, we must grab 'em while they're young and keep 'em pure. So, be sure to see Letitia or

Eliza before you go home."

Another drum roll heralded Amelia's dramatic exit from the bandstand. Peter Eliot's brass band members lifted their horns, eager to play at last, and launched into John Phillip Sousa's rousing new "Washington Post March." Fresh-faced youngsters, their parents helping them keep time to the music, waved tiny American flags courtesy of the D.A.R.

Farther up Front Street, north of the Triangle, Lawyer Thomas Schweitzer and his willowy wife Madge pedaled sedately on their tandem bicycle, looking elegant though warm in blue velvet outfits. Other cyclists in candy-striped shirts wheeled figure-eights and waved, happy not to be dodging the usual heaps of horse dung. For today, the mayor had banned horses from the area surrounding the Triangle. Many folks parked their rigs at homes of friends who lived nearby, and the Congregational Church offered its shed on a first-come, first-served basis. Those from the north end, from the Polish, Irish, German, and Italian neighborhoods, simply walked down to the Triangle, as they did everywhere.

"And now, folks, the event you've all been a-waiting." The megaphone nearly hid the chubby face of Mayor E. Christian, who was also the town's tailor. No one knew what the E. stood for, but the rumor was that it was "Ebenezer." He rose up to his full five-feet-five inches of importance and held aloft one of the most handsome of the baskets. "Remember, every penny you bid for one of these mouth-watering offerings goes to Charles McLaughlin's family. Now, this here basket," he fumbled for the tag in the blue-and-white-checked napkin, "is Ada Ruhlman's. You all know that Ada's momma Maybelle made piecrust as tender as a mother's love. So you can sure expect Ada's goodie basket to be a fittin' one. What do I hear for Ada's basket? How about a dollar?"

"I'll give 50 cents," came an opening bid.

"Let's make it 75," shouted another.

"Now, who'll make it a dollar?" puffed the mayor.

The first basket went for $1.25, and the buyer hopped up to the cashier at the bandstand steps to pay his due and claim his basket.

Stepping back against the shade of a building so a lady and child could see, Stephen listened sharply as the bidding continued. Four or five more baskets were bid upon and claimed, but there was only one name he wanted to hear.

"Now, here's a fine-looking number. This one's done up by Rose Wolinski. You all know Rose helps cook over at the City Hotel. She can make yeast rolls lighter 'n air. How much do I hear . . ."

Before the mayor could get the bidding started, Stephen heard his voice, hollow and strange, call out, "I bid one dollar." Heads turned, necks craned, townspeople's eyes met in faint surprise.

Stephen saw Mrs. Koeller toss her head slightly as if she'd sniffed in the air. Stephen realized he'd probably made a grave error. Jane Koeller must have a basket up there.

From the knot of quarrymen on the other side of the bandstand, a rough voice shouted, "One dollar, two bits." Stephen couldn't see the bidder but felt sure it was James Janek. He'd heard Janek was sweet on Rose.

"Two dollars," Stephen answered without hesitating.

"And two bits," came back the fiery voice.

"Three-fifty."

The quarrymen were getting riled now. "Go on, James."

"Make it four dollars."

"Don't quit, now, James."

But the bidder's voice remained silent. That would be more than two days' pay for a quarryman.

"Going once, going twice . . . sold to Mr. Stephen Ballard, superintendent of our Berea Quarries, for $3.50." A noticeable ripple went through the crowd.

After paying his tab and collecting the basket, Stephen lost interest in the rest of the bidding and wandered to the edge of the crowd near the carousel where pug-faced boys and little girls in starched pinafores waved to their parents like semaphores each time they spun past. Their glee captured Stephen, and he found himself waving back. Nearby, several couples near his own age had bought peanut brittle and were licking their lips and fingers with delight.

He recognized Pearl Chamberlain, one of the girl type-setters at the Berea *Enterprise,* and Carl Geiger, a clerk at Brightman & Lawrence Hardware store. Their care-free attitude and unfettered pleasure in such a simple act as sharing candy touched off a chain of questions in Stephen's brain.

"Is this really where I'm supposed to be?" Over and over he'd wrestled with this question like a recurring bad dream. Why was he picked to take over the bur-densome job of the Berea quarries for the Cleveland Stone Company? Surely there was someone, some-where in these quarries more experienced and qualified.

"How can I cope with this labor union thing that I know is coming as sure as tomorrow's sunrise?" Today's silent demonstration was only the beginning. He'd had no experience with labor problems. The Michigan quar-ries where he'd come from were isolated from the labor movement, but Berea's location near smoke-and-steel Cleveland made these quarries a prime target for the organizers.

"What kind of life can I have here?" Living in a rented room, even at the comfortable Koeller home, was a lonely existence. Stephen longed for social activity, even such simple exchanges as he saw among the candy buyers. Still, to the townspeople he represented the Cleveland Stone Company. He was one of "them," which meant he was supposed to confine his socializ-ing to the holy South Side.

Suddenly, Martha Adams was at his side. "Does that make you wish you were a little boy again?" Though her broad hat brim partly shaded her face, Stephen could make out her amused expression and the merriment in her eyes.

"You know, Martha, sometimes I wish there'd be nothing better than to know events in life are going to be just as certain as those children are sure they're going to see their parents each time the ponies come around . . . that nothing is going to change." Stephen had removed his straw sailor hat and turned it round and round in his hands as he spoke.

Martha's classic features grew more serious. "But, Stephen, surely you wouldn't want us to be little puppets on a stage, acting out a script." She smiled warmly, and Stephen sensed her earnestness as she spoke. "Decisions are often difficult, but we have the intelligence and free will to make them." Martha was aware of Stephen's anxiety about the quarry labor situation. "We have to remember where our help comes from and where our hope must be."

Stephen sheepishly remembered his mother's admonition—to rely on Divine help. And here was Martha Adams, a woman whose husband met his death by a runaway team of horses and a carriage on their twenty-fifth wedding anniversary—and she was talking about hope.

"I'm going home now. The Koellers have gone already. Leila feared she was getting too much sun.

Could I take your basket and put it on Koellers' porch?" Martha offered.

Stephen glanced down self-consciously at his feet where he'd set the basket while he watched the carousel. He'd stolen a look inside first, though, and the sight of the berry slump brought a mental picture of Rose's strong, yet decidedly feminine hands picking the berries, as he was certain she had.

"I promise I won't snitch any of Rose's goodies," she added, twinkling.

"That'd be fine of you, Martha. I'd like to stay around and watch the dancing groups for a while." The Polish, the Irish and the Italian groups were beginning to gather near the bandstand. If their dances were as intricate and colorful as their costumes, they would be worth watching.

"Enjoy yourself, Stephen. You work so hard. You deserve this holiday as much as the quarrymen." Martha turned and made her way through the crowd, a rather elegant figure that commanded respect. After all, Stephen thought, to win an office in the first local election in which women were allowed to vote in Ohio was quite a feat. He found her quite a remarkable person and determined to know her better.

He waited for the first group that apparently would be the Irish. Apple-cheeked young girls in tapestry-like pinafores gathered near the bandstand, chattering like sparrows as they waited for their cue to begin. Stephen wove his way through the crowd

over to the City Hotel, nodding agreeably at the townspeople, most of whom he could already call by name.
He thought that perhaps Rose would still be at the
hotel, and he could thank her for her effort in preparing the basket.

The City Hotel had recently undergone a facelift
and a name change under the direction of its new
owner, one Mrs. M. B. Longwood, formerly of Buffalo. It was a box-like, two-story brick building at the
corner of Church and Front Streets, just off the Triangle. On the first floor heavy velvet portieres
screened the sparsely furnished lobby from the street.
It boasted a popular saloon, the only one within the
town limits, and the wainscoated-paneled dining
room now sported new bentwood chairs and white
tablecloths.

The owner remained somewhat of an enigma to
Bereans. No one ever called her anything but Mrs.
Longwood, for no one knew what the initials M. B.
stood for. Some of the regulars that gathered at the
City Hotel's saloon secretly snickered in their suds
that maybe the letters stood for Madam of the
Brothel—that perhaps she'd had another career in
Buffalo. Sheriff Wallace Maxson kept a close eye on
activities at the City Hotel. It had been a respectable
establishment for a number of years, and the town
wished no changes in that status.

Mrs. M. B. Longwood was plopped in her commanding spot, a high stool behind an ornate brass cash

register. She was not close enough to the window that anyone could observe her money drawer but close enough to witness nearly anything that took place on the north end of the Triangle. As usual, she wore a dress of black bombazine in spite of the warm day. A cameo choker nestled in the fleshy folds of her throat, and a gold pendant watch decorated her ample bosom. At her elbow, a parrot, blind in one eye and wearing a ruby collar, occupied a willow cage.

"Good afternoon, Mrs. Longwood," Stephen remarked in what he hoped was a pleasant tone. One never wanted to get off on the wrong foot in a conversation with this lady. He'd learned this already. Once when he'd commented about missing fresh Michigan blueberries, she'd taken his remark as criticism of the buttermilk flapjacks served in the hotel's dining room.

"It's a marvelous day for the Summerfest, wouldn't you say?" Clutching his hat, Stephen felt himself give a slight, courtly bow to this imposing woman.

While eyeing him critically from beneath her hooded lids, Mrs. Longwood ignored his comment. "You look as if you took some sun this afternoon, Mr. Ballard. Better go in and have a drink and rest yourself." She fluttered her plump, fingers toward the saloon doorway from where a low drone of male voices and a blue stream of cigar smoke drifted into the empty lobby. Her nails punctured the air like talons. Her other hand clutched the handle of an embroidered silk fan that gently stirred the air in front of her heavily rouged face. Tiny beads of sweat marched across her upper lip, nonetheless, somehow putting Stephen more at ease with this rather formidable, somewhat mysterious woman.

"Thank you, no, I'm waiting for the dancers to begin." A pause hung between them, as wide as an open door. "I really, well, I wanted to ask if—" He broke off in mid-sentence as Mrs. Longwood snapped her fan shut and stared squarely at him.

"Come, come, Mr. Ballard, you're an important man in this town, even if you are young and new here. I've no time for someone who can't speak his mind." She picked up a biscuit from a small pewter tray and began poking crumbs through the slats of the parrot's cage. "We like people to speak up, don't we, Belvedere?"

"Speak! Speak!" croaked the wretched bird. Stephen felt his cheeks growing hot. "You see, ma'am, I bid on a basket at the auction and—"

"I know. I saw and I heard. It was Rose's."

"I just came by to thank her—if she's still here." The words tumbled out finally, and at last Stephen felt his knees stiffening with resolve.

"She donated the food, the same as you donated your money. You've no cause to thank her." The woman was speaking sternly now, her jowly face shaking as if her stool had suddenly started vibrating. "You're inviting trouble, Mr. Ballard, if you start chasing after Rose. She's a good girl, good help, and good to her mother. Yet, she's the daughter of a Polish quarryman, rest his soul, for he's been dead since she was a tyke, I understand. But her brother George is a quarryman and a hothead, as you must know, and he'll be more than just a troublesome worker if you start meddling with Rose."

She paused and eyeballed him to see if he was taking in her advice. Stephen stood stockstill, waves of disappointment flooding over him.

"Rose left here an hour ago," Mrs. Longwood's clipped words fell like knives. "She said she was going home to freshen up and come back for the open dancing." She paused emphatically. "She said she was coming to the dancing with James Janek."

Trying to compose himself, Stephen managed a weak smile. "Thank you, Mrs. Longwood. I appreciate the information—and the advice. I know you meant it in good faith."

"Certainly, I did." Her tone softened a trace. "You have yourself quite a job, young man. You don't need to complicate it by mixing it up with personal problems. Now, goodbye." She turned to her ledger, dismissing him without another glance.

Stephen left by the dining room's side door and headed toward the Koeller house. He had no heart for watching the dancing now. With his head throbbing to the beat of an imagined polka, twin images of Rose and James Janek, like twirling dolls in perfect step, spun in his consciousness.

* * *

Brass spittoons and cane-backed rocking chairs dominated the sparse décor of the lobby of the City Hotel. A thin curtain of tired cigar smoke veiled the entire room. Two dusty palms and an oversized mirror in an ornately carved frame struggled to supply touches of elegance. The well-worn floorboards squeaked under the heavy tread of houseman Caleb Barkham as he pushed a mop half-heartedly. Each time he neared a window, he stole a peek through the heavy portieres at the doings on the Triangle.

Squeaky-voiced Harlan Perkins, the room clerk, was issuing a key to a stout, officious-seeming man who had just arrived from the railroad station, traveling most of the way by single-seater deluxe. Mopping his florid face, the visitor appeared put out, probably because he'd had to walk the last quarter mile since horses were banned from the area for the day.

"You'll be comfortable there—in 27, sir. That room's on the back of the building, so the music and the crowd at the Summerfest won't bother you." Harlan peered through his spectacles at several keys, dropped one, and bumped his head on the counter as he leaned down to pick up the key. "I'll find someone to carry your bag, sir, and if I can't, I'll carry it up myself." He gleamed a wide smile of reassurance to the arriving guest. Caleb Barkham had curiously disappeared from sight.

Franklin Pritchett, organizer for the Knights of Labor, glanced around grimly. The City Hotel was not much like Cleveland's Forest City House. He'd come out from Cleveland to Berea on Saturday to spend the night so he could attend church here tomorrow, get to know some of the quarry folk, and gain their confidence a bit. Besides, he wanted to get permission to use St. Adalbert's school for a meeting to interest more quarrymen in joining the union.

He hadn't known a blasted street fair would be going on. On the other hand, there could be no better way to move about the town unnoticed with his ear to the ground.

"That's fine. I can manage." Pritchett nodded to the over-eager clerk and picked up his supple leather valise. He could manage more than this goon ever could dream of.

Three

"Hallelujah! What a grand day Saturday was," cried Franz Lieberharr, tossing his sweat-stained hat in the air. "A day away from the quarries."

"And a day to chase after Miss Gracey Shoe-maker." Beefy John Seidler taunted his fellow quarryman. "Did you get lovey-dovey, yet? I saw you two walking on the campus. You wouldn't have known if the church steeple had fell on you." John never had a girl of his own, but he enjoyed needling his friends.

Three short blasts of a shrill whistle nearly drowned out his last taunt. "Here comes the Dinky. Let's go." Franz yelled, happy to change the subject.

Franz, John and a half-dozen other young quarrymen hurried to gather their coats, picks, axes, and lunch pails as a squatty engine lurched around the bend, towing a string of gondola-like cars. The workers were lucky today. They could hitch a ride in one of the empty cars and let the Dinky haul them to the quarry operations, thus saving a long and dusty walk.

They piled onto the car, as the Dinky picked up steam and began winding its way toward the quarry. The air was heavy with the haze of midsummer and quarry dust. The noisy Dinky and the clattering of the empty cars it pulled drowned out the cawing of crows and the angry scolding of jays, the cheer-cheers of cardinals and the honking of a few geese that inhabited some of the already-abandoned quarries nearby.

Once at the quarry, the men would start their twelve-hour day's work while steam shovels heaped excess shale and dirt into the empty cars to be hauled off and deposited in some vacant place or fill a hole already quarried. The Dinky engines traveled on narrow, snakelike pieces of track, especially built by the stone company to reach dangerous sites of operation.

Once aboard, the quarrymen jostled one another for position in the car and picked up the thread of their conversation about the previous Saturday.

"What ab-b-bout Wolinski and Janek—that b-b-banner at the b-b-bandstand," pasty-faced, stringy-haired Anthony Carabelli stuttered.

John Seidler shrugged. He was always full of information, whether truth or rumor. "Just a stunt," he declared. They've heard about unions in Cleveland,

and they'd just like to stir up trouble for Mr. Ballard because he's new and not much older than they are. Hey, look over there," he shouted above another shrill blast from the Dinky.

He pointed as they passed a mill yard where piles of grindstones, round and smooth, stood stacked neatly like rows of giant coins. Tall, sentinel-like pine trees surrounded the mill where thousands of grindstones were turned out each year to be shipped all over the country. "Just think where all those stones are going," said John. "They say the Berea mills ship grindstones everywhere. I'd like to get on one and ride..."

He grinned, mischief lighting his ice-blue eyes.

Loud guffaws erupted from the group at the thought of hefty John Seidler riding a grindstone.

"It'd take a mighty big grindstone to hold you, John Seidler.

"And a derrick to get it off the ground." The young quarrymen laughed and taunted their friend good-naturedly.

The coolness of early morning was slipping away as the sun, like a dull, copper coin, burned its way through the ever-present scrim of beige-white dust that hung in the quarries. A screen of cedars, maples, and oaks, backlit by the morning sun, marched around the rim of the quarry. The train bumped and swayed alongside the Rocky River where the gray-green water rushed and leaped over stones, as if trying to hurdle its banks.

Spirits soared also this morning. As the train chugged past the Center Street footbridge, several shopkeepers crossing to the Triangle to open for business turned and raised their arms in salute to the carload of quarrymen. Saturday's holiday mood seemed to have carried over to Monday morning, at least.

Garrulous John Seidel doffed his battered hat and shouted, "Hal-lo, Mr. Carman. Good morning, Mr. Mattison," he shouted. "Ain't it a gorgeous day?"

When the Dinky pulled its string of cars into Big Quarry, the scene already teemed with the start-up of another week's work. Quarrymen of all ages scurried about everywhere like well-rehearsed characters on a stage. Hoists clanked and drills were already rasping. A steam-driven channeling machine had cut through exposed sandstone that had been marked off in 40-foot square sections. At the bottom of these channels, iron wedges were driven to separate the seam of sandstone. Slow and cumbersome though the channeling machine was, men no longer had to labor using picks and iron bars for this task as they had in the early days of quarrying.

After the channeling, each 40-foot section was then cross-marked into smaller sections. Steam-powered drilling machines bored straight down through the thickness of the seam.

"Hop to it there," the burly job boss called, seeing the carload of muscle power arriving. "Your holiday's over. Those rods won't run by themselves."

The young quarrymen hoisted heavy steel rods that had specially shaped heads from which spurs protruded on opposite sides. They drove these down through the holes to make a score mark in line with the holes. Then the explosive handlers arrived on the scene to place small amounts of dynamite in the holes. Dynamite was safer than the black powder formerly used, but this was still a dangerous operation. The blasting split the layout into accurate, smaller sections. Derricks then hoisted these and loaded the stones, like giant bars of soap, onto flatbed railroad cars that hauled them to the gang sawmills where they would become integrated parts of huge buildings as far away as Canada.

Once they finished scoring for the blasting, John Seidler, Franz Lieberharr and their fellow workers would wield sledgehammers to place short wedges into drilled holes separating smaller blocks of stone that would become paving and curbstones.

Most of these young men were sons of quarrymen whose fathers and some whose grandfathers had settled in Berea because of opportunity for work in the quarries. They recognized and respected the dangers of working there. The risk of being killed or maimed for life by blasting, flying debris, railroad accidents, or steam boiler explosions was ever present.

Every year quarrymen lost their lives in quarry accidents, leaving widows and small children to survive as best they could; the Stone Company provided no organized assistance for these families. And the ubiquitous, silent, beige-white specter — sandstone dust — threatened to stifle the workers' very breath with what was known as "grit consumption."

But, likewise, quarrying was the life breath of these men. Meager as wages were, quarrying was the mainstay of existence for about one-third of the town. Like all mining occupations, little opportunity existed to advance. Some people, like Stephen Ballard, who had learned about steam engines and boilers and possessed an extraordinary ability to supervise and direct an occupation that he knew well — these were the few who could expect to climb up out of the trenches and make a career of quarrying. For most, though, being a quarryman offered a bone-bruising, muscle-wrenching way of life — ten hours a day, six days a week for $1.50 per day.

A few years before, during the Panic of 1893, quarrymen's wages had been cut back from $1.75 a day. Although times were better once again, the wage remained at $1.50 a day. Many of the quarry workers' wives and even some children earned as much or more for a day's work during the onion harvest in the mucky fields around nearby Lake Abram. Thus, the families eked out an existence.

In a clearing away from the work area stood a crude wooden shelter where the quarrymen left their coats, lunches, and personal tools during the day. Here the water boys were balancing the yokes and buckets they would carry all day to keep the quarrymen supplied with water from the well at the top of the quarry.

Sam Mikolak, one of the oldest, most experienced of these waterboys, already looked forward to a day when he could be a real quarryman. "Look at James Janek, will you? He's about the best derrick man I ever seen. He gets up that pole faster than a squirrel." Sam reached over to help Jacob Zielinski tighten the strap that held the yoke on the younger boy's bony right shoulder.

"Hey, know what I heard?" Jacob turned a sunburned face toward Sam. "Out there around Lake Abram somewhere there's a cabin, practic'ly hidden by all the reeds and swampy grass. I bet that's where Fast Jack goes at night. Bet he keeps all that money there that he's s'posed to have. Whattaya think?"

Before Sam could answer, Chris Janovick chimed in. "Yeah, he always walks out Eastland Road direction. Then he just sort of fades away."

Just as every town seems to claim at least one curiosity-arousing character, Berea was no exception. Seamy-faced Fast Jack, as folks referred to him, strode the streets daily, whether they were shoetop-deep in mud or the temperature soared into the 90s. Even on those days, he wore a musty-looking, full-length Army coat, a throwback to Civil War days, but never a hat of any kind. His shoulder-length, yellowish, wispy hair streamed behind him as he walked. In three-foot-long strides, he loped from one end of the town to the other. The book he carried was possibly a Bible, but no one knew for certain because it had a plain black cover, and he never tried to preach or pray with anyone. If people spoke to him, he nodded and looked back at them with kind but rheumy blue eyes and kept on walking. People knew that the City Hotel owner, Mrs. Longwood, set food out the back door for him every day. Jack would lean against a barrel, use both hands to bolt the food down, and then keep on walking.

Jacob persisted. "Whattaya think, Sam? Would you go out there one day with me to look for the shack?" Jacob knew that he'd never get permission from his worrisome mother to go to Lake Abram alone. Although there hadn't been a wolf killed in that area for five or six years, the place was still wild-looking and remote.

"Hey, Jake, I'd go. Just lemme know," Chris said. Jake ignored Chris. He was only a few months older than himself. "I'll think about it," Sam said. "Probably I could on a Sunday afternoon." He hoisted his yoke into position, balancing the buckets with care.

"Yeah, let's do it." Jacob was brave and eager, now that he knew he had an older companion for the venture. He stashed his belongings under a bench in the shelter with an air of bravado and got ready for the first climb of the day. The spring that supplied water to the quarrymen was eighty-five steps above the quarry floor. Before the day was over the water boys would make fifteen or more trips up and down the steep bank, their bodies straining at contorted angles under the weighty yokes that bore their buckets.

"Rose, Rose, the Polka Queen," W. G. Frazer, the fire insurance agent, sing-songed as Rose Wolinski served up his flapjacks in the City Hotel dining room. He relished his leisurely breakfast on Monday mornings before beginning his round of calls. "You and your feller really showed the town how it's done last Saturday night." He drowned the flapjacks in pure Ohio maple syrup as he kept up his banter with Rose. "Guess that's sort of a national dance with you folks, though, isn't it? Heh-heh." He gave a patronizing smile, one great gold tooth shining like a beacon.

"I-I guess so. I never thought about it." Rose felt herself blushing, and her hand that held the coffee pot trembled slightly.

She didn't mind being complimented for her dancing. She knew she had looked fetching in her embroidered apron and blouse with the full, gauzy sleeves. And she and James Janek did make a great-looking couple on a dance floor; lots of people had told her that after Mass yesterday. The entire congregation of St. Adalbert's must have gathered at the sidelines of the Triangle Saturday night, clapping and stomping. Other dancers had cleared the roped-off dance space while Rose and James had whirled faster and faster, their feet flying as the music kept pumping and rocking.

Still, the way Mr. Frazer said "you people" bothered Rose, and she resented hearing people call James her "feller." She and James had been friends, almost neighbors, since her family came to Berea when she was just a tiny girl with blond braids and twin dimples. Yet, except when they went dancing, James was not exciting. When he took her hand as they were walking or tried to touch her cheek, his own hands were rough and clumsy. His speech was heavy with the Old Country accent spoken by his parents—and her own mother and brother. Since she'd been working at the hotel, Rose liked hearing the tradespeople and the college professors talk. She'd often find herself listening carefully to try to improve her own speech.

"The street fair was fine, wasn't it?" Rose ignored Mr. Frazer's compliment but tried to ease herself away from his table. "Excuse me. If there's nothing else you need, I'll be taking Mrs. Longwood her coffee."

Frazer nodded absently. By now he was trying to divide his attention between his flapjacks and his newspaper.

At Mrs. Longwood's high desk, Rose poured steaming, fragrant coffee into an English Spode cup that rested next to Belvedere's cage. "Thanks, thanks," the bird squawked.

Rose detested Belvedere and made a face at him behind Mrs. Longwood's broad back. Although the hotel owner was hard at work on her ledgers already during the early breakfast hour, upon hearing the tinkle of china, she swung her ample girth around on her stool and stared critically at Rose.

Without so much as a "Good morning," she announced, "Stephen Ballard came nosing around here for you after you'd left Saturday night." She sipped her coffee, arching a ruby-bedecked pinky finger. "M-m-m. No coffee tastes as sweet as the morning's first cup," she observed.

"Sweet. Sweet," Belvedere agreed. Mrs. Longwood began treating him to a biscuit, a few crumbs at a time. Rose waited, hoping Mrs. Longwood would keep talking about Stephen, her heart pounding like a triphammer at the thought that Stephen had been looking for her.

The hotel owner set her cup down with care. "I advised him," she said deliberately, her coal-black glittering eyes boring into Rose's expectant face, "that you were going to the dancing with James Janek." She stopped short of telling Rose the rest of the advice she'd given the young quarry superintendent.

Rose could feel her cheeks flaming. "Thank you for telling me, Mrs. Longwood," she said, trying not to stammer. Ducking her head, she painstakingly swept up the biscuit crumbs from around the parrot's cage. Then she looked up abruptly at her employer. "Did you know Mr. Ballard bid $3.50 for my basket?" She looked up with an ever-so-slight toss of her head.

"So he did." Mrs. Longwood's eyes locked with Rose's in a rock-hard gaze that spoke volumes; Rose could read the woman's thoughts as surely as if she had shouted them. She was practically forbidding any friendship that Rose might have with Stephen Ballard. In spite of Mrs. Longwood's serious manner, to her amazement Rose found herself contemplating Mrs. Longwood's double—or was it triple?—chins. Why do women let themselves go so? Her Grandmother Wolinski, determined to keep her looks, had worn a chinstrap when she slept. The first time Rose had seen her wearing it, she thought her grandmother had a toothache. Mrs. Longwood would need a super-sized chinstrap.

Two college professors, dressed in light-colored linen suits and deep in discussion, were approaching to pay their breakfast checks.

"That'll be all, Rose. Go tend to your duties."

Mrs. Longwood's demeanor changed instantly from one of critical judgment to cloying sweetness. "And how was everything this morning, gentlemen?" she beamed at her customers. "Were the flapjacks light enough?"

* * *

Footsore and nearly blinded by dust, Knights of Labor organizer Franklin Pritchett limped into the center of operations at Big Quarry. He'd had no luck finding someone with a horse and wagon to bring him from the hotel out to the quarry. Everyone in Berea must be back to work already on this Monday morning, he'd decided. With a plump, pink hand, Pritchett brushed a film of dust from the shoulders of his well-tailored suit of brown worsted and mopped his cherry-red face with an initialed linen handkerchief.

He saw George Wolinski striding toward him, pulling a bandana from his sweaty face. These quarry workers and their bandanas look like renegades, and Pritchett didn't believe that would help their cause. Still, one couldn't blame them for doing anything to battle this confounded dust—

"'Morning, Mr. Pritchett." Wolinski's hulking shoulders and strong eastern European features projected an aura of strength and authority. His wide-set, flinty blue eyes and his firm jaw shouted an attitude of defiance.

Eyeing this young man with interest, Pritchett decided he'd chosen an able lieutenant. "How long until their lunch time?" he asked George, nodding toward the workers. Pritchett was eager to meet with the men and then escape to his quiet office in Cleveland. Already the sun was pounding rivets into his skull, right through his natty bowler. Few factories where he went to organize workers were as gritty and unpleasant as this stone quarry.

"About eight minutes, sir. You can stand on that pile of flat stones over there and talk to them while they're eating. They've been told you're going to be here." Noticing the stranger, a few of the quarrymen had already slowed down their work.

"He's the guy what was at Mass yesterday," Harold Dombowski remarked, putting down his shovel and loosening his bandana. "I heard he's from the union."

"You're right. So he is." James Janek, who was already a union member, jumped to the ground from the lowest foothold of a derrick. His muscles rippled beneath his coarse homespun shirt, and his body was taut and lean as a young stag's. Deep brown eyes flashed in a tanned face weathered from quarry work. When James took off his hat to shake the dust off, his straight black hair lay perfectly parted on one side.

James Janek's job of guyer was one of the most demanding in the quarry. To "guy" the derrick, a worker had to know where to attach the guy wire at exactly the right place and at the right length and how to hook the chains around the sandstone. He would climb the spikes on the pole to repair the guy wires and cables on the derricks that raised the stone out of the quarries. The more dangerous the job, the more James Janek seemed to glory in it. Admiration of young boys like Sam Mikolak pumped James up. They would often huddle to watch him scale the derricks and fasten the cables. From the top he would doff his hat as they cheered, "Jan-ek, Jan-ek, rah-rah-rah." He only wished Rose Wolinski could watch him at work in the quarry. Maybe he could impress her more. Rose puzzled him. Saturday night, for instance, she seemed light-hearted and enjoying herself when they danced at the Triangle. And he was proud when everyone clapped and cheered for them. But later, walking home the long way through the German Wallace campus, Rose had seemed quiet and indifferent. She kept pulling away when he tried to put his arm around her waist or even take her hand.

James had always supposed he'd marry Rose someday, but he wasn't ready to think about settling down yet. Right now, he and Rose's brother George were bent on helping to organize the quarrymen. He really believed that joining together against the owners of the Stone Company was the only way quarrymen could better their lot. Already they'd had some success in getting some of the men to join. If he was going to spend his life in the quarries, it would be a better life than his father had. The grit consumption had killed him when James was fourteen, forcing James to quit school and go to work in the quarry as a water boy. The quarry was his life, just as it was George's, whose father had been killed when George and Rose were young children. He liked Rose, but helping to make life better in the quarries was nearly an all-consuming passion with him right now.

George was motioning for James to join Franklin Pritchett and him. Pritchett's round face looked like an overripe tomato about to explode. Dust coated his well-cut suit and shoes.

"Good morning, James." Still breathing heavily from his long walk, Pritchett held out a sweaty palm.

"Glad to have you here, sir," James said. He shook hands, awkwardly as if conscious of his grubbiness.

George Wolinski was taking charge now, directing the quarrymen into one spot where they could listen to Pritchett while they ate.

"George better hope Ballard don't get wind of this," Pavel Prohaska muttered as he picked up his lunch pail and moved to a spot farther from the blocks of stone Pritchett would use for a podium.

Otto Schnell, a channeler, was already munching on a hunk of rye bread and cheese. With his mouth full, he answered, "If we don't take some chances, we'll never learn how to better our lot."

Opening his lunch pail, the aging Pavel muttered inaudibly, but his tone clearly indicated his distrust of union activity being stirred up by these young bucks.

When George leaped up on the stones and began introducing Franklin Pritchett, his voice bounced back from the quarry walls with ringing authority. Up above, a hawk dipped and dived, then disappeared beyond the dense trees that rimmed the quarry.

"You all know," George was saying, "that workers in some companies in Cleveland, like the Rolling Mill, joined up with the Knights of Labor and have bettered their lot. Some of us have already joined up, but we need numbers to give us strength. Mr. Pritchett, here, is from the Knights of Labor, District Assembly No. 47, and he's going to tell us a little bit about how the union can help us." He turned to the visitor. "Mr. Pritchett, it's yours for 26 more minutes."

George and James boosted a puffing Pritchett onto the blocks of stone. Some quarrymen applauded, but most were rattling their lunch pails or busy eating. His dignity recovered, Pritchett peeled off his coat, handed it down to James, and launched into his task.

While the men dived into their lunches, he summed up the history of organized labor's activity in Cleveland. Pritchett regularly spoke to workers during their lunch times, and he knew just how to present his message. He knew they'd listen only passively while they were eating. As the men began shutting their lunch pails and wiping their faces with their bandanas, Pritchett launched into his practiced litany.

"What does the Cleveland Stone Company do for you if you're hurt?" he shouted.

Bitter laughter erupted. Voices rumbled from the crowd: "Nothing." "Not a damn thing."

Pritchett continued: "What did the Cleveland Stone Company do for the McLaughlin family when Charles McLaughlin gave his legs to this quarry?"

"Not much!" More voices, louder this time.

"What has the Cleveland Stone Company done about raising the daily wage that was cut three years ago when times were bad?"

"Nothing." The voices roared back. Pritchett sensed the animation of the crowd by now.

"What's been done about requiring regular inspections of steam boilers?"

"Nothing," The vehement chorus of voices trumpeted back from the stark, silent walls of the quarry.

"By joining together," Pritchett bellowed, "you will make your voices heard, just as you are doing right now. The leaders you choose will meet with the bosses of the Cleveland Stone Company to bring about changes. Collective action is the only way you can improve conditions for yourselves and your families." Pritchett mopped his face and stole a look at his gold pocket watch.

"But what if we lose our jobs?" A lone quarryman, Rudolf Zielinski, voiced the unspoken fears of his comrades.

Pritchett had known this question would come, and he was ready for it. "Faint hearts never won better working lives," he shot back. "Besides," he went on, motioning to include the whole group, "joined together, you are a threat to the successful operation of these quarries," he paused, "if you should choose not to work." The emphasis on this last statement made the word STRIKE loom up in the minds of the

Patricia Mote

quarrymen as clearly as if had been spelled out on the sandstone walls.

"Come to St. Adalbert's School Wednesday evening at eight o'clock to learn more, and to join up if you're ready. Thank you for your time, everyone." A hearty burst of applause accompanied Pritchett's ungainly hop down from the pile of stone. James and George caught him under each drenched armpit.

Wide smiles wreathed George's broad face. "You really fired them up, sir." He clapped Mr. Pritchett on the shoulder.

Despite the stifling heat, James helped Pritchett on with his coat. The chubby man buttoned the coat over his soggy shirt and took his hat from James. The group had seemed responsive, but Pritchett had no experience at organizing quarry workers. They were a hard bunch to read.

"We'll see how many show up at St. Adalbert's Wednesday night," he answered. "Then we'll know how bright the fire burns."

"Thank you, Mrs. Longwood. I'm just waiting for someone." Picking up a discarded copy of the Berea *Advertiser*, Stephen settled himself as comfortably as possible in a creaky rocker in the City Hotel lobby. Stephen felt that the cagey proprietor probably knew whom he wanted to see—and why. At least, though, she wouldn't think he was hanging around after Rose.

62

Stephen had seen the well-dressed, though slightly bedraggled, stranger leave the quarry shortly after noon. The man, whom Stephen was certain was from the union, had been trotting along as fast as his stubby legs would carry him, but there was no way he could avoid the swinging bridge near Stephen's office. Following him and confronting him before he left town seemed to Stephen to be the best plan. This would avoid a showdown in front of the quarrymen.

The stale air in the hotel lobby barely stirred the leaves of the dusty palms. The portieres at the long windows hung limp. There was no breeze from the half-open window. Stephen ran his finger around his shirt collar, conscious of his rumpled appearance. His dust-caked boots had made faint tracks across the polished wood floor, and his trousers were dusty as well. From the dining room doors he could hear the clatter of crockery and silver and the muffled hum of voices. The aroma of chicken and dumplings, the Monday lunch special, reminded Stephen of the untouched lunch pail back in his office — and the dessert Mrs. Koeller would have put in it from Rose's goody basket. He pictured Rose serving lunch in the dining room and strained his ears, trying to hear the music of her voice.

"Bye-bye." Belvedere, the raucous parrot, suddenly screeched from across the lobby. Stephen saw the stocky man in the brown suit settling his bill with Mrs. Longwood. "Come again, now, won't you?" Mrs. Longwood beamed. Easing himself from the ancient rocker, Stephen stepped out into the noontime sun, preparing to head off the man when he left.

"Excuse me, sir. I'm Stephen Ballard, superintendent of the Berea Quarries." Stephen's tone was matter-of-fact and curt, but he did not offer to shake hands. He intended to keep the intruder on the defensive. "Since you were in the quarries this morning, I'd assume you had some stated business there." Stephen paused, expecting an explanation.

"Why, I—uh," flustered, the man set down his valise with a thud. With no interurban car in sight, he'd intended to hurry to the livery stable for a ride to the depot. He hadn't expected this unwelcome delay. "My name is Pritchett. I represent the Knights of Labor, District Assembly #47. Just out visiting a bit with some of the quarrymen on their lunchtime, those who've shown an interest in the labor movement, you know. Heh-heh." Pritchett flashed a false smile and made a stab at lightness. Since he had brushed the quarry dust from his clothes and was on his way back to Cleveland, he now felt in control. More men in that quarry were interested than this superintendent dreamed.

Towering above the perspiring Pritchett, Stephen grasped confidence he was striving for. "Mr. Pritchett," Stephen spoke slowly and forcefully without raising his voice. People were passing by on the Triangle, and he didn't care to have this conversation repeated around town. "I'm going to say this to you once—and only once. You have no right to set a foot in those quarries. You are trespassing on the private property of the Cleveland Stone Company. If you so much as show your face in these quarries again, I'll notify the sheriff and have you arrested." Stephen paused, letting his words sink into the bold little man's consciousness. "Be so advised as of this moment. Good day to you."

With that, Stephen turned on his heel and strode across the Triangle toward his office, leaving Pritchett in the glaring sun, blotting his red face.

It wouldn't be the first time for Pritchett to be arrested. He plodded toward the livery stable, his bag bumping painfully against his leg with every step, consoling himself that he would have an organization behind him of nearly 100,000 Knights of Labor workers to bail him out.

Four

Their two heads bent together, Stephen's dark, wavy hair and Martha Adams' rose-ribboned hat brim were nearly touching. The two neighbors, who were becoming fast friends, were trying to finish a conversation they began as they walked to the Congregational Church at Seminary and Church Streets. Often the site for civic meetings and sometimes even entertainments, it was commonly called the Brick Church to distinguish it from the Methodist, known as the Stone Church.

Tonight, members of the WCTU would present their common concerns to the mayor and city council. While Martha Adams was not a WCTU member, she was attending as a school board member and a citizen who had a keen interest in all things that could better the community of Berea.

Out in her yard, deadheading her roses, Martha

had stopped Stephen as he was returning from work and pressed him to attend a community meeting that evening.

"You, too, Stephen, should take part in what goes on in town. Much of Berea depends your quarries." Weary and worn and longing to wash off the day's dust and dig into one of Mrs. Koeller's mouth-watering dinners, Stephen had planned to spend the evening reading the book of Tennyson's poetry that Dr. Koeller had loaned him. Fond of American poetry since his early school days, Stephen appreciated Dr. Koeller's introducing him to the British poets. "All right, Martha, I'll join you in a while," Stephen had agreed, flashing his neighbor a good-natured smile. He had come to respect Martha's views, as her finger seemed to be on Berea's pulse. He valued her friendship as well.

Perhaps that was why, on this short walk down Bridge Street to the Brick Church, Stephen had deftly steered their conversation around to Rose. When he mentioned the tasty desserts he'd enjoyed from Rose's goody basket all week, he soon found himself confiding to Martha that he wanted to see Rose, to get to know her better.

"She's such an alive person. The few times I've been around her she makes me feel buoyed up and carefree." Stephen took Martha's arm firmly to help her step around a deep rut. Even on Berea's South Side, dirt streets made walking hazardous.

"She's like that passage from Browning — in "Pippa Passes" — Stephen would have rushed on, but Martha's firm voice cut in.

"You must understand by now, Stephen," Martha said, nodding her thanks for his help, "something of Berea's mentality. To say there is a caste system here would be too harsh, but, I'm sorry to say, it is almost like that." Martha's own place on Berea's South Side among "Berea's 400," or upper social set, was her birthright. Some of the town's oldest citizens remembered her father, George Totten, long ago deceased, as "the town doctor." Her husband, Will Adams, had been a well-respected pharmacist until his untimely death. Yet, Stephen admired Martha for her open-mindedness and fair judgment in spite of her privileged background.

But now even Martha was echoing Mrs. Longwood's warning: "You would be inviting trouble if you began seeing Rose socially."

"I understand that, Martha." Before he realized it, Stephen found himself telling Martha of George Wolinski's threat and Mrs. Longwood's harsh words. He hadn't meant to do this but the words tumbled out like pent-up waters from behind a broken dam. They had walked in silence then, for they were almost to the church doors where other townspeople, who had left their supper tables and their evening activities, were filing in.

Inside, rows of townspeople, all appearing to be

from the comfortable homes of the South Side, more than half filled the sanctuary. In front, the cross and candles had been removed from the communion table for the evening's meeting. The last faltering rays of summer twilight filtered through the muted colors of the stained-glass windows.

Now Martha was leaning close to Stephen, trying to finish their conversation before the meeting began. "You will have to pay a price, Stephen, if you should become serious about Rose. Why not get acquainted with her at public affairs, where your intentions can't be misunderstood? There'll be talk, surely, about anyone you see socially. You're a handsome man, Stephen, with an important position, and you must know you're generally regarded as a prize catch."

Feeling his face redden, Stephen started to protest, but Martha had turned to speak to Mr. and Mrs. Simpson who were seating themselves behind them.

"What a grand turn-out we're getting," burbled Mrs. Simpson, a stalwart WCTU member. Stephen nodded to the Simpsons but hoped Martha would return to their conversation. He thought to himself that the hat Mrs. Simpson was wearing looked as if it were trimmed with kale, and bespectacled Billy Simpson looked stiff and bored. He'd surely rather be in his workshop trying to make his confounded engine run.

Martha continued, whispering now, "Why not invite Rose to the Arcade excursion a week from

Sunday?" Her face was so close to Stephen's that he could see the twin points of light dancing in her gray-green eyes. "The interurban company is running special cars from Berea with two hours to spend viewing the splendid Arcade in downtown Cleveland. There are four floors of gilded balconies with shops, musicians and cafés on the main floor."

Throughout the WCTU presentation, ably articulated by Amelia Pierce and others, Stephen's mind kept wandering. He pictured himself on the interurban with Rose, headed for downtown Cleveland. He'd only seen the spectacular Arcade once, gilded and towering, built largely with piles of Rockefeller money. He could see Rose and himself, walking together on the promenades or seated at a café, listening to lilting melodies by strolling musicians. Rose would surely be thrilled with such an outing. He wondered how many times she had even been to Cleveland...

"...and we thank you, Mayor Christian, for this great opportunity to voice some local concerns of our members." Amelia Pierce's sharp voice rang out. Her last name certainly suited her. She went on, warming to her subject. "Of course, our Number One concern is the Devil Drink, and while our village itself has no taverns, except the long-time, respectable one at the City Hotel, there is a growing number out near the Union Station. Our council and mayor have no control over these since that's Middleburg Township.

Thus, we wish to advise that our chapter will be joining with the Middleburg Township chapter very soon
to declare WAR on these dens of iniquity." Her voice
surely reached the highest timber of the vaulted ceiling to the delight of her fellow WCTU members. They
applauded with vigor, while the reaction of the rest
of the audience was more cautious and reserved.

Then one of Amelia's staunch lieutenants, Eliza
Sterling, rose stiffly, stepped to the lectern Amelia had
vacated, and adjusted her spectacles. Only the noticeable tremor of her leg-of-mutton sleeves and the tell-
tale crack in her voice betrayed her nervousness.

"Another of our concerns," she began, "is the in-
humane treatment of animals in our town. Horses are
left tied to hitching posts for hours, even entire business days, to endure insufferable heat and bitter cold.
We propose a two-hour limit for these poor animals
to be tied in the Triangle area. Furthermore, the horse
barn, owned by this hospitable Congregational
Church, where many people are allowed to leave their
horses on weekdays, is an odiferous disgrace and an
unsanitary menace. This building must be cleaned out
at least three times a week. At present, the church care-
taker shovels it out on Monday, following the Sunday
service. We recommend the town pay someone to
clean it on Wednesdays and Fridays also, since the
church is providing space for tradespeople's horses."

Her fellow WCTU'ers greeted Emma's proposal
with bold applause while a spatter came from the rest

of the chamber. The mayor and council sat, unblinking.

Martha whispered to Stephen, "If they can get the council to spend money for that, I'll be surprised."

"It's a good idea, though," Stephen replied. "That horsebarn is a disgrace." He had to respect the WCTU ladies. Their enthusiasm for their causes was genuine, and speaking out in public gatherings took courage for women, who only recently had been granted the right to vote in local elections.

Even Billy Simpson was muttering agreement. His shop was not far from that horsebarn.

"And now for our final item," another WCTU lieutenant rose to speak. This time it was Letitia Marks, a frail, putty-faced lady whose slight frame seemed to swim in her black-and-white gingham blouse and black moire skirt.

"Everyone—" she cleared her throat—"everyone knows that the pump at the Triangle is an unsanitary disgrace." She shuffled her notes tentatively and adjusted her gingham-trimmed hat several times as if she feared it would fly off her head.

The two-handled pump had been a fixture at the southeast angle of the Triangle for more than twenty years. Children stood in line to operate it, for it worked much after the fashion of railroad handcars. The well water was pure and cold. But two tin cups were chained to the pump, and Letitia droned on and on about these, warning of the horrors of the common drinking vessels, which, in her words, were carriers of dreaded disease and pestilence.

"We implore you, Honorable Mr. Mayor and esteemed council members, please declare such common use of this pump a menace—"

"There should be some easy solution to this," Stephen muttered to Martha.

"Such as everyone bring their own cup, maybe?" she suggested. "Seems to me we tried that, but people keep replacing—"

A sudden pounding of feet and excited clamor erupted from the vestibule of the church. Forgetting the pestilent pump for the moment, citizens craned their necks to look toward the rear doors.

"Fire! Fire!" Jacob Zielinski, wild-eyed, his face drained of color, burst into the hall. Following him was Sam Mikolak, shouting, "It's up by the depot, they say. Prob'ly the brewery."

This latter comment brought wide smiles of unrestrained joy from Amelia and her two fellow WCTUers at the front of the church. A few men, presumably volunteer firemen, dashed out to help form a bucket brigade. Berea's old pumper was only useful near the river where an adequate water supply was at hand. The area north of town, the location of the railroad station and Hoffman's Brewery, had no nearby water source. This area was actually outside the town limits, but Berea's firefighters would rally to help.

More shouting arose from outside in the streets, and the excited babble of the crowd in the sanctuary rose higher and higher.

The mayor, puffing and pounding for order, desperately tried to refocus attention on the town pump, but the noise level mounted, and he kept opening and closing his mouth like a starving fish.

"Thank you, ladies...take your concerns...next...." The mayor's voice rose only slightly above the excited clamor. As the WCTU ladies gathered their papers, the nervous audience began snaking its way to the rear doors, chattering like magpies.

Though the distance from the Triangle to the Hoffman Brewery on Depot Street was little more than a mile, few South Side residents stood among the rowdy crowd that watched it burn. Efforts of the bucket brigade grew almost ludicrous since the fire had evidently been burning for some time. Soon it was apparent that saving the vats of ale, porter and brown stout, not the building, was the real concern.

Jake and Sam watched the leaping flames from a safe distance, seated on the limbs of a sturdy oak tree. "What do you guess started that big of a fire?" asked Jake, rubbing his smarting eyes. A stiff breeze was now blowing billows of black smoke over all of the onlookers.

Sam shifted to a lower limb that felt stronger. "Most likely somebody didn't put out a rubbish fire all the way. That's what usually starts fires — unless," he hesitated —

"Unless what?" Jake demanded.

" — somebody done it a-purpose."

"Why in the world would anybody set a brewery on fire?" Jake wanted to know.

"Well, just listen — "

From the crowd of north end residents arose the cries, "Save the beer!" "Drink, drink!" More and more helpers joined in, but not, sadly to say, for the benefit of brewmeister Hoffman. As soon as kegs of stout and ale were pulled away from the blaze, the reveling quarrymen popped them open. Tin cups appeared from nowhere, and Berea's Greatest Beer Fest began. It was to last far into the night. Polish and Irish quarrymen, often at odds, flung their arms over one another's shoulders, raised their tin cups to their parched lips, and sang lustily.

According to the *Advertiser* the next week, the fire caused an estimated loss of $60,000. Most of the two-story brick building was destroyed. The newspaper account was vague as to whether this included the value of the liquid property, and the cause of the blaze was never determined.

Five

A gray-flannel sky shrouded the town the morning after the fire, as if the dense smoke had somehow snuffed out the sunshine and cottony clouds of the previous few days. Stephen thought he could even taste the acrid stench of damp, charred wood that hung in the air. To his happy surprise on this grim morning, he'd met Rose as he was heading across the Triangle to the bank. She was just leaving the bank, carrying an empty money pouch and a bank book. The pecuniary-minded Mrs. Longwood, for all her concern with her ledgers, apparently had utter confidence in her employee's honesty and entrusted her with depositing the hotel's receipts.

Perhaps the element of surprise was in Stephen's favor. He had no time to become nervous or tongue-tied about what was uppermost in his mind where this engaging girl was concerned. Before he realized what he was saying, the words poured out and he'd invited her to the Arcade excursion.

"I'd be honored to have your company, Rose. There'll be a crowd going. Two interurban cars, I'm told." Stephen felt himself twisting his hat around in his hands.

Rose's clear blue eyes widened in surprise, her brows arched, but she gave him a hesitant smile. Then the corners of her full mouth turned up in delight. "Oh, Mr. Ballard, how lovely! I've truly dreamed of seeing the Arcade one day. They say it's—"

Two sharp-featured women bustled past, staring pointedly down their noses at the pair. Stephen recognized them as WCTU members he'd seen at the previous night's meeting. "Excuse us," said Stephen, taking Rose's arm and guiding her under a tree, out of the path and earshot of passersby.

"I'll call for you at half-past one. That will give us plenty of time. Let's hope it's a pleasant day like we've been having—" Stephen checked himself, fearing he would rattle on nervously about the weather.

He had to lean down to hear Rose's low answer. She had ducked her head, and all he could see was the arrow-straight part in the middle of her honey-blonde hair. "I can't let you come to my house . . . my neighborhood, Mr. Ballard. People there would think—"

"Rose, begin by calling me Stephen, will you please? I hear enough 'Mr. Ballards' all week long in the quarries." He kept his voice low, his lips as close to her ear as he dared. "Second, when I invite a young lady to accompany me somewhere, I expect to call for her." He hesitated, longing to raise her face to his. "And yet—" Suddenly, he added, "I don't want to cause trouble for you."

"I'm afraid you'll cause trouble for yourself, Mr. B—Stephen." She said his name softly, as if she feared someone would hear. She'd lifted her head now, but her eyes reflected her apprehension. "My brother George gets furious about me talking to you, says I'm trying to put on airs, and James Janek has no right to be jealous about you outbidding him at the auction...but he can be mean sometimes."

"Rose, your brother has spoken to me, and I recognize his feelings. But he must realize you aren't a piece of family property. You have a right to choose your friends." Shifting the portfolio he was carrying to the other hand, Stephen steered Rose across the dirt street to a bench on the grassy part of the Triangle, making certain it was out of Mrs. Longwood's beady-eyed line of vision from the window of the City Hotel. He settled himself next to her.

Rose clasped her hands in her lap and turned to Stephen, her smooth face etched with relief, her clear eyes shining. "I have a splendid idea," she declared. "My cousin Anna Mikolak and her husband Viktor are going on that trip. They won tickets in the raffle at the Summerfest. She's the one who was telling me how grand it would be. I'll come down to the Triangle with Anna and Viktor. You'll be here, and then you and I will get on the interurban car together. People will see us together, but at least I won't get the neighborhood all stirred up with you coming there. Oh, it will be so delightful—" Rose fairly leaped from the bench, giddy as a five-year-old.

Stephen smiled at the young woman's winsome eagerness, her unbridled spirit of adventure. This was what had first drawn him to Rose—this aura of aliveness that surrounded her.

As Rose made her way across the Triangle to the hotel, Stephen admired her straight back, her slim waist, her swinging, blue-and-white gingham skirt. The thick braids she wore at work hung below her shoulders. Stephen wondered if on Sunday she'd wear her hair twisted on top of her head like the South Side ladies wore—

Heading back to his office, Stephen could feel that his step was more sprightly, his air more jaunty. "Good morning, Carl. Fine day, isn't it?" Carl Geiger was cranking down the awning at B & L Hardware Store. Stephen remembered seeing Carl and his girlfriend, Pearl Chamberlain, on the day of the Summerfest, enjoying each other's company and how he had envied them.

"G-good morning, Mr. Ballard." For a moment, Carl somewhat startled by Stephen's friendliness. He thought the quarry superintendent usually seemed rushed and pre-occupied. "I have those drills that you ordered. They came in yesterday."

"Fine, fine, Carl. I can always count on B & L Hardware to get items we need quickly. I'll send someone to pick them up shortly." Stephen strode on, a nameless, joyful tune playing in his head.

The day at the quarries proved less productive than Stephen would have wished. At least seventy quarrymen failed to report to work—the result of the previous night's beer debacle.

"They expect higher wages, yet they pull a stunt like this," Stephen thought to himself. He had hoped to meet a quota of stone today for the Stearns Mill, but that was virtually impossible with so many quarrymen off the job.

Another result of the high absentee rate today would be more pro-union activity. By afternoon, the quarrymen would have slept off the effects of the previous night and would congregate on the streets and in the taverns to "talk union" in their unexpected free time.

"You put down that union nonsense, Stephen, every chance you get. You're in charge there." Mr. G. H. Worthington had fairly shouted at Stephen over the crackling telephone wires when he'd reported to him of Mr. Pritchett's visit. Stephen could picture the stuffy Worthington in his cocoon-like office, high above downtown Cleveland, totally insulated from the rising labor unrest.

"Easy for you to say, G.H." Sometimes Stephen found himself interacting mindlessly with his dust-coated office walls. But he knew union momentum was building. Just this morning, Pavel Prohaska had shuffled up to him, wheezing between his words, bearing news of the meeting planned for St. Adalbert's School Wednesday night. Pavel had been a friend to Stephen since he drove the young superintendent around the quarries in a runabout on his first day. Today, between his distress and his breathing problems, Pavel could barely spit out his words. He'd worked thirty-seven years in the quarries, and given his age and his difficulty in breathing, he should be sitting on his front steps, telling stories to the neighborhood children.

His breath coming in short spurts, Pavel asked, "What if the Stone Company fires — the men who join the union?" A lingering cough rattled in his chest like dry leaves. "They're not thinking of their families. That Pritchett fellow — filled their heads with dangerous ideas." The elderly quarryman leaned against the doorframe, gasping for breath.

Firing the men raised a possibility that Stephen refused to dwell on — at least not yet. He spoke to Pavel with an assurance he did not feel himself. "Pavel, we have to take each day as it comes. Thank you for letting me know what's going on with the men. We can hope that perhaps it's only these young rowdies, like James Janek, who are going to be influenced by Mr. Pritchett."

Oblique shafts of late afternoon sunlight pierced the curtains of dust that hung in the quarry. White-coated leaves scarcely stirred on the mottled branches in a grove of sycamore trees. Below them sprawled three water boys, sweating, bedraggled, longing for the end of another workday.

"Whew! It must be 95 degrees even here in the shade," Sam Mikolak said. He was chomping on an overripe apple he had fished from his knapsack, spitting the seeds in Jake Zielinski's direction.

"Yeah, and those guys down there got holes in their cups," Chris Janovick put in. "I've lost track of my trips today."

The well on Prospect Street stood eighty-five steps above the busy floor of the quarry. Water boys, some as young as ten, filled their buckets and swarmed up and down the hill all day like coolies, the heavy yokes teetering on their bony shoulders.

"Hey, Sam, remember you promised to go out to Lake Abram with me — to hunt for Fast Jack's cabin." With a stubby thumb and forefinger, Jake flipped the apple seeds back at his friend.

"We could go out next Sunday, maybe. My parents are going on some trip to Cleveland on the train."

Sam stretched full length and studied the tip of his worn boot. "Lots of people will be gone that day. We probably won't even be missed. Don't be disappointed, though," he cautioned the younger boy, "if we don't find anything. I saw him out Fowles Road direction the other day — with a mangy dog."

Sam's warning failed to dampen Jake's enthusiasm. "Let's meet in back of Union School at one o'clock. Church will be over for everyone and —"

Sam sat up abruptly. "Oh-oh. Here comes trouble." He motioned to a tall figure climbing up the hillside, planting one foot after another resolutely, as if he could hardly wait to arrive at his destination. At once, the boys scrambled for their yokes and buckets. One of Chris's buckets broke loose and rolled downhill, coming to rest at the foot of a spindly poplar near the path of the oncoming visitor.

Purple-faced, James Janek towered over the water boys. His thick lips sneered. "You wretched, good-for-nothing scalawags. Men are slaving away down there, throats caked with dust while you loll about in the shade with no concern for the job you're hired to do." Heaving Chris's bucket that he'd grabbed on his way up the hill, he watched it land just close enough to the boys to frighten them even more. "What a bunch of no-good, lazy rascals." Janek hoisted his dust-coated trousers and whipped off the sweat-sodden bandana from around his neck. While he paused in his ranting and mopped his face, the cowering boys clambered up the hillside, dragging their yokes and buckets, desperate to get out of earshot of the raging Janek.

The quarryman kept on bellowing, his fierce words ringing through the trees. "I'll report you to Ballard, you dumbheads. You deserve to be fired." He shook a grimy fist at the retreating boys.

"Some days I'd like to get fired," Jake said. Out of Janek's line of vision, behind a stand of scrubby pine trees, the boys had halted to reposition their equipment. "I'd rather work at the hardware store, sweeping floors and sorting nails," he added.

"You know there's always work at the quarries, though," Sam said in a practical tone. He was ready to start up the hill. "If you work at a store, you get let go the minute business gets bad."

Slowly, the band of water boys snaked their way up the remainder of the eighty-five steps to refill their buckets from the deep, cool well. Then they would head back down to the floor of the quarry to cries of both grateful relief and scornful contempt from the quarrymen. Hasseling the water boys traditionally provided amusement for some quarrymen, and James Janek often spearheaded this diversion. His own memories of life as a lowly water boy rankled indelibly in his memory. Now, as a skilled and fearless guyer, it was his turn to hand out the derision to the underlings.

Slipping in the side door of the City Hotel, Rose heaved a sigh of relief to see that Mrs. Longwood had stepped away from her usual post at the desk in the lobby and was pulling aside the portieres from the long lobby windows. The sun's noontime glare flooded the room, waking a rumpled, bald-headed man snoozing in a corner. "We rent rooms for sleeping in, Mr. Curtis—$1.50 a night." Despite her curtness, Jedediah Curtis knew that Mrs. Longwood was only teasing in her blunt way. A permanent resident at the hotel since his wife Jenny died, Jedediah spent much of his days in the hotel lobby or walking around the Triangle, just to combat loneliness.

Her hands trembling, Rose laid the bankbook and money pouch on the hotelkeeper's desk. She dreaded to think what Mrs. Longwood would have to say if she had seen her talking with Stephen. Hadn't she practically forbade her to see him? Rose's family depended on her wages from the hotel, and she dared not lose her job by angering Mrs. Longwood.

She hurried to the kitchen and began measuring flour for the noon meal's batch of biscuits. Counting the cupfuls, almost aloud, she poured the flour into a huge crockery bowl and began to cut in the lard. Like a whiplash, her mind kept jumping back to the sunny scene on the Triangle and her surprise meeting with Stephen.

She thought she sounded like an idiot. She probably didn't make him understand why she doesn't want him to come to her house—that all her neighbors and friends would be so embarrassed to have him come there—and probably angry with her for bringing him there, to our homely neighborhood? But—an entire Sunday afternoon with him will be worth any unkind thing that anybody says.

Mrs. Longwood apparently had little time to be concerned about Rose on that day. A larger-than-usual lunch crowd, still somewhat in a holiday mood, occupied her at the cash register. Then two nattily dressed salesmen from different furniture companies began vying for her attention. She had made it known that she was seriously considering buying much-needed lobby furniture. Obviously delighted in the salesmen's politeness and courtly behavior toward her, her strident voice echoed around the now nearly empty lobby. She was prodding each of them to describe why his chairs were more durable, his sofas more inviting than the other's.

"You don't really expect me to believe that the springs in your chairs will last twice as long as his, Mr. Fischer? Now rea-ally." Mrs. Longwood waved her ever-present fan at first one salesman, then the other, fluttering her eyelashes in attempted coyness. "Show me some proof, both of you! Who else has bought from you, and how has the stuff held up?"

The salesmen donned their derbies, practically in unison, picked up their heavy sample cases, headed for the door. "She's one tough number," one muttered.

"Hey, you wanna have a drink?" the other asked him.

Smiling, Mrs. Longwood watched the pair detour from the lobby into the adjoining tavern.

The dusky sanctuary of St. Adalbert's wrapped Rose in welcome comfort after her tiring workday at the hotel. She looked forward to Monday afternoons when she came to tidy up the church after Sunday Mass, part of her tithe to her church. Latching the door softly behind her, Rose stepped to the votives, crossed herself, and paused to light a candle, whispering a prayer for the father she could scarcely remember.

Just as she had hoped, organist Karel Porubovich was still practicing as he did each weekday afternoon. Aside from his lamp near the organ, the only other light came from the slanted rays of the afternoon sun that streamed through the saffron-colored windows, catching dust motes dancing lazily. A thin, musky curtain of incense hung in the air. Resonant tones from the organ swelled and filled every corner of the cavernous sanctuary. Enthralled with the music's majesty—she recognized "How Lovely is Thy Dwelling Place" from Brahms' *Requiem*. Rose sank, relaxed, into a back pew. Since she was small, she had loved the organ music at church. "It tickles my tummy," she used to laugh when the low notes rumbled and nearly shook the building. Now, having heard organist Porubovich's repertoire all her life, she had learned the names of the works and the composers. One of her favorite daydreams pictured herself seated in a concert hall someday, listening to a symphony orchestra. Today, she envisioned the person seated next to her, who had heretofore been just a shadow. Stephen Ballard leaned his dark head toward hers and whispered — *Stop!* She doesn't even know if he likes classical music. But surely, he —

Sudddenly, Rose realized that the organ music had ceased, and Mr. Porubovich was gathering up his sheets of music. Rose sprang, moving quickly among the pews, replacing hymnals in racks, picking up lost buttons and hatpins and a few loose coins that she would drop in the poor box. From a cupboard in the vestibule, she pulled two new tall tapers and headed toward the altar. Rose waved goodbye to the organist as he left and, crossing herself again, set about replacing the tapers as she did each week. The partially burned ones would be melted down by the ladies of the Altar Committee and remolded into long tapers once again. The ladies insisted upon pristine, tall tapers for each Sunday Mass. She polished the candlesticks, careful not to touch the cross and other items on the altar reserved especially for the priest.

Turning onto Pulaski Street, where she lived with her mother Sophie and brother George, Rose tried to see her neighborhood as Stephen Ballard might see it if she allowed him to come here. The street was little more than a wide trail, but even the streets on

Berea's fashionable South Side were not paved, she reminded herself. Here, the houses were one-story, a few two-story, gabled, mostly frame, squarish and neat. A number had been built by the parents of the present occupants, who had come over from Poland and found work in the quarries. Many of the men, including Rose's grandfather, had come alone, living in boarding houses in Berea and saving their money until they could afford to bring their families over. Some of them lived in "company houses" for a time until they were able, with justifiable pride, to move their families into houses they had built. Owning their own homes was a great source of pride with these immigrant families. Rose was proud of their home that Grandfather Rosckiewicz had built, and she happily helped her mother keep it neat and clean. Recently, she had sewed new curtains for the parlor from material she had saved for from her tips at the hotel.

She sidestepped two dust-caked boys playing mumble peg. One eyed her with a wide, toothy grin. "I saw you Saturday night, dancing with James. You dance good together." He rubbed his face with a dusty hand. "Are you going to get married to him?"

"Don't you know you shouldn't ask ladies personal questions?" Smiling, Rose gave the boy's cap brim a playful tug to show him she really wasn't angry and headed toward her cousin Anna's house. She had time to stop in before going on down the street to her own house. In the pit of her stomach was a gnawing dread, the knowledge that she would have to share with Anna her daring plan to spend next Sunday with Stephen. She should not have been so bold. Of course, her mother will hear about it. Even the small children know everything about everybody on our street. And George will be furious. The knot in her stomach tightened as she neared Anna's blue-painted door. When she lifted the black iron knocker, she noticed for the second time that day that her hand was trembling.

Six

"Rozmary, you're wearing your best dress on that train trip?" Sophie Wolinski rested her stout body against the door frame of Rose's tiny bedroom and looked at her daughter with a mother's critical eye. The cornflower blue of Rose's simple shirtwaist matched her eyes, and her thick honey-blonde hair, loosened from her weekday braid and piled on top of her head, gave her a regal air. The fringed silk shawl draped over her shoulders added a bit more elegance.

Rose turned slowly, assessing her looks as best she could in the cloudy mirror that hung next to her bed. Her real reason for adding the shawl was to detract a bit from her shoulders, which she felt were too broad compared to her narrow waist. But there wasn't anything she could do to disguise the slight gap between her front two teeth. Even though Mama said it was hardly noticeable, it troubled her when she let herself think about it. She sighed and pinned a cluster of silk roses at her throat. Anna had made them from scraps she'd saved at her job at Mrs. Avis Meacham's, Fashionable Milliner. Tacked next to the mirror a newspaper clipping advertised today's excursion to the Arcade. FOR A MEMORABLE OCCASION — the headline declared. Rose was picturing Stephen's strong, erect figure, and she could almost hear his even voice saying —

Her mother's voice filled the room. "Roza, didn't you hear me? You're surely not going to wear your Aunt Nell's shawl. On a train trip? Maybe you'll lose it and then have nothing to remember her by, God rest her dear soul." With a worried glance at the crucifix at the head of Rose's bed, Sophie crossed herself, her smooth brow furrowed in lines of worry.

Whirling around, Rose, who stood a head-and-a-half taller than her plump mother, smiled and said, "Don't worry, Mama. You know, I'm very careful with things." With that she kissed her mother's warm cheek and picked up her bag and the cream-colored parasol trimmed with a blue grosgrain ribbon, another remnant find at Mrs. Meacham's. As she waltzed out the door to meet Anna and Viktor, she feared her mother might see the telltale pounding of her heart through the soft material of her shirtwaist. Of course, she planned to tell her mother about being with Stephen on the train and at the Arcade. She just hoped she could get home in time to tell her before someone else did. But no one else that she knew of from her neighborhood was going. Anna and Viktor had won their tickets or else they couldn't afford to go. Rose had simply said to her mother that someone at work had offered her a ticket. Not altogether an untruth.

Pulaski Street lay under a cover of Sunday afternoon slow motion; it was the only day of rest for the quarrymen. Mass was long since over and families had gathered around their tables, joining hands in thanks for their many blessings and their Sunday dinners. Now wives were hanging out their dishcloths and drawing long breaths. Sunday afternoon offered a brief respite from their work also, but on Monday morning, after they'd cooked breakfast for their families, many would head to work in the marshy onion fields around murky Lake Abram. There they would earn $1.00 to $1.50 a day, almost as much as their quarrymen husbands.

Today young fathers played catch with their sons or staked tomatoes in gardens or repaired loose shutters or boards in their fences. Single men, like George and James, were off fishing in the Rocky River or Lake Abram. Pavel Prohaska, the oldest man in the neighborhood, leaned against a beech tree in his front yard, coaxing plaintive Polish folk tunes from his buttonbox accordion. If people stopped to listen, he would tell them over and over how he had played these same tunes on the long-ago voyage across the Atlantic. He had lulled babies to sleep and lifted the spirits of his sea-weary shipmates with music from the homeland they were leaving.

Anna, in a rose-print waist and a watered silk skirt, and her husband Viktor, still wearing his Sunday church suit and twirling a straw boater with a checkered band, were waiting for Rose in front of their trim, hollyhock-bordered house. They had taken their two little daughters, Ruth and Frieda, to Anna's Aunt Ivana's house for the afternoon while they went on this very special excursion. As they saw Rose's graceful figure coming toward them, Viktor remarked, "She looks mighty pretty today. Wonder if she's meeting someone special."

Anna turned away to pick off a few dead hollyhock blossoms, hoping her husband did not see her knowing smile. She knew she would have to admit to having a part in Stephen and Rose's plan, but she would do it later. She knew how to handle Viktor. He was a true romantic at heart, and besides, he admired Mr. Ballard. "He's a prince of a man," Viktor had said a number of times since Stephen Ballard had taken over the quarries. He respected him for his even temper and his fair method of handling the quarrymen.

"He'll be tested soon though," Viktor had recently remarked at the Carpathian Village tavern when some of the quarrymen were discussing the union activity. "This union thing is bound to break loose." Viktor and his friends, most of whom were married with families, were not part of the pro-union group that

George Wolinski and James Janek were spearheading.

The Cleveland Berea Railway train jostled across the Superior Viaduct into downtown Cleveland. Sitting next to the window, Rose peered down at the winding loops of the Cuyahoga River, thinking how smart the Indians were who named it: *crooked*, she had learned in school. Today, all was quiet in the steel mills that lined the river's banks, but the whole valley looked like a giant stage set, ready to spring into action when, in a few short hours, the players — the steelworkers — would pour onto the scene. Rose's only other trip to Cleveland was last year when she and her mother and brother went to the Polish National Singing Concert that took place every two years. She still shivered when she remembered those vibrant Polish voices raised in the powerful anthems of their native land. Even the massive rafters of the Gothic St. Stanislaus Church had seemed to tremble.

Although the view out the window was exciting, nothing could equal Rose's pure joy at Stephen's presence beside her. True, some passengers' heads had turned when the two of them had mounted the steps of the train; there was no mistaking that they had planned to make the trip together. Stephen had firmly but gently handed her up the steps and then led the way to a seat for the two of them.

Now Stephen's voice broke into Rose's thoughts. She heard him saying. "I'd consider it an honor, sir, to serve on the safety committee." While the scenery flying past had absorbed Rose, he'd been talking earnestly with Councilman John Sterling, who was seated across the aisle with his bird-like wife Eliza.

When Stephen turned away from the councilman. Rose caught her breath as he leaned nearer to her to point out the Standard Oil Refinery in the valley below. "That's Mr. Rockefeller's. It's partly his money that built the Arcade where we're going."

Rose kept trying to keep her heart from pounding so. She tried to ignore Mrs. Sterling's darting attempts to see around Stephen and get a better look at her. Perhaps she didn't recognize Rose without her braids and apron. Rose stifled a giggle, and Stephen looked at her, as if puzzled.

"I can't tell you right now," she whispered, "but I will later." Her smooth, oval face flushed slightly with embarrassment as she turned back to face the window. Just then the train lurched around a curve, and Stephen's shoulder and his thigh pressed against hers. "What industry is that over there?" Rose pointed out the window, trying her best to make her voice sound normal.

Able now to straighten in his seat, Stephen replied, "That's the Cleveland Rolling Mill. A lot of Polish people work there since they helped break a strike some years ago. They were such good workers that many of them were hired on to stay." As he spoke of a strike, Stephen's expression grew somber. Then, as if determined not to let worries about the quarries spoil his day, he hastily changed the subject. "We should be getting to Public Square in a few minutes. Then it's just a short walk up Euclid Avenue to the Arcade. It runs the entire block between Euclid and Superior."

Rose did not miss the shadow that crossed Stephen's finely chiseled features. She had heard bits and pieces about a possible strike when she was serving at the hotel. And hadn't her own brother stood up there on the bandstand with that silly banner at the Summerfest and told quarrymen to come to a meeting about the union?

Rose turned just then to flash Stephen an impish grin, her eyes shining with delight. "Oh, I do think it's going to be a lovely afternoon."

Standing just inside the Arcade's massive brass doors, Rose felt as if her feet were planted in wet clay. For as far as she could see stretched four levels of golden-filigreed balconies. "Like yards and yards and yards of golden lace," she exclaimed.

Looking up, she saw the ceiling of the Arcade rise to a vaulted skylight. Sunlight reflecting through hundreds of panes of opaque glass shed a golden aura upon the gaily clad visitors, who were strolling, mostly in pairs, along the tiered levels. The ground floor shop windows vied for displays of the most elegant merchandise imaginable. At the second level, small tables and chairs offered spots for strollers to rest and have a root beer or an ice cream sundae. Hundreds of American flags festooned the top level.

"It reminds me of a picture my grandmother had of a great hall in a castle in Poland. Stephen," his name was coming more easily now, "this is magnificent." A bit breathless, Rose clapped her hands to her mouth.

"There probably aren't usually this many flags," Stephen remarked, looking up. "I believe they are hung because of the Cleveland Centennial this year."

Stephen had only seen the Arcade once himself. Several weeks ago he'd had occasion to visit the office of an equipment manufacturer located on the top tier of the Arcade. Fascinated with its concept and construction, he'd spent as much time there that working day as he dared and, as was his habit, read everything about it that he could find. He was delighted to return so soon.

"It took a bridge builder from Detroit to erect this structure," he told Rose. "No firm from Cleveland would even bid on it."

"Come, let's look in the shop windows." Rose grasped Stephen's hand without thinking. She was relieved to be off the train and feeling that they could seem alone together in this massive place. Others from their train had scattered and gone their various ways. When Stephen felt her strong, capable hand on his, a sensation of warmth and contentment swept over him.

The brass-encased show windows held more finery than Rose had ever even dreamed of — supple kid gloves, hats with dipping ostrich plumes, gossamer-like blouses with huge puffed and billowing sleeves.

Standing before a window filled with hats, Rose was trying to memorize details that Anna might use in her work at Mrs. Meacham's. Stephen waited patiently, enjoying Rose's enthusiasm and wanting her to savor every moment. Then he turned briefly to watch people milling through levels of the Arcade. On a mezzanine toward the Superior Avenue end of the Arcade, a group of stringed musicians concluded the program of classical music that had been floating over the strolling visitors. A nervous, penguin-like conductor with flapping arms bowed to the spattered applause the cavernous Arcade seemed to swallow. Then another man joined him, gesturing up the steps with a baton. Stephen watched curiously, hoping the musicians would resume. He enjoyed classical music whenever he had opportunity to hear it though, truthfully, he didn't know one composer from another except Brahms and Mozart; those were the two that he'd grown up hearing his mother play on the squarish Story & Clark piano back in Stone City. As more people began drifting toward the mezzanine, Stephen pulled out his watch.

Taking Rose's elbow, he said, "We have a real treat in store. The Cleveland Singers Club will perform at three o'clock."

Rose turned away from a shop window where she'd been memorizing the lines and trimmings of a dress. The nervous conductor was arranging a group of some forty dark-suited men on the two levels of steps above the mezzanine. Stephen and Rose moved as close as they could in the crowd that pressed in on either side. Allowing Rose to step in front of him, Stephen could see over the top of her blond head. Just then he fought back a wild urge to put his arms around her waist, right here in this crowd, and pull her close to him.

She turned to him to ask, "Do you see Anna and Viktor anywhere? I hope they get to hear this." Stephen caught sight of Viktor across the mezzanine-turned stage and nodded. Rose, standing on tiptoe, tried but couldn't see her cousin. Voices of the crowd were dropping now to a lower pitch as the string players resumed their seats. The other man Stephen had seen with a baton was mounting a podium before the Singers Club. Using a pitch pipe, he was putting them through their warm-up exercises.

The Singers' Club, first organized and sponsored by the YWCA in 1890, had become in only a few years quite an elite, sought-after group for Sunday afternoon concerts. Their repertoire ranged from classical to popular tunes, from Brahms to the "Battle Hymn of the Republic," and men of various ages made up the group. As the stringed musicians broke into "America," voices of the crowd joined in to soar to the peak of the Arcade's vaulted roof. The final note seemed to hang there like a single invisible star.

The program began with some light selections from Stephen Foster, then presented spirited selections from Gilbert and Sullivan and highlighted the Swedish composer Sibelius' newest composition *Finlandia*. Brahms' stirring *Academic Festival Overture* concluded the program. At the opening bars, Stephen heard Rose catch her breath. Stealing a glance at her face, he caught her mouthing the words with the Singers—though they were singing in Latin.

Gaudeamus igitur,
Dum iuventes sumus,
Post iucundam iuventutem,
Post molestam senectutem
Nos habebit humus.

Vita nostra brevis est,
Brevi finietur;
Venit mors velociter
Rapit nos atrociter;
Nemini parcetur.

Afterwards, Rose explained, "I knew that song because we learned it in eighth grade. Sister Christina loved it. That was the only time we ever learned anything in any other language—except Polish." When she translated the words, Stephen laughed and said, "I like the beginning, anyway. 'Let us rejoice, therefore, while we are young.' The rest about old age and death doesn't seem to fit with that spirited music."

Rose laughed. "The rest of it does get pretty morbid. 'After our youth, after a troublesome old age, The ground will hold us.'"

Her heart raced. Everything was converging upon her—the thrill of the music, the majesty of this wonderland of a place, the nearness of this attractive man who had sought her out from dozens of eager young women in Berea.

As they headed back to the parade of shop windows, Stephen saw George Worthington and his wife approaching—Worthington, immaculate in pearl gray and his freshly trimmed chin whiskers, Mrs. Worthington in a cloud of mauve chiffon. Having once spent a very stuffy dinner hour at their home, Stephen would have been just as happy not to meet them today. But since the Cleveland Stone Company was one of the sponsors of today's event, seeing the Worthingtons here was no great surprise.

"Good afternoon, Ballard. Glad to see you enjoying a Sunday outing." George Worthington nodded as his eyes flicked over Rose with perceptible interest.

"Mr. Worthington, Mrs. Worthington. May I present Miss Rose Wolinski?"

Rose smiled and nodded graciously. Truth be told, she felt as if she should curtsey after Stephen's so-proper introduction. To think, she was meeting George Worthington, president of the Cleveland Stone Company!

"The Singers were splendid, didn't you think?" Worthington carelessly twirled the carnation he'd removed from his lapel.

"They were outstanding," Stephen replied quickly. "This entire event is a very fine gesture for the Company—"

Mrs. Worthington, who had given up surveying Rose through her lorgnette, making Rose feel as if she were a display of pears at the market, was craning her chiffon-swathed neck, searching the crowd. "George, there's Sarah Wilton and her husband. We should greet them. He's the new president of the Commerce Bank."

"I'm acquainted with Malcolm Wilton, my dear. But as you wish—Good seeing you, Ballard. Goodbye, Miss—"

"Wolinski," Stephen reminded him distinctly.

George Worthington spoke directly to Stephen in parting. "I'll phone you tomorrow morning at ten o'clock sharp for an up-to-date report on the union situation. Be in your office at that time."

"Yes, sir. I'll manage that," Stephen answered easily. He refused to let George Worthington rattle him.

"You and the young lady enjoy the rest of the afternoon." Mr. Worthington, still twisting the battered carnation, gave Rose another curious look. His wife nodded as if she had a stiff neck, and they swept off in an aura of rosewater and expensive pipe tobacco.

"Of course, my name told them I am Polish. He had to know I have family working in the quarries," Rose declared. She was sipping a root beer while she and Stephen sat at one of the tables for two on the first balcony.

Stephen heard her voice, but he was watching her capable, firm hands on the glass. "So?" He searched her questioning blue eyes for some clue to her distress.

"Well, what do you suppose your employer thinks of you keeping company with a Polish girl?" She set her empty glass down defiantly. "And that wife of his! If she'd looked down her nose any farther at me, her eyes would have dropped off. Neither of them said a word *to* me. They just looked right *through* me." Rose's face was flushed, her speech animated.

Stephen took her hands firmly in his. "Rose, your brother works for the Cleveland Stone Company, and your father and his father before him worked in the quarries. It's hard work, but it's honest work. Without quarrymen, there'd be no jobs for a Mr. Worthington—or for the likes of me either, for that matter." He searched her face—that lovely face that was beginning now to replace Sally Westin's in his thoughts and dreams—to be certain she was following what he was trying to say. "People aren't always going to be only with people who work where they do or whose names sound the same as theirs."

Rose's eyes darted to the passing parade of well-dressed people, people who seemed to know they fit in this gloriously ornate place with its tantalizing shop windows, its aura of wealth and beauty.

Looking down in her lap, she began smoothing wrinkles from the soft folds of her skirt.

"More than anyone in town, Rose," Stephen's voice dropped low and earnest, "you've made me feel welcome. You've helped me forget disappointment and endure loneliness—and believe me, I've spent some lonely, sad Sunday afternoons. Seeing your smile each morning at the hotel helps me start my day out looking for the best in the people I have to deal with. This afternoon has been a carefree, pleasant time, and I've been able to put anything that's troubling or distressing out of my mind." He hesitated, realizing his words were tumbling out. When she still didn't respond, Stephen said softly, "Can we have more Sundays like this, Rose? Please say yes—that you enjoy being with me."

Swallowing hard, for she could hardly speak, Rose squeezed his hand, ignoring the strolling passersby. In fact, while he was speaking she had virtually forgotten her surroundings. It seemed that she and

Stephen and their little table were floating, completely detached from the excitement and the milling crowd.

His earnest brown eyes met hers with a look so forthright and sincere that she felt a tremor slither down her spine. She didn't know whether it was a thrill of delight in his feelings for her or if it was fear for what a relationship with this man might bring.

"Stephen, I—I do enjoy being with you, and I thank you for this—this golden afternoon." She looked about, once again conscious of others nearby—of elegant skirts sweeping near her chair, a mix of low voices in intimate conversation, notes from the stringed musicians filtering across the gilded Arcade.

She met his gaze squarely, saying, "I've never been one to be afraid to do something I wanted to do if it seemed right, no matter what others thought. I graduated from high school when many people thought it was foolish for a Polish girl to do that. Then my mama and brother didn't want me to go to work at the hotel. But I did—partly to be around lots of different folks. Oh, it's not that I don't respect my family and my neighbors, you know—"

Stephen nodded. "I know, Rose. You want to stretch and grow a bit?"

She nodded. "But I know there may be trouble for both of us, Stephen. People won't understand—not your people, nor my people." She shook her head slightly, and her face clouded.

Stephen stood up, helping her to her feet. "You said it all: 'If it seems right.' Being together is what seems right to me."

Rose's heart seemed it would burst, that she could never be any happier. Yet, she couldn't bear any more of this conversation. She took Stephen's arm and looked up at him impishly. "Do you think an ice cream sundae would be bad on top of root beer?"

Seven

Union School playground lay forsaken in the dusty stillness of early Sunday afternoon, and the building's windows stared down at it like sightless eyes.

Sam Mikolak and Chris Janovick had veered off Front Street and were plodding across the playground. Sam gave a push to a makeshift rope swing drooping from a beech tree and dropped his knapsack on the ground.

"You really think Jake will show up?" Chris asked.

"He will, but he'll most likely have to sneak off," Sam answered. "His folks are mighty strict." Sam kept swinging the rope carelessly, a bit higher each time. "Shoot, my folks don't ask no questions. They're just glad to get me out of the house on Sunday afternoons. They don't usually do nothin'. Surprised me they went on that train ride." He gave the swing a last push.

Chris was whistling to an unseen phoebe up in the maple tree. "Fee-bee, Fee-bee," they whistled back and forth to each other. "Phoebes are noisy, but they're hard to see," Chris remarked.

"That's because they're so drab and — hey, there's Jake now. But who's that with him?" Sam squinted at the two boys trudging over the grassy bank that bordered the playground. Alongside Jacob waddled a tubby boy with flame-orange hair. He was wearing a striped shirtwaist and short pants and licking a lollipop that he promptly dropped in the dust when he reached Sam and Chris.

"This is my cousin, Whitney Prentiss," Jacob rushed to explain. "His family is visiting today from West View." Jacob scowled sideways at Whitney who by now was picking the dust off his lollipop. "The only way I could come was if I'd bring him." Sam shot a quick look at Whitney and then at Chris, who shrugged resignedly.

"Well, Jacob, you're the one what had the idea for us to go find Fast Jack. But just remember if Whitney gets tired and wants to go back, you'll have to take him by yourself." He looked at Whitney's stubby legs sticking out of the short pants. "Can you run fast, Whitney?"

"I can run fast as the wind," Whitney declared. Flinging the lollipop down, he began trotting toward the other side of the playground.

"Come on back," his cousin shouted. Whitney

turned around, a puzzled frown on his face, and started back.

"Let's get going," Sam said. "Time's a-wastin'." He picked up his knapsack and swung it over his shoulder. "I've got water for us and a few other goodies."

The nearer the four boys got to Lake Abram, the marshier the ground became. The mucky land was the reason that onions, as well as celery, grew so well here. Thousands of tons of onions were shipped out all over the country from these fields every year. Tilling this soil was tricky. Sometimes the horses got mired in the muck in spite of the burlap that was placed over their hooves. More than once, a horse panicked when this happened and had to be shot.

Dense woods of walnut, beech, butternut, oak, and hemlock ringed the lake. On a number of clearings stood curing sheds with open slats and onion storage houses. The air, heavy with the pungent odor of the mucky soil, pricked the boys' nostrils as they tramped along the mucky bank. Cattails and dog-lilies lined the edge of the water. Since the other side of the lake was the best fishing area, the boys had purposely planned their route to avoid it. Besides, Fast Jack's place wouldn't be near where a lot of people came to fish.

"Look at that big frog," Jacob cried. *Ker-plash*. The frog disappeared. "Whitney, you quit throwing stones at critters. How would you like it if somebody threw a stone into your house?"

"I wish I still worked out here," said Chris. "I liked it a lot better than the old quarry, in spite of the muck. At least, there aren't bossy people like James Janek around." Only young children worked in the onion fields alongside their mothers, on their hands and knees during the growing season, pulling weeds and thinning out the excess onion plants. After his tenth birthday last March, Chris had gone to work as a water boy in the quarry.

"My father says that James Janek isn't gonna to be happy until he gets all of the quarrymen to join the union," said Sam. "And then there'll probably be a strike, even if a few don't join."

"What happens when there's a strike?" Jacob asked. He was listening but keeping a wary eye out for snakes. There were a lot of them out here. He could just imagine what Whitney would do if he'd see a snake. Truth be told, Jacob didn't much care for them himself.

"Nobody works. Nobody gets paid. 'Til the workers and the owners can agree." Sam was glad his father talked to him about these things. He felt a little more important than just a water boy. Mr. Ballard liked him too, he could tell, by the way the superintendent would get that warm, kindly shine in his eyes when they would talk.

"Wa-a-it for me!" Whitney wailed. He had lagged about forty paces behind the other three, and a wild grapevine had snared his foot, throwing him down. Black muck streaked his shirtwaist, and each of his plump legs bore a patchwork of angry scratches. He was a pathetic sight.

"Go get him, Jake, and we'll rest a bit." Sam dropped down and began rummaging in his knapsack. "We should have realized he couldn't go at our pace." He brought out a canteen and passed it to Chris. "Did you ever hear about that worker out here—a man, sorta old—he picked up a jug he found at the end of a row of onions? He thought he'd found somebody's half-full jug of whiskey." Sam chuckled. He gloried in telling stories to his younger friends. "Well, he looked around to be sure nobody was close by, then he up and drained that jug."

"Did he get drunk?" Chris asked, handing Sam the canteen.

"Drunk? Sam echoed. "I guess not." He took a mouthful of water and spit into the lake. "I heard he was as green around the gills as a seasick sailor. He'd a' died if the foreman, Malcolm Smith, hadn't 'a tore into town with him in a buggy to Doc McKelvey's. Seems like that 'whiskey' was formaldehyde they use to treat the seeds so the onion louse won't eat on 'em. That dumb worker owed his life to Doc McKelvey for gettin' him to throw up that poisonous stuff."

By the time they reached the north end of Lake Abram, the boys were growing discouraged at not seeing any signs of a hut or a cabin. As they left the onion fields behind, their path veered toward Podunk Swamp. This area lay north and a little west of Lake Abram, and the boys knew very little about it. They walked carefully, single-file, like young Indian braves, on a narrow strip of ground next to the swamp.

"Stop!" Sam commanded. He sniffed the air around him. " You can't smell the onions any more, but what's that smell?"

"It's fire," Jake said, scrunching his face as he looked toward the dense woods beyond.

"I don't see any smoke—" Whitney said.

"It's back in there someplace," Sam declared. "Let's head into the woods."

They pushed on, even Whitney. Unknown to Sam and Chris, Jacob had whispered to Whitney, "If you don't keep up, we'll leave you here forever in the swamp—and it's full of snakes."

The acrid smell of smoke was sharper now. Sam kept spitting into the brush. "That smoke sure is funny. It almost *tastes* bad. Don't smell like any wood fire I ever smelled before."

"Maybe Fast Jack's back here cookin' him a wolf. That's what he lives on, they say." Jacob was determined that Fast Jack would be part of this adventure.

Just then an eerie howl erupted from deep in the woods. Jacob's face paled, his eyes round as silver dollars. "See," he cried, "he's probably killing one now for his dinner."

"Naw, that's just an old coyote," Sam protested. "Don't believe those stories 'bout wolves. There ain't been one killed out here for years. Jack gets his food from behind the City Hotel—what Mrs. Longwood sets out there for him."

Sounds of the woods surrounded the boys with mystery and loneliness—a pileated woodpecker boring like a jackhammer, squirrels chattering angrily, the gentle humming of bees working the mounds of trumpet vine, and in the far distance, a haunting hoot of an owl. Patches of metallic blue sky flashed through the dense canopy of pine and oak trees. Hardly any sun was visible now, and the woods were growing less friendly by the minute.

"Stop!" Sam ordered, holding up his hand in warning. "I heard a voice."

He leaped up on a huge trunk of a fallen tree and peered ahead. Chris could see Sam's knees trembling the slightest bit, and his voice had a jagged edge.

"There's a shack yonder. That's where the smoke's a-comin' from—the voice too, probably."

"Lemme see, lemme see," Whitney pouted, kicking the tree trunk, nearly causing Sam to lose his footing.

Jacob grabbed his cousin around his chunky middle. "Shut up, you little fool. If there's smoke, there's somebody there. We want to see them, but not let them see us." He pushed Whitney down into a dense patch of mayapples.

"Baw-w-w." Whitney began to wail loudly. "I want to go home. Don't want to see no shack."

"Shut him up, Jake," Sam hissed. "Someone's coming out the door right now." He shifted his weight to keep his balance on the tree trunk. As the sagging plank door of the shack opened, a figure emerged. Beneath a rumpled felt hat was a craggy-faced man with a beard stained with decades of tobacco juice. Sam couldn't see his eyes, but he felt sure they'd be harsh and steely. The man's clothes hung on him like potato sacks and had blackened holes in them. He walked to the edge of the clearing with a decided limp and looked out into the woods in the boys' direction.

By this time Jacob had his hand clasped over Whitney's blubbering mouth, but the boy kept kicking his chubby legs in protest.

"Sit on 'im, Chris," Sam whispered. "You cut that out, Whitney." Sam continued watching. "There must be two of 'em. He's talking to someone inside."

Hardly were the words out of Sam's mouth when the man with the seamy face ducked into the shack and then back out again. He hoisted a shotgun and fired three times into the air, the sound ricocheting through the woods.

"If there be anybody out there in them woods," he bellowed, his misshapen face the color of an eggplant, "let this be a warning to ye." He paused, letting the echoing shots die away. "Stay away from this cabin.

This here is private propity." He spat out the last two words as if they were sour grapes.

"We'd better go, Sam," Jacob whispered, still muzzling the struggling Whitney.

"Wait, I want to see what he's — he's got a table set up there, outside, and he's pounding or punching something. I can't tell —" Sam squinted harder, trying to make out the man's actions.

"B-but he's got a gun," Chris murmured. "He ain't no Fast Jack anyhow."

Sam gave in and jumped down from the tree trunk.

The hike back was a century long, it seemed, and the sun cast long violet shadows across Lake Abram by the time they reached it. The three explorers, dragging Whitney in tow, headed toward town and their respective homes. At Front Street, Jacob and Whitney headed toward Adalbert Street where the Zielinskis lived.

"You think you want to come exploring with us again sometime, Whitney?" Chris laughed, rumpling the boy's red hair and chucking him under his plump chin.

Whitney looked down at his ruined striped shirt-waist and his shoes that were caked with muck. "My m-mama will k-kill me," was all he could say.

At the hoot of a train whistle, Sam and Chris dashed for a pile of grindstones across from Union Station. Hunkered down behind the stones, they waited to watch the passengers step off from the excursion train as it made a stop at Depot Street.

"I'll watch 'til my folks get off," Sam said, "then I can still beat 'em home, running across back lots."

"Look," Chris said, "there's Councilman Sterling. He looks half-asleep. Probably missed his pint of brew and his Sunday afternoon nap."

"Hey, there's Mr. Ballard—and who's that with him?. . . Why—it's my cousin Rose," exclaimed Sam.

"You mean Rose what works at the hotel?" Chris asked. "She sure looks pretty—and see her looking up at Mr. Ballard and laughing—like they're all lovey-dovey."

"I've never seen Mr. Ballard smile so much either," said Sam. "Oh-oh, there are my folks, right behind 'em. See you tomorrow, Chris. Don't tell nobody about what we saw in the woods."

Sam dashed home, leaping across carefully tended flower gardens and shushing friendly dogs along the way, while Chris headed on to his home on Berea Street.

"Walk slower, Viktor," Anna Mikolak scolded her husband. "I loved seeing the Arcade, but my feet are used to these shoes only for sitting and kneeling in church." Anna kept her eyes straight ahead on the erect figure of Stephen Ballard with the laughing Rose on his arm. She'd hung back deliberately to give them a few last minutes together.

"Why do I think, Anna," Viktor chided his wife, "that you knew Rose and Mr. Ballard planned this outing?" He didn't wait for her answer. "What will your Aunt Sophie have to say if the superintendent of the quarries shows up on her doorstep?"

Anna watched, mischief dancing in her dark eyes, as Stephen and Rose turned down Pulaski Street.

"Well, Viktor," she said firmly, "you know how Aunt Sophie always says Rose is an exceptional girl? Well then, she shouldn't be surprised that her daughter has attracted a very exceptional man."

As Rose let herself in the front door of her home, she was surprised there was no lamp burning. Late-day shadows filled every corner of the tiny box-like parlor, and a nameless feeling squeezed her heart. At first she thought it was the amazing echo of Stephen's voice as he said at her front gate, "We can have times like this again and again, Rose." But now she sensed another presence in the room. Her mother? But Sophie went on Sunday afternoons to her sister Ivana's to sew. Anyway, why would she be sitting in the dark if she were home? Rose moved toward the unlighted lamp, barely able to see its outline in the dim room.

A rough, menacing voice cut through the stillness. "Well, aren't you the fine lady, though, keeping company with the quarry superintendent, no less?" Her brother George's hulking figure stepped toward her out of the shadows. "What do you suppose he wants with the likes of you? A Polander, a serving girl in a hotel? It's not hard to figure out . . ."

Rose clapped her hands over her ears. "I won't have you making something cheap out of my friendship with Stephen. He—" She stopped short.

"Oh, Stephen, is it? When he's Mr. Ballard to everyone else of our people?" George was snarling, mocking now, his words hitting Rose like small, sharp stones. "You can't give the time of day to James Janek, one of your own, who'd marry you one day. Now I see why." George's meaty fingers clutched the back of his mother's rocking chair and caused it to tilt at a crazy angle.

"George," Rose's tone was sharp though her eyes were filled with tears, "you don't care a fig for what I might want. But I'll tell you this: I am not your property," she said, unknowingly echoing Stephen's very words to her brother a few days earlier. "I have feelings whether you realize it or not."

"Feelings," George spat the word at her. "You'll be feeling all right—feeling left out in the cold when the whole quarry goes against Ballard and the Stone Company one day soon. Folks here won't have no use for you."

Rose was struggling to light the lamp. "Stephen Ballard is not the Cleveland Stone Company as far as I'm concerned. He's an attractive, interesting man who knows how to treat a lady."

She turned the lamp up, revealing George's angry,

mottled face. His bulky shadow loomed on the wall like that of an unwanted intruder.

"You'll see." George was determined to have the last word. His attitude toward Rose ignored the fact that he was two years younger than his sister. Wasn't he the man of the house? He squared his shoulders and pushed past Rose, lunging toward the front door.

As the door banged shut, Rose stood perfectly still, allowing her brother's mean-spirited words to prickle her scalp and churn in her stomach. The mood of the magical afternoon shattered, Rose admitted to herself that George made some sense. If there was to be trouble in the quarries . . . and she still had Mama to face.

"Scoot, Tabitha." Stephen shooed the Koellers' handsome Persian cat out of Dr. Koeller's wicker rocker. Knowing that the Koellers wouldn't be coming home from Sunday night services for another half an hour at least, he was enjoying the spacious front porch, sheltered by Mrs. Koeller's rose-covered trellises. One trellis at the end of the porch had blown down in a storm nearly two weeks ago, and Stephen made a mental note to offer to help Dr. Koeller put it to rights.

Other things were on his mind. For one, this town of Berea that he'd come to — that he'd hardly heard of before. Here, several thousand people seemed divided into three camps that moved independently of one another, like planets around the sun, each in its own orbit. At the center was the great unifying force, the quarries. There was the tight-knit neighborhood around St. Adalbert's, the first Polish Catholic congregation in the state. The Irish, German, and Italian neighborhoods clustered around St. Mary's Church, a little father south.

Then there was this side of town, the South Side or "God's side of town," where business and college people lived comfortably, many in imposing residences. Stephen cringed inwardly, remembering Mr. Worthington's sardonic advice to him that he should live there. He thought of the trim, neat houses and yards he'd seen on Pulaski Street when he walked with Rose to her home. He admired how Rose and her brother supported their mother and kept up the home their father, Frederic Wolinski, had built when they were young children. Actually, Rose had told him, their grandfather had built the front part of the house a few years after he came from Poland to work in the quarries. He had lived with other quarrymen in a company house until he could build the home. Then he sent for his wife and small son, Frederic. Until he had a home to bring them to, Grandfather Wolinski would not uproot his family from their native Polish soil. When Frederic married and brought Sophie to the family home, he had added the kitchen and another bedroom. Stephen admired industrious folks like that. Although they were not highly educated or wealthy,

Stephen recognized them as honest, resourceful people, nonetheless, who enjoy life on modest means.

And Rose—with her love of beauty and music—and she likes poetry too, Stephen mused. She expresses a love of life in everything she does, whether she's experiencing something new like the Arcade today or the way she goes about her daily work at the hotel, serving folks with her easy friendliness and calm, efficient ways. Being with Rose for an entire afternoon had left Stephen with a sense of aliveness he had not felt for months. Sadly, Sally Westin's sudden breaking off of their engagement had left him an empty, hollow shell of a man. He had seized the opportunity to leave Stone City to avoid seeing Sally take her place as the Banker's Wife and feel the pitying glances of townspeople when he met them.

With each of his brief chats with Rose, he'd had a surge of energy, a challenge to know this young woman better. Rose was lively and delightful company, and she was physically exciting as well. Stephen recalled how he literally had ached to put his arms around her waist and draw her close during the Singers' Club concert.

Despite warnings from Worthington, from Mrs. Longwood, even measured words of caution from Martha Adams, Stephen would continue to see Rose Wolinski, regardless of the town and the Cleveland Stone Company.

Eight

"Sam, Sam, here's your lunch bucket. It's time we're off." Viktor opened the back door to find his son Sam knocking dried black mud from his boots. "I don't have to ask where you went yesterday to get in muck like that. What were you doing at Lake Abram, son?"

Sam ducked his head lower, still pounding his boots together.

"Answer me, Sam. That's a long way to go on a Sunday afternoon hike, I'd say."

"Me and Jake and Chris were trying to find where Fast Jack lives." Sam mumbled the words very fast, as if his mouth were full of hot mush.

Viktor tapped his foot. "Come, now, let's be going. And did you?"

"Did I what?" Sam looked up at his father, blinked, then bent down and began to pull on his boots.

"What you set out to do. Find Fast Jack's place?" Viktor's tone was patient.

"We saw a shack, but we didn't find him." Sam was determined not to tell everything—about the man with the gun. His pa would probably forbid him to go out there again. He wasn't sure he wanted to go, but he didn't want his pa getting riled about it.

Both picked up their lunch buckets and headed through the hollyhock-bordered fence. Viktor stopped, turned toward his son, and put one hand on the boy's slim shoulder that was nearly even with his own. "Sam. I'm going to say this just once, and it should be enough. Forget about finding where that man goes when he's not walking up and down the streets of Berea." They resumed their pace toward the quarry. "Fast Jack, as everyone refers to him, has been around the town for as long as I can remember. He's likely harmless as a kitten. Most towns have their town characters and people like to make up stories about them, just because they don't know much about them since they keep to themselves. He's entitled to live the way he wants to without a bunch of rag-tag boys chasing after him."

"Yessir." Sam avoided Viktor's eyes, wondering what his pa would have said if he'd dared to tell him about the man with the gun and the strange smell in the air near that shack. Probably he should tell some-one about it.

* * *

"Mr. Ballard! Mr. Ballard! Come quick. There's a fight goin' on in the quarry." Pavel Prohaska pulled the quarry's two-seated runabout as close as he could to the open door of Stephen's office. He was panting, his rumpled hat askew.

Startled, Stephen jumped up from his cluttered desk, fairly overturning his relic of a chair. Pavel's cries had jolted him out of his woolgathering; his mind had been far from affairs of the quarry as he recaptured his Sunday afternoon with Rose. Grabbing his hat from a peg on the wall, he leaped into the runabout, and Pavel turned his horse back toward Stearns Quarry.

"You say it's a fight?" Stephen shouted above the horse's clattering hooves and the runabout's rattling seats. "Is it a two-man fight or a free-for-all?"

"When it started, it was just James Janek and Harold Damboski. But no telling what it may be when we get there." It looked like it was gonna get real ugly."

Coarse shouts pierced the scrim of flour-white dust that surrounded the work area of the quarry as Pavel drove his horse hard into the scene. About twenty quarrymen had moved away from a wiry figure, lying moaning on the ground, his face buried in the dust, his right arm at a rakish angle from his side.

Stephen stooped down and spoke quietly to the quarryman. "Looks as if you'll need Doc McKelvey to look at that arm, Harold. Pavel will take you. Can you stand?"

While two other quarrymen stepped forward to help Harold into the runabout, Stephen's eyes roved about the group, searching for James Janek. He spotted him, huddled on a pile of stones, trying to stanch the flow of blood from his split lip. The low murmur of voices from the men revealed nothing as to what had prompted the fight.

Standing nearby, staring hard at the dusty ground, were John Seidler and Franz Lieberharr, usually reliable, diligent workers. Stephen was surprised that they were part of this group that had stopped to watch a fight in the middle of the workday.

"What got this started?" Stephen asked. Franz waited for John to speak, since he was usually the more forward.

"Sir, there's been talk, almost threats, all day from Janek about how all us will have to join the union. I guess Harold just got sick of hearing it. I don't really know who struck first." John's round face wore an earnest expression, but he seemed hesitant to say more.

"Thank you, John. That's helpful." As Stephen strode over in James' direction, he shouted, "Back to work, now, all of you. Enough time lost today." He looked down at James, who still nursed his split lip. "As for you, you are suspended from this quarry without pay for three days—the rest of today, Tuesday and Wednesday. Fighting has no place in the quarry." Stephen's voice was calm, but his tone was firm. "You do your union organizing and aggravating elsewhere and on your own time. Is that clear?" He stared hard at James, sparks fairly shooting from his dark eyes. "Damboski will probably lose more time than you by the looks of that arm of his."

James Janek made no effort to stand when Stephen spoke to him, only looked over toward where the men were picking up their tools and returning to work.

"Janek, are you clear on what I said – about your union activities?" Stephen heard his own voice sounding like brittle glass breaking. He felt the muscle in his left cheek begin to twitch, a sure sign his anger was reaching the boiling point.

"Yeah, I hear you," James muttered, still not looking at the superintendent.

"You will get on your feet, and you will speak to me by name." Stephen had to restrain himself from jerking the surly quarryman to his feet.

James labored to his feet. His eyes were as cold as steel, but his split lip gave him a half-pathetic look. " I said I hear you – Mr. Ballard." The slight emphasis on the Mr. sounded a tinny, false note that Stephen chose to ignore. As he turned away, James stood statue-like, fists clenched, his eyes boring into Stephen's back.

* * *

Their skirts and boots coated with black muck, Lucy Zielinski and Gretchen Janovick stretched out beneath a willow tree near Lake Abram to enjoy their lunches. They'd been on their hands and knees all morning, thinning out onion plants so a healthy crop would develop. The pulling was not hard, only the kneeling, but what they earned helped give their families a decent living. Altogether about twenty women had fanned out beneath the trees to enjoy food and conversation.

"Chris told me him and Jacob came up here yesterday. I asked him how he got so muddy." Gretchen offered Lucy some of her ginger cookies.

"Thank you, Gretchen. These are so crispy and good." Lucy answered between bites, "I wasn't pleased they took my nephew Winston that far. His family was visiting from West View, and they were ready to leave long before Winston got back—and a muddy mess he was too."

"Chris says they're trying to find a shack where they think someone lives—"

"Oh, you know, that old man with the white hair and the long coat who walks around—

"What would he do if they found him?" Suddenly Gretchen's face darkened. "Do you suppose he'd hurt the boys?"

"Probably not," Lucy said, "but I'm going to ask Jacob's father to speak to him about going so far." Lucy was peeling a ripe, juicy peach.

"Something else Chris told me about yesterday—"

"Chris talks to you a lot, don't he?" Peach juice was dripping from Lucy's chin, and she wiped it away with a clean place on the hem of her skirt. "Well, he has no brothers and sisters, you know. I guess that's why."

"What'd he say anyway?"

Gretchen leaned closer and lowered her voice. "The boys were by the station when the excursion train came in—you know, the one that went to the Arcade in Cleveland? Well, who got off but Mr. Ballard, the quarry superintendent—and can you guess who was with him?" Gretchen was stringing out her story, obviously enjoying every word.

"How should I know any of those South Side ladies by name?"

"Not a South Side lady. One of our own," Gretchen said with pride. "None other than Miss Rose Wolinski herself. And that's not all. He walked her to her house, so it wasn't no accidental meeting."

"Well, Rose is a pretty thing, and she's nice to everyone." Lucy paused. "And remember how he bought her basket at the Summerfest? He's probably had an eye on her for a while. But there'll be trouble if they keep seeing each other. Folks on the South Side will make trouble, for both of 'em probably."

Lucy rolled her eyes. "But— mm-mm, he'd be worth getting into trouble for."

Anna and Rose were making their way up Front Street late in the afternoon after work. Shopkeepers were closing up for the night. Mr. Carman trundled barrels of potatoes and onions inside his store. At the hardware store, Carl Geiger cranked up the awning and wiped the glass in the heavy oak door. Paul Machovina was arranging a display of five-dollar-a-pair work boots in his clothing store window.

"Oh, I caught a peek of the two you several times yesterday and again in front of your house before I went inside. He is so – so—" Words failed Anna for once.

"I can't think of enough words to do him justice either," Rose said. "I never knew a man could make me feel so grand."

They walked on in silence for a few minutes. Rose seemed lost in her own thoughts, but Anna was impatient to hear more.

"Did Aunt Sophie see him? What did you say to her?"

Rose drew a deep breath. "I told her when she came home from Aunt Ivana's that I'd spent the afternoon at the Arcade with Mr. Ballard and that he walked me to my house and that he wants to see me again." Rose spit the words out in a rush just the way she'd said them to her mother, as if she feared she wouldn't get them out otherwise.

Her mother had clasped her dimpled hands to her cheeks. "Holy Mother of God," she'd cried. Then she started babbling in Polish. "Why my daughter of all women in Berea? But I should know, working down there at that hotel, men would have their eyes on you. What are you thinking of? A man like him can have his pick of women—women of his own kind. What does he want with you?" Her voice rose an octave. "Jesus, Mary and Joseph, it's not too hard to figure." Sophie had shaken her head sadly and headed for her bedroom.

Before her cousin could object, too, Rose tried to explain. "But Anna, he does like being with me, and he doesn't seem to care that I'm Polish and work in a hotel," Rose said, brushing aside a willow branch that overhung their path. "I wish Mr. Christopher would trim these trees. Stephen told me when he came to breakfast this morning that he couldn't remember when he'd enjoyed a day more than yesterday."

Anna turned to face Rose, searching her joy-wreathed face. She had always known her younger cousin would be attractive to men, but she never would have wished for her a dilemma such as this. Not only would she be envied and gossiped about by the South Siders, but also her own people wouldn't understand.

"You've got to be prepared, Rose, to find out that people can be cruel. Even our own. There's talk of strike in the quarries, and your friend Stephen—Mr. Ballard—will be against us."

Rose looked wide-eyed, then shivered. Clouds had slipped over the late afternoon sun. From behind the two women came the familiar thuds and pounding of blasting in the quarries that shook the rock-hard clay surface of Front Street beneath them. They continued on their way, not talking any more. When they reached Adalbert Street, Rose said a quiet goodbye and turned toward the church and her regular Monday duties.

"Wait, Rose," Anna called after her. She ran toward her cousin and hugged her until Rose felt her bones would pop through her shirtwaist. "Please don't be angry with me. I understand how you are attracted to this man. I saw the two of you together yesterday enough to know you already have feelings for each other." Anna's eyes sparkled with tears. She herself didn't know whether they were tears of joy for Rose or were out of fear for what Rose might bring upon herself. "But I can't help being afraid for you. Things may get ugly in the quarries, Viktor says, and with George so involved in trying to get the union going—"

Rose stopped her. "George talked mean to me last night, but I know he'd never hurt me." She gathered her skirts. "I must run on to the church or I'll miss Mr. Porubovich's practice." She hugged Anna. "Thank you for your love and concern, Anna. I'll be fine."

Watching her cousin head toward the church, Anna said a silent, earnest prayer for her safety.

* * *

"Ballard, Worthington here. I called promptly at ten as I said I would. I got no answer." George Worthington's voice bristled with agitation through the crackling telephone wires.

Stephen had started counting to ten mentally as soon as the telephone rang. "I was called out to a quarry site, sir," Stephen said, "to resolve a problem." He hoped the company president wouldn't press him for details.

"What I want from you, as I stated yesterday," Worthington rattled on, "is an accurate picture of the union activity that's going on out there. How many have joined? What are they planning? Who are the leaders? You surely have your ear to the ground, know which people you can trust to give you accurate information. After all, you've been here nearly four months." Worthington stopped his rapid-fire monologue, presumably to re-light his cigar. Stephen's mind backtracked over Worthington's words. He'd been looking out his office door at the cloudless sky that lay over the quarries today, thinking how it reminded him of Rose's clear blue eyes.

Worthington went on. "I'm here to tell you, Ballard, we can't have any nonsense out there like a strike, for God's sake. We've got orders for sandstone from all over the country, from Canada, from England even..."

Stephen had heard this same tirade a number of times before. Carefully, he cut in. "I can tell you that after the meeting at St. Adalbert's School, I'm told 18 have joined, according to what I was told by two different quarrymen that went but have no intent of joining. That's a pretty small percent so far, but you're right, we have to keep on top of this, and I certainly intend to." Stephen hoped his tone sounded authoritative and convincing.

"Humph," Worthington snorted. "Rabble-rousers. They aren't grateful for good honest work. I want that movement stopped." He lowered his voice to a syrupy tone. "By the way, that was an attractive young lady with you yesterday. What did you that say her name is?"

Stephen felt a flash behind his eyes as if he'd had a sudden shock. "Her name is Rose," he said coolly. "Rose Wolinski."

Worthington's how-dare-you voice fairly leaped over the wire. "Ballard, I don't want to tell you how to spend your free time, but a man in your position in Berea should find some young ladies on the South Side to keep company with. The Polish are pretty content to keep to themselves as long as we don't give them ideas about mingling. You think about that, young man. I'll say good day now, Ballard."

A metallic click signaled the end of Mr. Worthington's wisdom for the day. Stephen was glad that he didn't wait for a reply. The way he was feeling this morning, remembering yesterday with Rose, he might have gotten an earful, and Stephen would have probably regretted replying that way to his superior.

Foreman Rufus Warner trudged through the door to Stephen's office, layers of quarry dust caked on his clothing and shoes. His face wore a haggard expression, and his gnarled hand clutched a crumpled piece of paper that he thrust onto Stephen's desk.

"I thought ye ought to know them union blokes'll be meeting' again next Wednesday night. Same place. St. Adalbert's School."

Stephen pored over a crudely lettered handbill, his fingers drumming the top of his scarred desktop. Francis Pritchett and union members from Cleveland will be present," he read. "So," Stephen muttered, more to himself than to Rufus, "they're bringing in the troops. It's to be expected, I guess, what with success unions have had in some other places.

Steeped as he was in the small town ways of Stone City, Michigan, Stephen struggled daily to cope with the social hierarchy of Berea. In Stone City, the population was made up of a few immigrant families who had come there to work in the quarry, but the sons and daughters of those families had intermarried with the offspring of the native folks. There weren't any separate Polish or Italian sections of town, although the Catholics tended to stay to themselves, for the most part. Here there were many more quarries and the labor movement in nearby Cleveland influenced attitudes of the workers.

Stephen rose and strode to the door of his office. Sounds of blasting and drilling echoed along the walls of the quarry, pounding a threatening tattoo into his brain. He felt helpless to, as Worthington put it, "put down this thing." The quarrymen deserved a decent wage for the dangerous work they did. If other trades were joining together to better their lot, weren't the quarrymen within their right? But he knew he should be thinking as a representative of the Cleveland Stone Company, not as a quarryman.

He turned to face his foreman, who was shifting uneasily from one foot to another, clutching at his dust-caked hat. Stephen scanned the man's weathered face, his bruised hands. Rufus was looking at Stephen expectantly as if he thought he could utter some magic words to cancel out the planned meeting.

"There's a movement afoot, Rufus, that's bigger than I am. Although I'm supposed to stop it, the men are within their right. What they do in their off hours and out of the quarry, I'm not at liberty to interfere with." He stepped over and clasped Rufus's sagging shoulder. "Thank you for keeping me informed though. This thing is swelling, and it will peak soon, I'm thinking."

Nine

Editor Elijah Peebles had just put his Berea *Advertiser* to bed for the week. While locking the door to his newspaper's cluttered office, he gave himself a mental pat on the back. Elijah enjoyed the feeling that he acted as Berea's mouthpiece, broadcasting the town's triumphs and bringing to light its shortcomings. Last week his write-up of the Summerfest had heaped praise on the town for its compassion for the McLaughlin family. This week's editorial, demanding the scrapping of the unhealthy town pump on the Triangle, might bring him ridicule, but he had vowed to the WCTU members he'd champion their cause.

Heading toward his Spring Street home, he retraced his steps to the City Hotel. Momentarily, the lobby seemed cool and refreshing as he stepped in out of the glaring afternoon sun. Mrs. Longwood sat behind her high desk, bending over her ledgers and seeming oblivious to anything else. But she probably knew exactly who just walked through door of her hotel. Elijah considered her a crafty one, but since she's running a decent place here, the town should be grateful for that.

"Hel-lo. Hel-lo," squawked a one-eyed parrot with a ruby collar from his cage on Mrs. Longwood's desk.

"Good afternoon, Mr. Peebles. How may I help you?" The hotelkeeper turned to face him. Her heavily rouged face and lips and masses of dyed black hair gave her the appearance of a very large, aging vaudeville actress.

"Mrs. Longwood." Elijah gave a courtly nod. "Your hotel is looking fine and doing a brisk business, I trust."

"Tolerable, Mr. Peebles. Tolerable. What can I do for you?" she repeated. Small talk was not in Mrs. Longwood's repertoire.

Elijah dug into his pocket and brought out three silver dollars and aligned them on the edge of Mrs. Longwood's desk.

She looked at him, her dark brows raised like question marks. "And what is this? Some sort of magic trick?" Her voice carried a bit of an edge.

"I'd like you to pick up each coin separately, examine it, weigh it in your hand. Then see if you have any comment to make." Elijah gave the lady what he hoped was a charm-laden smile as he pushed the coins closer to her.

Mrs. Longwood's beady eyes and pudgy, ring-bedecked hand meticulously assessed the coins as Elijah had directed. Looking up, she declared flatly, "The one in the middle could be a fake. It is noticeably lighter in weight than the rest. The color's a dab darker as well." She pushed the coins back toward Elijah as if dismissing him.

"Three different shopkeepers have discovered these in their tills this week," Elijah said, holding up the middle coin. "Be on the lookout for them. This could mean there's a counterfeit ring operating hereabouts. I'll be putting a notice about it in this week's paper." Elijah bristled with the importance of his message.

Mrs. Lockwood's florid countenance seemed to blanch slightly at this news, but she quickly assumed her customary aloof façade.

"Thank you, Mr. Peebles. You are kind to alert me."

"Kind. Kind," the parrot squawked. Mrs. Longwood nodded a dismissal and poked a piece of biscuit between the slats of Belvedere's cage.

Squinting up at the waning rays of the sun, Rose gathered clippings from the lilac bush she'd been pruning. Since it had grown so tall that Sophie could no longer reach the upper branches, Rose had taken over this task for her mother. Sophie, an immaculate housekeeper who regarded her home and yard as a sacred trust she had inherited from her long-ago husband, seldom asked for help from Rose and George. Grateful for their financial support and devotion, she happily did the household chores.

Aware of a figure approaching from the end of the dirt street, Rose suddenly felt a cold sense of dread. She hurried to finish picking up the clippings, but she knew James Janek had seen her and was walking toward her. There would be no way to avoid him. As he drew nearer to her front yard, Rose stood, a basket of clippings on her arm and a friendly smile pasted on her face. But beneath her gingham shirtwaist her heart was pounding and her knees were shaking under her muslin skirt.

"Hello, James." She was determined to start on a friendly note. Clearly, James was not just passing by; he had come purposely to see her, or he was on his way somewhere else. Gone were the day's layers of quarry dust. His clothes were clean and pressed, his hair slicked down and parted arrow-straight. But his facial muscles were taut, and his eyes narrowed as he looked at her.

"Rose. Come. Walk with me." His tone was demanding, not inviting, but she knew she owed him this much.

"Wait until I get rid of these," she motioned to the basket, "and I'll let Mama know I'm leaving."

They walked in silence for a bit, and James made no move to take her hand. They headed toward nearby St. Mary's Cemetery where they had often walked. Somehow it didn't seem disrespectful to walk for pleasure among the gravestones of people who were not your own ancestors, people with names like Brennan and Murphy and Hagan, not Roskiewicz and Bednarski.

When they came to a low stone wall, James pulled her down beside him, then let go of her hand quickly and stared straight ahead in stony silence. Finally, he spoke. "I just want you to know, Rose, you've made a fool of me, and I ain't happy about it. The men in the quarry look up to me. I'm becoming a leader. But you — you've made me look like a weakling who can't keep his woman from dallying around with somebody that don't even understand us. I can't—"

Rose could listen to this no longer. "James," she said, her words fierce and her eyes blazing, "where you are wrong is that I am not your woman, nor am I anyone else's. I'm my own person, free to do what I like and see whoever I like." Her tone softened slightly. "We've always been friends, James, but you've no claim on me."

James leaped up, then leaned down, taking her by the shoulders and shaking her harder than he probably realized. "You keep on seeing Ballard, and you're going to bring trouble on all us quarry people. You're probably running to him with every piece of news you hear about the union."

Rose wrenched away from his grasp and jumped

to her feet. "I don't talk to him about his work," she retorted, stamping her foot. "He respects the fact that I'm Polish and my family has always worked in the quarries." Her fists clenched, now Rose was screaming at James. She looked squarely into his eyes that were smoldering like cinders. "I've no interest in your foolish union. Do you really care about the men—or do you just like the feeling of power you have over them?" She whirled around, leaving James sputtering out more words of contempt.

"You'll see. You won't have a friend left. Everyone will hate you for putting on your fancy airs and strutting around with Stephen Ballard, the flunky of the Cleveland Stone Company," he shouted.

Still resenting the pressure of his hands on her shoulders, Rose picked up her skirt and ran toward her home, determined to put as much distance between herself and this hateful man as she could—this man who no longer seemed like the friend she'd known most of her life.

Terrified that he might be following her, Rose glanced over her shoulder. In that split second, her foot struck a melon-sized stone, and she went down in a heap. Behind her, the path was empty, only a gray squirrel scampered to the base of a towering oak tree. Rose loosened her high-topped shoe and rubbed her ankle. Bracing her self against a tree trunk, she managed to stand, gingerly putting her weight on her aching foot. Brushing off her skirt, she looked up at the leafy branches that fingered the darkening sky and breathed a thankful prayer that her ankle did not appear to be broken. Aloud she said, "Oh, how can I be so gloriously happy one day and so confused and miserable the next?"

Franklin Pritchett, organizer for the Knights of Labor, puffed and mopped his face for the third time since climbing the stairs to Sister Agnes' sixth grade area in one-fourth of the upstairs hall of St. Adalbert's School. When he'd asked why the meeting couldn't be held on the first floor where it might be cooler on this muggy June night, George Wolinski had answered, grinning, "The men won't fit in the primary grade desks."

Now the quarrymen were filing in, most still in work clothes. They'd probably stopped off at home to eat a quick supper on their back steps. George looked at the dusty footprints on the varnished floors and realized he'd need to get someone to mop the floors and dust the desks tomorrow. He'd ask his mother. Certainly he wouldn't ask Rose.

A spiffed-up but sullen James Janek had arrived and thrown open all of the tall windows, but as more and more men crowded into the room, the air grew fetid with a curious mixture of last-day-of-school lunches, sweaty feet, and quarry dust. Outside, branches of the beech trees that separated the school from the church caught the tender evening breeze, and the soft cooing of mourning doves floated upward. The message still on the blackboard in Sister Agnes' sloping penmanship wished students, "Happy Vacation Days." The hands of the clock had halted at a quarter past four, as if it knew when school was out for the summer. Tonight a blue drape covered the statue of the Blessed Mother in the front of the room, apparently to shield her from the secular goings-on that were about to transpire.

Warming to his leadership role, George had skipped his supper in favor of splashing off the dust and donning clean work clothes that he would wear tomorrow. He'd removed his hat as had most of the quarrymen, and his ash-blonde hair, still wet and slicked down, looked dark.

"After you get a count, George, of how many are here, then go down the list of things we're demanding." Pritchett spoke in a gunfire-like staccato as he removed his coat and draped it over Sister Agatha's desk chair.

George nodded, eyeing the American flag that covered half of the wall above the blackboard. "Uh—" he hesitated, "I'd sorta like to begin with the Pledge of Allegiance since there's a flag in the room." He looked at Pritchett for approval.

"As you wish. Some do. Some don't," Pritchett staccatoed again.

By the time George called the meeting to order and led the group in the pledge, a scowling James

Janek, hunched on a stool in the back of the room reported 42 present. Men filled every seat and lined both sides and the back of the room, and some of the smaller, wiry quarrymen, like Peter Serafine and Anthony Carabelli, sat two to a seat.

"The first and most important thing we want from the Cleveland Stone Company is that they recognize our union. Once we get that, then we'll have what Mr. Pritchett here calls bargaining power. These men up here are from another union in Cleveland—at the Rolling Mill. They're going to answer your questions later on about what union membership has done for them." He pointed to two stalwart strangers in the first row.

George cleared his throat and looked down at his notes. "Once we are recognized, the union will then speak for all of us about the following matters:

First, we want our wages restored to what they were before they were cut in 1893 because of the Panic.

Second, there'll be no more taking money from our paychecks without our consent, even if it is for a worthy cause.

Also there'll be an end to holding back several weeks' pay. Paydays will take place on a definite schedule.

Another thing, any workers who have been fired for union activities will be rehired. Even though firing hasn't happened here yet, it has happened at other places.

And finally, we want an end to mistreatment of workers by bosses. Mistreatment is common practice in some quarries, though not in ours, either when Mr. Carstairs was superintendent or since Mr. Ballard has been here."

George sensed a stirring and a low rumbling in the room. "Any questions about these demands? Do you think they are reasonable?"

"I have a question, George. What happens if they choose not to listen to us?" Power driller Anthony Carabelli rose. His dark eyes flashed, circling the room with a stony glance. Anthony supported his crippled mother and a little sister.

George looked at Pritchett, who nodded to him to go on. "The last resort, of course, is a strike. But they don't want that any more than we do. There's thousands of dollars of orders for Berea sandstone sitting in their offices right now, and they can't fill them if we don't work. Anything you'd like to say, Mr. Pritchett?" With beads of sweat popping out on his forehead, George seemed eager to turn the meeting over to someone else.

Pritchett stepped forward and raised one stubby arm in an affable salute. "Evening, gents. Appreciate you coming out on a warm night like this."

But Peter Serafine didn't wait for Pritchett to go on. The feisty Italian channeler was already on his feet, his cheeks flaming. "Tell us, Mr. Pritchett, what happens if the Stone Company lays us off? I've got a wife and five kids to feed."

An undercurrent of assent rippled through the room. Peter evidently bespoke the fears of other quarrymen.

"Now, men," Pritchett's tone was fatherly, "the big thing, as George says, is to get you recognized. With a union your jobs will be secure. We'll put that right into the contract in big, bold print." His glance skipped around the room as if searching for approval. "You'll eventually work less hours for more money. And we'll demand safer conditions, too, so there won't be as many accidents. I tell you, men, there's no limit to what the union can do to make your lives better. The days of being bullied by the Cleveland Stone Company will be over." He whipped out a sodden handkerchief and ran it around beneath his limp shirt collar.

Driller Fred Skirts lumbered to his feet. He was powerfully built with a shock of iron-gray hair that added to his commanding appearance. Muscles on his arms rippled, testifying to the bone-wrenching work he'd done for two decades.

"But you don't say, Mr. Pritchett, what happens if they don't recognize us."

Pritchett opened his mouth as if gasping for air but Fred Skirts held up a beefy hand in protest. "Never mind, Mr. Pritchett, we all know. You'll tell us to strike. Then you'll go back to your fancy office somewhere and light a cigar, and they'll hire people to take our places—they call them scabs. Whenever the strike ends, we'll be out of a job. They'll hire the scabs for good. We know other places where that's happened."

"Yeah, you're right."

"Hear, hear."

"Good going, Fred." A few quarrymen voiced approval of the big driller's bravado.

Pritchett inched his way along the aisle between desks until he stood waist-deep among the quarrymen. He began reverently, "The Declaration of Independence of this country states that every person is entitled to life, liberty, and the pursuit of happiness. Well, you don't have much of a life—working ten hours a day in unsafe conditions. You don't have the liberty to speak collectively to better yourselves, and you don't have free time or money enough to pursue much that will make you happy. Don't you think these things are worth a risk?" He paused. "The Minute Men thought so when they fought on Lexington Green. Your grandfathers and fathers who fought at Gettysburg did. For others of you, think what your forefathers risked to leave their homeland and cross the ocean to America. Filth, storms, seasickness, and a language they couldn't understand, once they got here. Some of you are still struggling with that, but you don't give up. Are you any less men than those who came before you? I don't think so. Deep down, you have the same fire in the belly that fueled their bravery. And don't you ever forget it." Pritchett lowered his voice and bowed his head as if pronouncing a benediction. He stood, unmoving, amidst the quarrymen, like a beacon of hope, or so he intended.

George took charge again. "Now if you are with us, see Mr. Pritchett here before you leave and fill out a union card. Zeke and Wally here are going to stay around to answer questions any of you might have about the benefits of belonging to a union."

Without a glance in Pritchett's direction, a straight-backed Peter Serafine and a small cluster of quarrymen headed for the door. A few of those who stayed stopped to talk with the visiting union members, but the line in front of Franklin Pritchett stretched out into the hall.

"It's all for one," Pritchett intoned as he busily passed out enrollment cards.

Ten

The stained glass windows of the Congregational Church, the Brick Church, as Bereans called it, virtually trembled as organist Rudolph Graham pulled out all stops on the pipe organ to lead the congregation in its final hymn:

Once to every man and nation
Comes the moment to decide,
In the strife of truth with falsehood,
For the good or evil side.
Though the cause of evil prosper,
The truth alone is strong;
Though her portion be the scaffold,
And upon the throne be wrong;
Yet that scaffold sways the future,
And behind him the dim unknown
Standeth God within the shadow
Keeping watch above his own.

The words resounded a challenge to Stephen as he followed the Koellers and Martha Adams from the church. In the vestibule, hands of fellow townsmen, were reaching for his.

"Hold fast, Ballard." Carman, the grocer.

"This town's counting on you to keep the quarries running." Mattison, the druggist.

"The paper's behind the Stone Company, Mr. Ballard. All the way." Peebles, editor of the *Advertiser*.

"These riff-raff strikemongers have to be dealt with," Mrs. William Simpson announced from beneath her hat-of-kale, addressing anyone within earshot.

"Good morning, Reverend Beard." Stephen gripped the pastor's palm that stuck out from his clerical robe. "Fine sermon today." The text was 1 John 3:23: *"And this is his commandment: that we should believe on the name of his Son Jesus Christ, and love one another, as he gave us commandment..."* [KJV]

"Always remember, Mr. Ballard, the Lord is on our side." Reverend Beard bestowed Stephen with a toothy smile.

Stephen liked Reverend Beard in the pulpit, from on high, as it were. But up close, he came across a bit like a frog puppet on a string, mouthing platitudes. Was Father Suplicki over at St. Adalbert's preaching to his flock this morning that the Lord was on *their* side?

Beneath the shade of towering oaks, knots of people gathered to chat outside the Brick Church. Sarah Carman and Jane Koeller, who taught at the Union School, especially enjoyed their time together during summer vacation.

"Such a charming hat, Sarah. Those mauve-colored rosettes are exquisite. Wherever did you get it? In Cleveland, I'll bet. At Halle's?"

Enjoying her friend's burbling praise, Sarah, who had the most fashionable wardrobe of any South Side young woman, answered coyly. "Jane, you've guessed wrong. Anna at Mrs. Dunham's did it for me. She's such a talent." She turned, letting Jane look more closely at her hat, then whirled around and putting her face close to Jane's, she whispered, "There goes that handsome quarry superintendent, Mr. Ballard. You're so fortunate, Jane, to have him living under your roof." Sarah's breath came in short puffs, her eyes trailing Stephen's tall figure across the lawn.

"A lot that means to me," Jane remarked, pursing her lips. "Any time he's around the house he spends talking poetry with my father or chitchatting across the hedge with Martha Adams. He's hardly said more than 'Good day, Miss Koeller' to me in six months."

"Seems he has more than that to say to Rose—from the hotel," Sarah hissed. "My parents said they went on that Arcade trip together."

"I guess he likes gingham dresses and the smell of yeast dough," Jane said, wrinkling her nose. "You'd think he'd stick with his own kind, though, wouldn't you? A man in his position."

"We're almost there, Jake—to where we turned off and found the shack." Sam Mikolak shifted his knapsack to his other shoulder and lifted his feet like a soldier on maneuvers on marshy ground. The early afternoon sun piercing through the humid air caused the boys to rest more often than they'd planned. Still, they'd made better time than on the other Sunday when they'd come out to Podunk Swamp with Chris and Winthrop, that pesky cousin of Jake's. Sam had to laugh to himself when he remembered the sight of Winthrop in his ruined clothes. "Hey, Jake, ain't you glad we don't got Winthrop along today? We wouldn't be this far."

His face beet-red from the tiring hike in the muggy heat, Jake answered, "That kid was a pain. It's a wonder he didn't get us caught by those men we saw at the shack. Wish we'd a ' seen a snake on the way back, though. He'd a probably peed his pants."

Determined to find out what the men they'd seen camped in the swamp were doing, Sam and Jake had turned their Sunday fishing trip to Lake Abram into another foray to Podunk Swamp. But they'd long ago stashed their fishing poles in a dense growth of reeds.

Stopping short, Sam sniffed the heavy air. "Smell that, Jake? That's that funny smell— sort of like a blacksmith's shop but different somehow."

"We must be getting close now," Jake panted.

Since few people ventured into Podunk Swamp, the wildlife creatures that inhabited it seemed to resent intruders. Gulls dived and squealed. Geese flew up from nowhere, startling the boys whose nerves, as they neared the site of the shack, were like taut wires. Every so often echoes of the sharp drilling of a woodpecker on a dead tree stump was an eerie reminder of the gunshots they'd heard the last time they were here.

Wood smoke rising from the clearing ahead, mixed with that other mysterious odor, meant they were close to the shack.

"Here's the fallen tree I stood on," Sam whispered, hoisting himself up on it again. "I can't see no one at all, but there's a fire going outside."

Boards were stretched across upright logs in front of the weathered shack that looked to be leaning even more than the previous time. Sam squinted, trying to see what it was on the boards that glinted in the weak rays of sun that filtered through the trees. A large wash boiler sat upon a now-smoldering fire, but the strange metallic odor filled up the whole area.

"What else do you see, Sam? Tell me." As hard as he tried, Jake's legs were not long or strong enough to boost him up on the tree. When Sam leaned over to whisper to him, he nearly lost his balance and tumbled from his lookout post.

"Here comes someone out the door. That man what shot the gun last time. And there's someone else. They're pickin' up things off those boards and puttin' 'em into bags." He watched silently as Jake waited to hear more. "It's money! That's what they're doing, Jake. Making fake money!" Sam whispered hoarsely.

The taller of the two men, who wore a bandana around his face, tied up the bag he'd filled with what looked like silver dollars. Sam could see his huge hands, knotted and blackened, jerking hard on the cords. He shivered, knowing what else those hands could do if the man discovered Jake and him.

Just then, the tall man spoke in a muffled voice from behind the bandana. Sam caught the words "suspect" and "leave." He watched as the stocky man with the tattered straw hat reached into the fire pit with long-handled tongs. Although he longed to know what Sam was seeing, Jake waited quietly. He didn't want to be a pest like Winthrop. Looking up at the patch of glaring sky, already Jake began dreading the long trek back to town.

Suddenly, Sam leaped down from the tree trunk, rolling on the swampy ground. He looked at Jake, his eyes wide with the knowledge of what he'd seen. "Now we know for sure," he whispered. "They're making fake dollars and firing 'em."

Wishing he'd see this with his own eyes, Jake hesitated to believe his friend. "How can you be so sure? You ain't seen 'em up close."

"Hush! They're talkin' now."

155

The boys could hear the low rumble of the men's voices but couldn't make out what they were saying. They feared the men had heard them from their lookout spot at the edge of the woods. "Let's lay low here for a bit," Sam said.

When they could no longer hear the men talking, Sam was adamant, his wide-set eyes popping. "I seen all I need to see. We got to tell somebody about this."

Treading gingerly across the swampy ground, the two friends headed back toward Lake Abram.

"Hope nobody stole our fishin' poles," Jake muttered.

Sam plodded on ahead resolutely, without a thought for fishing poles. He knew who he wanted to talk to.

They'd met several times at the corner of Front Street and Bagley for early evening walks on the German Wallace campus. These were times when Stephen and Rose were growing to know each other. Few persons were about on the campus during the summer, and they had found the gazebo near the chapel a pleasant place to sit. They had shared knowledge of each other's families, their love of literature and music.

The weekly band concert at the Triangle had delighted them both tonight. Although Peter Eliot's musicians had struggled a bit in the beginning with selections from Gilbert and Sullivan's *The Mikado*, the latter part of the program had the audience tapping their toes and swaying to such favorites as "Bicycle Built for Two" and "Sidewalks of New York." People had spoken cordially to Stephen and greeted Rose politely, but what they would say among themselves later, Rose knew. Her smiles felt painted on. She was perfectly at ease with these people when she was at work at the hotel. But here she feared she seemed gawky and self-conscious, knowing that they probably did not approve of seeing her with Stephen.

Afterwards as the chapel bells rang out across the campus, couples strolled leisurely along gravel paths lined with borders of purplish phlox and brilliant petunias. Ladies' plumed and ribboned hats bobbed and nodded as their wearers spoke in rippling tones to their smiling gentlemen friends, who twirled their sailor hats and struggled to make interesting small talk.

"What do they teach here, anyway?" Rose gripped Stephen's arm as they crossed a swaying footbridge over a meandering stream.

"Lots of religion," he said, "and philosophy, German, literature—and beyond that I can't tell you myself." He gave her hand a playful squeeze and smiled into her upturned face. "Both colleges, this one and Baldwin University, educate lots of preachers."

"I can't—" Rose bit her lip as if to cut off her words. Then she plunged ahead. "I can't imagine training preachers to treat some people like they're worth less than others."

Stephen turned to face her, his left eyebrow raised questioningly. "Whatever do you mean, Rose?" He bent down to push a fallen branch out of the way of her skirt.

"It's common knowledge—we Polish are not allowed to set foot on the sacred grounds of Baldwin University." She stared straight ahead and began walking a bit faster, as if keeping pace with her mounting temper. "The Germans here are not as uppity as those Methodists."

"What? Stephen's face was frozen in disbelief. "Are you sure that's not a legend? An old wives' tale? I've read where John Baldwin founded the school with the idea that anyone could attend, regardless of race or nationality. And one of the first people to graduate from there was a lady!"

She whirled around to face him. "Well, old John Baldwin must be spinning in his grave then. I'm positive—that school has no use for us Polish. We all know that. Why, my own cousin's boy, Sam—you know him, he's a water boy in the quarry—he tried to get a job there last winter. There was a notice posted at the *Advertiser* office for someone to shovel the walks. He went over to the campus, but when they learned his name was Mikolak, they told him to leave." Rose's tone was razor-sharp.

Stephen said nothing more but kept pace with Rose's rapid steps. Nearing the wisteria-sheltered gazebo where they often sat, he drew Rose out of sight of other couples passing by.

"What's so holy about their precious campus?" Rose persisted.

Stephen put his arm around Rose's trembling shoulders and turned her troubled face toward his own. "Rose, there are some things I don't understand about this town. I've been here only a few months, and I've met fine folks—who live in all parts of the town." He held her shoulders tight and refused to let her draw away. "All I can say for myself is, I try to live my life founded on what I believe is right as I see it. Shakespeare said it best, and I try to follow this: "This above all, to thine own self be true." I'll associate with whom I please—and you're at the top of my list, Miss Rose Wolinski." He put both arms around her and held her close as if to banish her doubts and unhappiness. Burying his face in her thick, tawny hair that smelled of rainwater and sunshine, Stephen tried not to think of the smooth, firm body beneath the folds of the rose-sprigged dress. But for an instant he could see himself lifting Rose and carrying her off to some distant joy-filled place where they could be together. Her soft dress would trail behind them, bidding farewell to Berea's naysayers and busybodies.

Rose sniffed and lifted her head from his shoulder. "I wish everyone believed as you do, Stephen. No wonder people in the quarry feel that you are very fair, that you treat everyone alike." She looked up at

159

him, and a smile swept across her now-calm features. "And I'm glad you like being with me, Stephen."

"We're good together, you and I, Rose," he said, holding her close again and brushing his lips across her temple.

Although this end of the quadrangle seemed empty of curious eyes on this early Sunday evening, Stephen drew back, keeping his feelings in check and helping Rose to her feet. No need to bring criticism down upon Rose and himself by behaving unseemly. He had tried to heed Martha Adams' advice about the wisdom of being seen together in public places. But these walks on the campus were where he and Rose were growing close, sharing the ebb and flow of their commonality and admitting their differences. Let people say what they will, but he would not fuel their gossip.

Rose, trying to regain her composure, had turned to watch a pair of cardinals. The brilliant-plumed male was high in a tree, cheering his heart out, it seemed, to the drab female pecking in the grass below.

"His song is so cheerful. I hear one each morning as I walk to work. It starts my day out on a joyful note."

"So that's your secret—Pippa." Stephen's eyes shone fondly and his lips curved in a gentle smile.

"Why do you call me Pippa? I hope it's a nice name," she teased.

"It's a lovely name of a young girl in a poem by Robert Browning. She makes the poet feel this way:

The year's at the spring,
And day's at the morn;
Morning's at seven,
The hillside's dew-pearled;
The lark's on the wing;
The snail's on the thorn;
God's in his heaven –
All's right with the world!

"How lovely, Stephen. That's a joyous thought and a beautiful compliment."

"I've been reading a lot of Browning lately from a book Dr. Koeller loaned me. I'll bring it along next time. I think you'd enjoy it, too."

Rose smiled and took his arm. She nearly said *I hope there's always a next time* but pressed her lips together to keep from seeming too bold.

When they turned down Pulaski Street, Rose could see her mother in the tiny front yard, watering the rose bushes that bloomed at either side of the door. "Stephen, you can—" she began, starting to head off a meeting between Stephen and her mother. She could go the rest of the way alone.

"I can meet your mother at last is what you were going to say." Stephen's voice had a strong, determined note. He covered her hand with his own to keep her from letting go of his arm. "It's time," he said firmly.

"Mama," Rose called, her voice had a nervous edge. She hoped George was not in the house. Seeing them coming, Sophie had turned to go in the house. "Wait. I want you to meet my friend, Stephen Ballard."

Sophie rubbed her pudgy hands on her faded dress and kept looking up and down the street as if half-hoping, half fearing that neighbors might be watching this unbelievable scene in front of her house.

Stephen was courtly and proper. "How do you do, Mrs. Wolinski. It's a pleasure to meet you. Your roses are lovely." Rose hoped her mother's discomfort would dwindle in the face of Stephen's kind manner. "I enjoy your daughter's company very much." He smiled at Rose.

Sophie, a shrewd judge of people, noted that gentle smile, yet the presence of this important man at her home seemed to unnerve her completely. She kept rubbing her hands against her skirt and then began chattering in Polish, her face reddening with embarrassment.

Rose put her arm around her mother's shoulders, saying gently, "Mama, just give Mr. Ballard your hand and say hello."

Sophie looked from her daughter's smiling face to Stephen Ballard and back to Rose again. Tentatively, she stretched out her hand.

"Hal-lo, Mr. Ballard."

Eleven

Outlined against purplish banks of clouds, the Triangle buildings cast long shadows, their windows blank in Sunday inactivity. Sam and Jacob, panting and parched from their final dash down Front Street, headed for the Triangle's pump. Sam helped man the pump and then threw himself on the grass while Jake drank first, slurping like a racehorse.

"Jake, quit that. You'll make yourself sick, drinkin' so fast." Sam stretched out and looked up at the evening star. His young friend sometimes didn't show good sense. Jake had been quiet though, out at the shack. They were sure lucky the two men hadn't heard them. And there was no gun fired this time. But Sam was risking getting home late in order to tell Sheriff Maxson about the men in the shack and what they were surely doing.

Jake had fretted about hiding their fishing poles, once they'd got them out of the reeds. "Nobody'll find them if we stow them in the hedge by the schoolyard," Sam had told him. "We can pick 'em up on the way back. Don't be such a worrier."

He took the bent tin cup from Jake and filled it halfway for himself. Truthfully, he wanted more, but after his warning to Jake, he didn't dare.

Although the single, weathered door to the sheriff's office was locked, the boys could make out a sign in the window. AT EVENING CHURCH SERVICE.

Jake and Sam looked at each other, saying, "What church?"

Sam, trying to be resourceful, said, "Let's try the Brick Church. It outghta be over a'fore long. I hear 'em singin' already. If he's not there, somebody'll tell us where he goes to church."

As the organ pealed forth, voices, some quavering, some rumbling, floated in the honeysuckle-laden summer air.

Softly now the light of day
Fades upon our sight away;
Free from care, from labor free
Lord, we would commune with Thee.

"They sing funny music at that church, don't they?" Jake said.

"Guess it suits them," Sam answered, shrugging. "They probably wouldn't like our Polish chants."

The boys huddled on the sandstone steps, waiting for the service to end and hoping Sheriff Maxson would appear in the doorway.

"My Pa'll whup me," Jake said. "I shoulda went on home." He sounded tired and worried.

As people began streaming through the heavy double doors, the level of chatter rose. Thin and rangy, Sheriff Maxson loomed behind his buxom wife. "Wouldn't surprise me if it'd rain tonight," he was saying to Mr. Mattison, the druggist. "We sure do—hello, who are you?" Sam had leaped up next to the sheriff. "Whoa, there, son. What's going on with you?" Sheriff Maxson sounded half annoyed.

For a moment Sam's customary bravado escaped him. He stammered, "Sir—sir, Jake and me need to tell you sump'n important."

Sheriff Maxson searched Sam's earnest face that he could barely make out in the shadows. He turned to his wife. "Lucinda, you walk on home with the Simpsons. Let me see what these boys have on their minds."

Mrs. Maxson threw the boys a curious glance as she moved to join Billy Simpson and his wife.

"Now, what's going on with you boys?" The sheriff's tone was more patient.

"Sheriff, we seen some men out at Podunk Swamp. They got a shack, and they're making things in a fire."

"What things? When were you out there?"

"Just this afternoon. But we was there two weeks ago too, and they was doin' the same thing. They thought they heard us that time, and they shot off a gun in the air, probably trying to scare us away."

"What exactly did you see them doing?" The words "making things in a fire" raised a red flag in the sheriff's mind.

"Money, sir. They was makin' money and puttin' it in sacks." A huge weight had rolled off Sam, just telling the sheriff about what they'd seen.

"Did you see this going on, too?" Sheriff Maxson turned to Jake, who hadn't said a word but just stood by, nodding in the darkness.

"Sir, I'm too short. I couldn't see it all, but I heard 'em talk, and I smelled their funny fire. It smelled like sumpn' metal."

The sheriff scratched his head and pulled his tie loose. He acted as if he'd been handed a puzzle and didn't know how to put the pieces together. "Why didn't you tell anyone about this the first time you saw these men?"

"We wasn't really sure they was doin' any bad thing," Sam answered, his voice wavering. This question had been certain to come.

The sexton shuffled out to lock the church, probably surprised to find the sheriff and the two boys still on the steps.

"We'll be going along now, Josiah," the sheriff

said. "Come on, boys. I'll get my trap from behind the office and take you home. Your folks are probably plenty worried about you. Who are your folks, anyway?"

Sam and Jake told him their names, while nudging each other and grinning in the darkness. All of their friends and neighbors who'd see them pull up with the sheriff in his trap would be green with envy.

As they sped up Front Street, the boys were bursting with importance. The hardware store, the hotel, the livery stable— all seemed to fly past. Unhappily, few people were out on the street to witness this sight. When Jake spotted Fast Jack loping along, he stifled an urge to call out to him. The sheriff followed Jake's directions to his home on Berea Street, then headed the buggy to Pulaski Street.

Reining in his horse in front of the Mikolak house, Sheriff Maxson called to Anna and Viktor, who were sitting on the front step, undoubtedly watching for Sam. "He's all right, folks. Not hurt or in any trouble." Turning to Sam, he said in a fatherly tone, "Son, I'll have to take some men out there tomorrow morning to see if we can flush out those counterfeiters—if that's what they are. I feel sure you're right. Folks have been seein' some questionable looking silver dollars showing up hereabouts." He leaned closer to Sam. "Would you go with us and guide us to the place? I'll speak to Mr. Ballard, and the town will pay your wages for the time you miss at the quarry." The horse stamped and switched his tail impatiently. "Hold on there, Big Bob. We'll be on our way in a minute or two."

In his mind's eye Sam pictured himself tomorrow, leading the sheriff and his men through Podunk Swamp to rout out the counterfeiters. But would he be able to find the place again? The sheriff believed him, but would the others? After all, he was a boy — and a Polander, at that.

"Yessir. I'd be glad to help," he managed to say.

"Fine. I'll pick you up here at six o'clock. We can ride at least to Lake Abram, though I know we'll have to walk to the swamp. I'd better get me some able-bodied helpers, hadn't I?"

"Yessir," Sam agreed. "That's tough walking around that swamp. Thank you for the ride, sir. I'll be ready." Sam jumped down. After telling this story to his parents, Sam would be lucky to sleep at all between now and six o'clock tomorrow morning.

"Evening, Mr. Ballard. It's a warm one, wouldn't you say?"

Stephen nodded in agreement with friendly Carl Geiger from the hardware store and tipped his hat to a beaming, beribboned Pearl Chamberlain who clutched Carl's arm. The pair continued up the dusty surface of Bridge Street, their voices low and intimate. Stephen had watched them at the Summerfest, how they enjoyed each other. Strange they didn't marry. Maybe it was religion. He'd seen Pearl often at the

Congregational Church. That was about the only place Carl wasn't with her, except when she was type-setting at the *Advertiser,* of course.

Stepping off the road, Stephen tried to avoid a cloud of dust thrown up by a passing carriage. Inside he could see the handsome profile of County Commissioner Edward Kennedy. A former state legislator and mayor of Berea, he still maintained his imposing home on Prospect Street, although much of his time was now spent in Cleveland. Stephen hoped sometime to learn more about this man's life because he'd heard he was a true hero of the Civil War and had become a leader in many of the successful business ventures in Berea.

While many South Siders attended Sunday night church services, Stephen preferred to walk, gathering his thoughts and praying for guidance in the week ahead. More workers had joined the union this past week, and the possibility of a strike loomed like a gathering thunderhead. Tonight, though, he was deeply troubled at some things he'd just seen. At the end of a side street of less imposing, yet comfortable homes, he had come upon a cemetery. He'd known it was there but had never before taken time to follow the cinder path that wound through it. He could make out some familiar names—Baker, Hulet, Perkins, Lang—etched on the weathered stones that studded the coarse grass. Other markers were mossy and hard to read. Few graves were marked with flowers or any kind of remembrance.

The path halted abruptly, and Stephen looked down into what had unmistakably been a quarry operation. The earth had been clawed at as if by a vicious fiend. Desecrated grave markers lay scattered about like broken toys. Weathered, splintered pieces of wood could only have been the remains of coffins. Beneath were undoubtedly the bleached bones of their occupants.

The woeful cooing of doves echoed the sadness Stephen felt smothering him. Before he had come to Berea, he knew that streets had been destroyed and houses moved that were in the path of the Cleveland Stone Company's progress. But he had never heard that a cemetery had fallen victim to the Stone Company's greedy practices.

Seeing this caused Stephen to ask himself what sort of people he was working for. Retracing his steps among the remaining graves, he had to wonder why the good people of Berea would tolerate such a sacrilege unless they are that fearful of and enslaved to the Stone Company.

In that plateau between daylight and dusk, crickets were chirping and fireflies began winking. Stephen walked slowly back to the Koellers', partly because of the warm evening and partly to rummage through his troubled thoughts about what he'd seen.

"Hal-lo, there, Stephen. Come give me a hand, will

you?" Stephen could barely make out the shadowy figure of Dr. Koeller, standing on the railing of his front porch, clutching the fascia board with one hand and holding a hammer in the other.

"Hold on." Stephen ran to help the older man, who could easily lose his balance and plunge into the shrubbery.

"I promised Leila I'd get this trellis put back up. Wind blew it down a couple weeks ago. She'll be back from Christian Endeavor soon, and I don't want to have to hear about it any more, you see." He chuckled and shifted his weight from one foot to the other. "I was waiting till it got cooler to do it, but I dropped the confounded thing. . . You came along just in time."

Picking up the fallen trellis, Stephen tried to avoid the thorny rambling roses he knew were there but could barely see. He steadied the trellis against the porch while the professor pounded it securely, then gave him a hand down.

Dr. Koeller carefully wiped his spectacles and then his bald head with a rumpled handkerchief. "Now," he said, opening the screen door and ushering Stephen into the cool, dim hallway, "we will have a brandy together for all your trouble — before Leila gets home from church," he added with a sly grin.

The professor's paneled study was sheer delight to Stephen. The room wrapped him in an aura of learning. Shelves of bound volumes reached to the ceiling. A handsome globe stood before one long window, and a thick dictionary on a stand faced the other. On the wall behind his burled walnut desk, Dr. Koeller's framed diplomas and awards announced his prestige as an educator. He had taught at an eastern college for a number of years before taking an appointment at German Wallace and moving his wife and daughter to what they had believed was the wild frontier.

While the professor poured two brandies from a small crystal decanter concealed in a lower desk drawer, Stephen took a seat in a leather-padded platform rocker beneath two Audubon prints of blue jays. He reveled in the inviting atmosphere — the smell of the leather bindings, the pungent aroma of the professor's pipe tobacco, the heady fragrance of a summer bouquet on a small stand near the desk. Leila Koeller graced every room of the house with fresh flowers from her garden, and her husband's study was no exception although she seldom ventured into it otherwise except to check on her housekeeper's work.

Stephen's eyes roved over the spines of some of the books. Since Dr. Koeller taught mostly English literature, some were not familiar; Milton, Donne, Burns he hadn't yet explored, but Dr. Koeller had kindly loaned him volumes of Tennyson, the Brownings, and Wordsworth. Broad, unexplored vistas had stretched before him as he read, carrying him far from his daily mundane surroundings at the quarry.

He had always loved books. Being an only child, he had spent countless hours listening to his mother read fairy tales, poems and tales of adventure. In high school, he had thrilled to American poetry and prose. His favorites were some of the raw, earthy verses of Whitman and the spare challenging prose of Thoreau.

Living here in a college town, Stephen was beginning to have shadowy doubts whether he was cut out to follow his father into quarry management. True, he knew every facet of quarrying from working alongside his father since he was twelve, after school and every summer. It had always seemed like an exciting job, full of risk and challenge—

"There's a book I'd like to share with you," Dr. Koeller said. He paused to light a meerschaum pipe. "This book is sweeping the country like a rampant south wind. I'd like to know what you think of it." The professor's words were clipped and terse.

Opening the slim volume the professor handed him, he saw it was entitled *In His Steps*. Stephen noted the author's name, Charles Sheldon. He looked questioningly at the professor, who was swirling the golden brandy in his glass.

"You've not heard of it? Good. Then you can give me your honest, unfettered reaction."

"I'll try to do that, sir." Stephen settled back to sip his brandy. He hoped to engage Dr. Koeller in a conversation about some of the English poets he'd been reading in a purple, velvet-covered volume Dr. Koeller had loaned him called *Gleanings*.

Twelve

Relentless as a steam-powered quarry drill, the early morning sun bore through the rumpled hat Sam had pulled down around his ears. The air was dense and still; even the wild creatures around Lake Abram were strangely quiet. Sam sat up tall in the sheriff's runabout, trying to hear any sound from the direction Sheriff Maxson and his two deputies had disappeared into the woods. Sam didn't think much of the two men the sheriff had deputized and brought along. Will Conner had such a potbelly, he'd never be able to escape if they had to run for it, and Denby Whitlock had weighted himself down with a long rifle that looked as if it hadn't been fired since Gettysburg.

Riding alongside Sheriff Maxson, Sam had sat up tall and proud although he was nervous about finding the place where he and Jake had entered the woods. Right away he'd recognize it, though, by a leaning, shaggy sycamore. Now he was stuck minding the horses.

"You stay here, Sam," the sheriff said, reining Big Bob to a halt and handing Sam the reins. "You're not gettin' nowhere near those men. I promised your daddy this morning that I'd keep you safe."

Sam had watched with a curious mixture of envy and relief as the three men disappeared into the gloomy woods—Sheriff Maxson leading his posse— rotund, puffing Mr. Conner and Mr. Whitlock, clumsily struggling with his ancient rifle.

"Quiet, Daredevil," Sam muttered. Conner's handsome sorrel, hitched to a flatbed wagon and tied to the sycamore tree, pawed the ground nervously and whinnied. Daredevil was as foolish a name for that horse as deputy sheriff was for Mr. Conner, Sam thought. The animal seemed too skittish to be very daring.

At least this beats sweating it out in the quarry today for fifty cents and putting up with James Janek's tommyrot. Sam scrunched down in the seat and picked absently at the callus on his thumb. What would the town be like, he wondered, if there'd be a strike? His father, he knew, wouldn't want any part of it. He'd feel he had a responsibility—to his family and the Stone Company. His dad was big on responsibility. But was it right—for the quarrymen to do such dangerous work for so little pay? What about Charles McLaughlin, the engineer who'll never walk again, and that Reuben Steinhoff, who died when he plunged from a derrick last year. And poor old Pavel Prohaska, who can't draw a breath without wheezing from breathing decades of quarry dust. Wonder what Mr. Ballard really thinks of some of the dangerous stuff that goes on in the quarry.

What'll I be doing twenty years from now? Sam wondered. He kept picking at the callus until he drew blood. How his mother hated seeing him do that. "You'll make scars on your hands, that's certain," she'd say. Scars or calluses, Sam thought. What's the difference?

A snapping in the underbrush startled Daredevil again, and his whinny echoed across the lake. Big Bob stood staunchly at attention, as if mindful of his master's caution to "Stay, now." Sam could hear voices and strained to see the sheriff and his men, hopefully with two counterfeiters in tow.

Instead, only Sheriff Maxson and his two deputies trudged out of the woods. They had no prisoners.

The sheriff called out, "You got us to the right place, son, but they was out ahead of us. They must've known someone was on to 'em." Reaching the runabout, he looked up at Sam's crestfallen face. "But don't feel bad, son. It was probably you and your friend that skeered 'em off. They went in a hurry because they left a lot of their junk behind. I'd bet they hitched on to the CC&C & St. L when it went through here in the night." He reached into a vest pocket and drew out a silver dollar — or at least what looked like a silver dollar.

"They were in such a rush, they dropped a few of these." He handed the coin to Sam. "Here's a souvenir for you. But don't you ever try spendin' it."

Turning the coin over and over in his hand, Sam had to marvel to himself at the skill of these men, although he knew they were wicked.

Conner and Whitlock were climbing into the spring wagon they'd brought, hoping they'd triumphantly bring prisoners back into town for everyone to see.

"It's good they've gone from here, at least," Sheriff Maxson said, urging Big Bob along. "You boys can figure you did your civic duty. I'm just glad you didn't get caught. No tellin' what those confounded varmints would have done with you." He handed the reins to Sam. "Here. You drive old Bob home. That hike in the woods plum wore me out."

As they trotted along the edge of Lake Abram, Sam tried to watch for any other signs of a path that might lead to a camp. He still didn't know where to find Fast Jack.

George and James were on their way to the quarry to work. George carried beneath his shirt a carefully folded copy of the demands the Quarrymen's Union would make upon the Cleveland Stone Company — the demands that George had read at the meeting at

St. Adalbert School. Since then, he'd had reports from the other quarries that brought the membership total to 129, enough Franklin Pritchett assured him, to make a strong showing to the owners. But Pritchett had advised George and James that neither of them should present the demands; he saw them as too hotheaded and likely to arouse negative feelings on the part of the owners. George readily agreed, since it was Stephen to whom the demands would be given, and James also had no desire to face up to the superintendent who, by this time, he was growing to despise.

"So who'll we get to read 'em?" James kicked a dirt clod along as they walked down Front Street.

"I wondered about John Seidel. Let's get some of those younger ones into it. What do you think?"

"He'd do OK—and he's sure got a big voice—matches the rest of him."

"I'll give it to him to read over at lunch. Then all us union men in this quarry will march up to Ballard's office when the quitting whistle blows."

George felt relieved to have a plan of action. He called out, "Good morning, Mr. Carman." The burly grocer was busy setting out barrels of potatoes and onions and scarcely nodded as the two quarrymen passed his store.

Today had started much the same as any other day in the quarries. A cobalt-blue sky blanketed the trees around the rim of the quarry, for there had been no quarrying weather, but the farmland surrounding Berea was parched, and every evening ladies on the South Side watered their roses and quarrymen's wives and children carried water in wooden pails from their pumps to the garden plots they depended on to help feed their families.

The steam-driven channeling machines were already at work this morning, marking out more sections to be blasted with gunpowder. Iron wedges were being driven at the bottom of the marked off channels to separate the seam, a backbreaking and bone-wearying job. John Seidel laid his pick aside, took off his bandana and mopped his face. On these days the heat, even this early in the day, as well as the ever-present, infernal dust, made quarrying almost intolerable.

But winter would be worse, for there would be little work for any of the quarrymen. Often wages, for those who were called to work, went down to ten cents an hour. A quarryman was lucky to draw an average of $13 a month throughout the year. If the women and children didn't have work in the onion fields in the early summer and fall, many families would not survive. John and his brother Daniel, as well as their father Joseph, all were quarrymen, and there were no young children in their household. His mother Christina, a talented dressmaker, had found hers was a skill for which a demand went on all year. In fact, winter was her busiest time with all of the party gowns the South Side ladies ordered. She would trudge from one imposing home to another, measuring and fitting, then work late into the night, stitching elegant creations on her treadle sewing machine in a corner of her parlor. Usually, the customers would send a deliveryman to fetch the dresses when they were finished, although Christina sometimes delivered them herself, carrying them in a folding case of muslin that she had created for this purpose. The income she received, as well as the high regard the South Side ladies had for Christina's talent, gave the Seidel family a slightly higher level of living than other quarrymen's families. Yet, they were always quick to aid those in their community who were in need and they tithed to St. Mary's Church.

Though it started like a usual day, this would not end like one. George Wolinski and James Janek had spread the word among the union members in the Berea Quarries—now nearly forty—that Stephen Ballard, as appointed agent of the Cleveland Stone Company, was to receive their demands at the close of work tomorrow. John Seidel, after some objection, had agreed to read the demands.

"But George, you read them fine at the meeting. You should be the one to speak for us." John was holding the painstakingly printed list of demands in his ham hock-like hand. His round face wore a bewildered look. "Why me?"

"You've a big voice, John, that carries good. We want all the men to hear these one more time, as well as Ballard." George refrained from saying that the union organizer, Pritchett, had advised both himself and James Janek that they would be looked upon as agitators by the Stone Company since they were the ones who had initiated the union movement. Big, affable John Seidel never caused any trouble. "Besides, John, you've had more schooling than me. You can say all those big words better."

John grinned, showing the gap between his teeth, and folded the paper into fourths. "I'll do my best, George." John's huge chest seemed to swell a few more inches as if an awesome knot of responsibility had settled there.

"I tell you, Mr. Ballard, there's something brewing. The men are keyed up. That scoundrel James Janek is up on his pole singing in Polish at the top of his lungs. And George Wolinski runs from one bunch of men to another like a drop of lard on a griddle." Foreman Rufus Warner feared this union stuff and felt that the young superintendent didn't realize what havoc idle workers could wreak in a town. Rufus had heard stories about the Rolling Mill strike in Cleveland. Young men had gathered in saloons, then turned to stealing. Older men had grown despondent, and hollow-eyed women and children begged in the streets.

Pushing back his spindly chair carefully, Stephen stretched his long arms and walked to the office door. Sunlight splashed in upon the dingy walls but failed to lighten the mood of either man. Stephen shared his foreman's apprehension although he'd had little firsthand experience with labor unrest. Sleepy, isolated Stone City on the mitten of Michigan, and Berea, only fifteen miles from on-the-rise industrial Cleveland were chasms apart in mentality.

"Rufus, we'll have to take each day as it comes. There's no way we can head this movement off." Running his long fingers through his jet-black hair, Stephen turned to face his foreman. Years of quarrying had left their mark on Rufus even though he'd worked his way to foreman eleven years before. Grim-faced, Rufus' shoulders sagged as if they carried an invisible weight. One finger was missing at the knuckle from his left hand, sacrificed to the black powder that was used for blasting before gunpowder. He had a permanent squint and the frequent rattling hack so common to men who had survived work-weary decades in the quarries.

Stephen went on, "God knows, the Cleveland Stone Company pays me to run these quarries, Rufus, but I have to say I feel there's justification for these men wanting a better lot. Look at the accident record. Look at the pitiful wages they're paid. These are people we're dealing with, Rufus, not parts of a machine. They have families who love them, many have homes they cherish that were built by their fathers and grandfathers. Their wives and children all work to help keep the families together. On Sundays they worship, not the same way we do, perhaps, but to the same God. They may eat kielbaski instead of roast goose, but they are people, just the same."

"What can you do?"

"How do I know what I can do?" Stephen's tone was exasperated. "All I know is that I have to take my orders from Mr. G. H. Worthington—that is if I want to keep my job." His expression softened. "Thanks, Rufus, for listening to me rant and rave. Now you'd better get back—but please know I appreciate that you keep your ear to the ground." Stephen put an arm over Rufus' brittle shoulder and walked out the door with him into the brilliant sunshine.

Midsummer days were the longest. Daylight stretched out like an uncharted map. After suppers were over, young boys who had strained all day, climbing up and down to the well on Prospect Street to slake the thirst of drained quarrymen, welcomed a short space of time just to be boys.

Sam and Jake and a half-dozen other water boys headed for the playground at Union School to play baseball until dark. Here for a brief hiatus, they were out of reach of quarrymen's taunts and demands as well as their parents' concerns. This was not their school; they were Polanders. They went to St. Adalbert's, but nobody seemed to mind if they played here where the swings would swing higher and the schoolroom windows were farther away from the foul line.

"Hey, Sam, lookit who's laying over there on the bank—Fast Jack!" Jake had that you'll-never-believe-this sound in his voice.

On one of the grassy banks that edged the playground, indeed, stretched the motionless form of Fast Jack. His lank hair, which looked yellowish up close, fanned out against his rusty-looking coat that was bundled, pillow-like beneath his head. His shirt and trousers, usually covered by his coat, were ragged but reasonably clean. The upturned soles of his broken-down shoes attested to his miles of fast walking; there was a hole in each one.

"He ain't movin' a whit and his eyes are shut," Jake whispered as the two boys inched closer. "Maybe he's dead."

"We oughta' get Sheriff Maxson." Jake had loved the important feeling of riding in the sheriff's runabout.

"Jake, use your head. Can't you see his chest going up and down?"

They crept closer, their searching eyes locked on the man's closed ones. A voice, crackling like hot wires, startled them, and they jerked back in fright.

"What do you think you're doing, pestering an old man who's taking a nap, not bothering a soul?"

The always-eager Jake spouted, "We never seen you stop walkin' and lay down before. We thought maybe you was hurt and we should get you some help." He inched closer, Sam following like an over-cautious parent.

"We're sorry to bother you—" Sam began.

"But we want to know—" Jake started, but Sam cut in.

"Don't mind Jake, Mr.___" Sam stopped short of calling him 'Jack', realizing he didn't know the man's real name.

Turning his watery blue eyes on Sam, the man pointed a bony finger at Jake. "Let him talk. Most people never bother to ask me questions. They just stare right through me—and then probably make up stories about me." He propped himself on one elbow and stared hard at Jake. "I bet you've heard I have lots of money hid somewhere—and I eat wolves." When he spoke he showed yellowed, uneven teeth. "But I don't care what folks say so long as they leave me be."

Jake was nodding. Sam stood behind him and kicked at his heel.

"I'll say," the man went on, his voice growing stronger now that he was wide awake, "I did used to eat rabbits and squirrels until that nice hotel lady come to town. She puts food out for me every day, and if it's raining, she lets me come in on the back porch of the hotel to eat. She's a good woman, she is."

"How come she does that?" Jake asked. Sam gave up. The boy would never quit.

"I guess she thinks she's got plenty and I don't got much."

The man sat up and scratched his arms through his thin shirt as if they were covered with mosquito bites.

"Don't you even have a house?" Even Sam could control his curiosity no longer.

"I got me a place out in the woods. That's all you need to know, boy." The blue eyes were harder now.

Sam's father always said that people make up stories to explain others' actions that they don't understand. If the hotel lady could be kind to this old man, why couldn't other people?

Picking up the black book that lay beside him, the cadaver-like man pulled himself to his feet. "Always remember, no matter how little you have, you'll always meet somebody with less. Don't judge them for that. Things are not always what they seem."

A puzzled Sam and Jake watched the man lope across the grassy expanse of the German Methodist Orphanage grounds toward Bagley Road. They still didn't know his real name.

Thirteen

"Come on, men! We don't want to look like a bunch of beat-down ragamuffins when we make these demands. Step up, now." George Wolinski's voice rumbled through the lines of the quarrymen as he ran alongside them.

Old Jumbo had sounded the end of the workday, the end of the work week, in fact, since it was Saturday. Union members at Big Quarry were marching, although sluggishly, toward Superintendent Ballard's office. Other quarries would send delegates with their demands, but here, where the Stone Company's office sat like a beacon between the town's business district and the quarry itself, the members had planned this demonstration.

Ignited as they were with union activity, nevertheless these men had channeled and drilled and guyed and blasted for ten hours. This was the end of a grueling 60-hour week. Hot suppers, precious time with bright-eyed children, soft beds, and loving wives were on their minds. Yet fear surely must clutch at the hearts of some who believed the Stone Company would fire them if they would join the union. And then how would they feed their families?

Stephen Ballard heard the stamping of heavy boots and the muffled voices approaching his office. His eyes and ears in the quarry—Sam Mikolak and foreman Rufus Warner—had prepared him for a confrontation with the quarrymen today. Now Rufus stood in support at the right of the wooden steps on which Stephen waited, erect but tense, hoping he appeared more at ease than he felt. A burning knot of apprehension rose in the middle of his chest, and his scalp prickled in the heat of the late afternoon sun. Could he meet this challenge? How could he answer these overworked, poorly paid men who toiled each day in this dangerous place? For a more mature, authoritarian look, Stephen wore the spectacles that he normally used only for reading. His white shirtsleeves were rolled to the elbow, his vest dangled open, and his coat and tie were inside, flung across his desk.

Quietly, the men stood in rows as John Seidel stepped forward directly in front of Stephen. "Here are the demands of the Quarrymen's Union," he boomed forth, startling a robin nesting under the eaves of the office building. The bird fluttered off into a grove of poplars, setting off a low rumble of laughter among the men.

John continued, "The restoration of the 1893 wage scale...the Company will meet with a duly accredited committee of employees...no more withholding several weeks pay—" He continued on with the list, and he was especially emphatic with the final point, "the ending of firing employees without good cause."

When he finished and handed the paper to Stephen, a tentative cheer erupted from the men.

"Let's hear it, men. Union! Union!" James Janek, at the rear of the group galvanized their enthusiasm into a hoarse, short-lived chant. They quickly quieted to hear Stephen's response.

"Thank you, John, for speaking up so forcefully for your fellow quarrymen." John Seidel stood eye-to-eye with Stephen, but he had trouble meeting the superintendent's dark, flashing eyes. Stephen went on, his voice reaching to the back row. "Be assured, I will convey your wishes (he was careful not to say demands) to Mr. Worthington, the president of the Cleveland Stone Company. I thank you for your hard work today—and every day. You and your families are a credit to this community."

With a nod of dismissal, Stephen disappeared into his office.

"Well done, Mr. Ballard. They know that you're not the one that will make the decisions, anyway," Rufus gathered his cap and his lunch pail and headed for the door. "I'll say good day, now."

Stephen nodded to him and slumped in his chair. Footsteps and voices faded in the distance as the quarrymen headed to their homes on the north side of town. Through the sand-smeared window the sun's rays managed to capture dust motes that danced crazily around the room. Outside, doves cooed in what often seemed a soothing chorus, but today their music seemed sad and oppressive.

The dingy walls of the office were closing in on him. Stephen drew himself to his full height, put on his coat, stuffed his tie in his pocket, and stepped to the telegraph to relay the information to Worthington.

Lumbering through the kitchen of the hotel, Mrs. Longwood stopped to stir a kettle of wedding soup and to give it a taste. She nodded approval to the cook who stood anxiously nearby. One never knew when Mrs. Longwood might find something that totally offended her standards of what should be offered in her hotel dining room. Those "mistakes," as she called them, provided they were edible, were never thrown away but instead were distributed to less fortunate people than those among the City Hotel's customers.

One of these gracious receivers was presently leaning against a pickle barrel, devouring a plate of beef tips and noodles as Mrs. Longwood stepped outside behind the hotel to check the appearance of the place.

"Oh, hello, there, Willem." She was not surprised to find the white-haired walker, the same man Sam and Jake nicknamed Fast Jack. He was one who benefited daily from leftovers and "mistakes" in the hotel kitchen. In fact, Mrs. Longwood had learned that his real name was Willem de Huis, and the two of them had formed a curious acquaintance of sorts; both were newcomers that the residents could not quite figure out. Although the hotel proprietor was a respected, if somewhat baffling figure, Willem de Huis was a curiosity who evoked ridicule rather than pity.

"Nice evening, wouldn't you say, Mrs. L.?" The man dug into the beef tips and noodles as if there would be no tomorrow. "This is really tasty, ma'am. I do so appreciate it."

Mrs. Longwood leaned her bulk against a stone wall that separated the small service yard from the area where horses and wagons pulled in to make deliveries. "Willem, you are indeed welcome. But I'd be happier to give you some sort of a job if you could ever bring yourself to live in town like ordinary folks and stop wallowing in the abyss of grief you've let yourself fall into."

Mrs. Longwood, who had lived in Berea only slightly more than a year, had learned more about this man than anyone in town had bothered to find out. Talking with him any number of times, when she had found him out here eating, she had pieced together his story.

More than thirty years before, at the close of the Civil War, Willem had been a Confederate prisoner of war at Camp Chase Prison near Columbus. A native of Georgia and a member of the Georgia 35th Infantry, he had been captured by the Union forces during the bloody days of Gettysburg. Though he had no physical wounds, he was deranged from the horrors of battle and lay listless and uncommunicative for months in a Union prison. He remembered little about his home or family. Finally his captors released him with nothing but the clothes upon his back. He was completely disoriented as to his whereabouts and remained mentally damaged by the carnage and inhumanity he had seen in the war.

He became a vagrant, staying in crude shelters that he built himself. For the past few years he had been in and around Berea, finding its people uninterested enough in him that they left him alone.

Perhaps because she was something of a loner herself, Mrs. Longwood didn't pressure Willem to change his pattern of living. She felt sure that some of his relatives could be found by contacting the Georgia company that his dog-eared papers said he belonged to, but she would make no effort to do so unless Willem agreed. For the time being, she would see that he didn't go hungry or cold. Last winter she had insisted on giving him some blankets from the hotel linen press.

"Bless you, ma'am," Willem would always say softly, his blue eyes filling up. In his speech there remained a slight trace of his southern way of speaking. "There ought to be more folks in this world who care about other people the way you do."

"You paid a price, Willem," Mrs. Longwood said, taking his empty plate and preparing to go back inside. "You served your country, the one you were part of, as you were called to do. What the war did to you was dreadful. Although you've lived many years almost like an animal, that isn't to say you have to live the rest of your life that way." Her tone softened and she looked at the broken man almost fondly. "Think about that, won't you?"

Rose's nimble fingers braided the chrusckis just the way her grandmother had taught her when she was hardly tall enough to reach this same kitchen table but insisted on helping. All those things she had learned from her grandmother were skills that helped her to get the job working for Mrs. Longwood at the hotel. Rose enjoyed her work there and liked feeling a part of the town. Better than working in the onion fields, certainly. Rose didn't think she was better than other people, but she had some feelings and aspirations that she couldn't share with anyone else—until she'd met Stephen Ballard.

Rose lifted the chrusckis one at a time from the kettle of boiling fat and laid them on a towel to drain. Stepping to the window of the steamy kitchen, she let a gentle, late afternoon breeze cool her cheeks.

Next door Pavel Prohaska had come home from

the quarries and, coughing and wheezing, was pounding the dust from his boots. On the other side, Feliks and Jan, Lon Sobieski's two lively boys, clung to him as he appeared near the back door. Quarrymen were arriving in back yards all around the neighborhood. The work week had ended.

Rose was watching her mother in the garden, tying up tomato plants, when she saw her brother George, washing up at the pump in the back yard.

George and Rose had scarcely said anything to each other since that tense Sunday evening in the parlor when George had been so critical of Rose for seeing Stephen. George left nearly every evening right after the meal, so avoiding a conversation with him wasn't difficult. He usually bolted his food, then headed for one of the taverns to meet with other quarrymen who might be interested in the union.

Almost before she realized it, George's solid form filled the tiny kitchen. He settled himself at the table and poured a glass of cold tea. "What smells so good?" he asked. His features were relaxed in a pleasant expression, and he regarded his sister as if nothing unpleasant had ever gone on between them.

She turned her back to drop another batch of chrusckis into the kettle. "Chrusckis—to take to the dinner after Mass tomorrow. It's the 130th anniversary of Poland's Christianity."

George shrugged. "I'm glad somebody keeps track of those anniversaries." Then he added, "Gives us a chance to have a really big feast."

Rose sat down across from her brother. "Glad to be through for the week, eh, George?" If he could be pleasant, so could she.

"And the week had a good ending, Rose." George poured himself more tea and swirled it around in his tumbler.

Rose's brows shot up, questioning. "How so?"

George puffed up the slightest bit. "John Seidel read the union's demands to the superintendent. Now the Stone Company will surely listen to us." He drank his tea, avoiding looking at Rose.

He hadn't called Stephen by name, but perhaps he was sorry for the hateful things he'd said that night in the parlor.

"And what are the demands?" Rose asked evenly.

George explained how the quarrymen's wages had been cut a few years before and never restored and how safer working conditions were so important to everyone whose family depended upon the quarries for their livelihood. And this, he assured her, included shorter work weeks.

Patiently, he explained to his sister the whole idea of collective bargaining.

Rose listened carefully. She had never seen her brother so animated and passionate about anything.

"So who will decide — whether these demands will be met?"

Rose jumped up and began washing up her

cooking things. She didn't want George to see the tell-tale expression that had to be on her face.

"I wish I could say it would be Mr. Ballard," George answered. "But it will probably be that hotshot Worthington from downtown Cleveland. And he knows about as much about quarrying as an organ grinder would."

Rose hung onto George's every word as she wiped an earthenware crock over and over. He went on, with a note of respect in his voice, "Ballard took a copy of what John read, then he spoke very kindly to us—even thanked us for our good work this week and every week. Said us and our families are a credit to the community. Those were his words." George was on his feet. "I tell you, Rose, that man understands us. You'll agree with that, I'm sure. He was raised with quarrying. He'd give us a fair shake. I hope he has some clout with old Worthington. I only saw that old goat once, but he seems like a real stiff neck."

Rose kept her knowledge and feelings about Mr. Worthington to herself, but she hoped her brother's admiration for Stephen as his superior was George's way of telling her he could understand why she liked being with him.

She kept her eyes lowered, busily sifting powdered sugar onto the chrusckis. "It will be splendid, George, if the Stone Company listens to those things you've asked for. You're only wanting things to make a decent life for folks, it seems to me." She looked at her brother squarely. "I'm proud of you for working so hard to help everyone. I really hadn't understood what you were doing."

George colored slightly at the praise. "But, Rose, you've got to remember, it's like Mr. Pritchett, the union man, says, those are things that take money away from the Stone Company — a shorter work week, raising pay, paying for inspections. And to agree to a union that can bargain for us, as I've told you, will take power away from the company and give it to us quarrymen."

Rose began laying the table for their evening meal. She was glad Sophie had stayed outside, probably visiting with neighbors. George would have hesitated to speak so openly in front of his mother. With her limited English, she would have trouble understanding. It would take time and patience for her and for many others in the neighborhood to understand what would be happening.

"Oh, George," Rose called to him as he headed to his bedroom to change clothes. "Did you hear about our cousin Sam? He's going to get some kind of award for being a good citizen — for helping run off that bunch of counterfeiters out at Podunk Swamp. I heard about it downtown today."

George's reply was muffled but clear enough to understand. "It's about time people realized us Polish — Polanders as they always call us in the newspaper — can be good citizens!"

Fourteen

Stephen had to duck slightly to miss the doorframe of the Wolinski's home. Sophie had greeted him, smiling shyly, then looking down ruefully at her apron, she disappeared to find Rose. Although she had told him, "Siedziec, siedziec," and motioned to a carved walnut rocker, Stephen remained standing and looked around the simply furnished, squarish parlor, eager to learn more about Rose. A picture of Kosciuszko, the Polish patriot and soldier of the American Revolution, stared over a small gateleg table. A crucifix hung on another wall, and on the stand beneath it a Bible lay open. Stephen bent down to see if the words were Polish. They were. He straightened up quickly, prepared to be courteous if George appeared. He hadn't forgotten George's warning about seeing Rose, but by now Rose clearly was willing to take the risk of criticism from her family and her neighbors that seeing him might bring.

He turned toward a rustle from the parlor door-way. "Hello, Stephen." That lilt in her voice, just say-ing his name, tugged at the very core of Stephen's being. She stood, poised and expectant, her blue eyes dancing, her face glowing. The dress, a pale green lawn that she'd borrowed from Anna, clung softly to the curves of her breasts and dropped in graceful folds over her hips.

Before Stephen could speak, she handed him a small basket. "I made some chrusckis. We may get hungry out in the fresh air."

Sundays in Berea were made for outings at "The Rocks," a waterfall on the Rocky River just north of town. Easily reached by a path that dropped down from the road, massive rocks piled below the falls, creating a theater-like backdrop for pleasure. At times, water rushed over the falls with a deafening roar amplified by the canyon. Occasionally a train would lumber over the bridge, drowning out all other sounds.

Today, with no rain in several weeks, the water dropped almost languidly over the falls, darting skit-tishly around the large stones in its path.

Stephen pulled the horse and single-seater he'd rented for the afternoon off the road at the clearing nearest to The Rocks. Other rigs were already there, and small boys, eager to earn a few coins, swarmed around to watch the horses.

"Careful, Rose." Stephen handed her down, lifting her skirt slightly.

"Stephen, you treat me like a grand duchess—and I love it." She squeezed his arm as they started toward the path leading to The Rocks.

He looked down fondly into her face that was flushed with excitement. On the path, wellworn but steep, Stephen went first, taking Rose's hand as they made their way down.

For several generations, young couples from the South Side, dressed to the nines on Sundays, had made this their special social gathering place. To drive out to The Rocks and spend a leisurely Sunday afternoon denoted a very special outing. A young man who invited a girl to The Rocks on a Sunday signaled that he had fallen for her.

Stephen found a smooth, flat rock and spread out an India print throw he'd borrowed from Martha Adams. She knew where he intended going this afternoon, but he could trust Martha to keep that to herself. Rose stood captivated. The sun lit up the sparkling water as it cascaded over the falls, turning it into a brilliant string of diamonds. There was an earthy, sensuous aura about this place where Nature had sculpted its patterns for generations, and young lovers had carved their initials in the stones.

Couples clustered along the banks, the young women in their frothy shirtwaists of dimity and organdy with voluminous sleeves, their male friends in

Sunday-best striped madras shirts and embroidered suspenders. Most sported straw boaters with colorful bands.

"Listen," Rose said. "Some people are singing. Do they always do that down here, do you suppose?"

Stephen cupped his ear and leaned in the direction of the sounds. "I think I know what music that is, Rose. A quartet is practicing for the barbershop contest at the county fair next month. I heard Carl Geiger talking about it in the hardware store the other day. He's one of a quartet—he and Louis Webster. I don't know who the others are."

The harmonious strains of "The Sidewalks of New York" drifted across the rippling water, adding to the magic of the place. Farther down the bank, three young men had whipped off their coats and were skipping flat stones across the water to the squealing delight of their female companions.

Rose reached in her basket but instead of chrusckis, she brought out a square carved box. "I thought we might have a game or two," she said, opening the box for Stephen's inspection. In it was a set of dominoes and a hinged board that Rose unfolded, saying, "My grandfather carved these while he was aboard the ship that brought him to this country. When he got here and could afford paint, he put the dots on. Mama probably would weep and wail if she knew I'd brought them, but I think he'd like to know we're using them."

"Rose, you're so full of surprises." Stephen leaned

on one elbow in her direction. "There's so much to know about you, and I want to learn everything — "

"Let's play," she said, starting to set up the game. Clearly, she was not ready for any serious talk.

Stephen hadn't played dominoes since he and his mother often played when he was a boy, but he managed to beat Rose one game out of three.

"I guess you deserve a chruscki, after all," she said, handing him one, along with a napkin. "You'll need this, the powdered sugar gets all over." As their hands touched, and their eyes caught each other's, the two exchanged knowing smiles. Simple pleasures, shared by two who were drawing closer to each other with each meeting, were becoming exceptional rather than ordinary.

But moods are as capricious as the summer winds. When they had finished their chrusckis, Rose's expression changed as abruptly as if a curtain had dropped.

"I hate to spoil this lovely afternoon," she began, her voice trembling a bit. She drew back as Stephen reached for her hand. "But I need to tell you something." She hesitated, groping for words, refusing to look directly at him. "I don't see how we can go on seeing each other, Stephen." Every word pounded on Stephen's heart like a jolt of muffled thunder. She rushed on before he could protest. "Of course, you know that my brother George is one of the leaders of this union business. If there's trouble between the union and the Stone Company — "

Since her talk with George in the kitchen the night before, she understood more about the union position, and she found herself agreeing with the things they were striving for. Up to that point she had only heard about the union activities from Anna's husband Viktor, who believed the Stone Company would never bend to the demands of a bunch of "hotheaded rabble rousers," as he called them. In fact, he felt they were jeopardizing their jobs and their families' wellbeing.

Stephen busied himself folding a napkin around the remaining chrusckis and replacing them in the basket before he spoke. When he did, his words were deliberate but kind. "I've told you more than once, Rose. I'm my own person. I'm grateful for this job that's been handed to me, but I will not go against my conscience to let it dictate to me who I associate with." The muscle in his jaw tightened, and his left eyebrow rose as if to emphasize his words. "There's a vein of snobbery that runs through this town, Rose, and I don't like it."

"That's very noble of you, Stephen, and I admire you for your principles, but there may be circumstances in which your idealism won't work." She turned away and watched the stone-skippers.

Another couple had seated themselves on a rock nearby. Stephen recognized Jane Koeller's friend, Sarah Carman, and a young man who was a teller in the bank. Miss Carman occupied herself with arranging her linen skirt and taking off her leghorn hat trimmed with lavender ribbons. Once she had arranged herself on the cushion her partner had brought, she stared in Stephen and Rose's direction. Promptly, she moved her cushion, turning her back toward them. Her escort looked their direction, then shrugged his shoulders and did likewise.

Both Stephen and Rose caught the sharp thrust of Sarah Carman's action. That same young woman had behaved unseemly only the day before in the hotel dining room. Twice she had demanded Rose replace her tea, declaring it was only lukewarm. "You'd think getting a cup of hot tea to the table wouldn't be so difficult," she'd declared to her friends and people at nearby tables. Rose had replaced the tea each time and said nothing.

Stephen cupped Rose's chin in his hands, so she had to look directly at him. "Our friendship, Rose Wolinski," he said quietly, "is far too important to me to let anything, I repeat, anything—unions or the Stone Company or snobbish people—come between us."

Rose looked back at him without seeing him for the tears that filled her eyes. No words would come. She felt as if someone were tying a scarf around her throat and pulling it tighter and tighter.

Fifteen

Stephen had dreaded this moment, dreaded it so much that he had rehearsed the scene he was now playing time and again in his mind, ever since he had pressed the telegraph key to send the quarrymen's list of demands to Mr. G. H. Worthington.

He creased and re-creased the special delivery letter that a curious Postmaster Meacham had just handed him. It bore the letterhead of the Cleveland Stone Company; its florid signature was that of George H. Worthington, President. From the crisp, creamy vellum screamed the order:

FIRE THE QUARRYMEN WHO ARE ORGANIZING THE UNION – TODAY! This will show these scoundrels their actions won't be tolerated. AND even more importantly, the entire quarry operations will take notice and understand that the Cleveland Stone Company is not about to take its orders from a bunch of ignorant laborers.

Bewildered, not even realizing he'd left the post office, Stephen found himself sitting on a bench in the Triangle, the letter dangling from his long fingers. He stared across the grassy space without seeing the cluster of young children playing nearby, probably while their mothers filled their shopping bags at Carman's Grocery. Their happy squeals failed to penetrate his consciousness. He scarcely spoke to Mr. Peebles, editor of the *Advertiser*, as he passed by, nodding a brisk good morning.

A pall of gloom settled over the young superintendent. He had no choice. For all his highfalutin talk about being true to his own principles, how could he not carry out the orders of his superior? But Rose— Stephen mentally shook his head emphatically. He had to keep Rose out of this. But what he would have to do was sure to affect his relationship with Rose. She is a part of the Polish community and is loyal to her family and her neighbors. This is what she had tried to warn him of that day on The Rocks. Stephen berated himself for his naïve idealism—vowing that nothing could come between them, just as they were growing closer and realizing their feelings for each other.

Someone was hightailing it across the other end of the Triangle toward the hotel. Only because the person was moving so fast did Stephen come out of the cocoon of his tumbling thoughts and notice. That loping gait could belong to none other than Sheriff

Maxson. Mrs. Longwood probably called him because someone had skipped out on a hotel bill. That seemed to happen with unfortunate frequency in spite of Mrs. Longwood's (and Belvedere's) diligent surveillance of the hotel lobby.

"You had better get some officer of the law in here, right now, or I shall spread the word everywhere that this clap-trap hotel isn't safe for women travelers." A wasp-waisted, heavily rouged and powdered woman in a stylish black moiré traveling suit stood before Mrs. Longwood's desk. Her glossy auburn hair was piled high, and in it perched a hat on which a velvet bird of paradise nested. Her appearance attracted a second look, but when she spoke, her harsh words and strident voice did not match her well turned-out appearance.

Mrs. Longwood, who seldom met a situation she couldn't handle, was struggling to keep her customary poise and aloofness. "Now, Mrs. Millett, I've sent for Sheriff Maxson. You can tell him of your difficulty and register a complaint if you so desire. Meanwhile, why don't you have a chair over there by the window?" Mrs. Longwood motioned with her ever-present embroidered silk fan.

The woman called Mrs. Millett eyed the fan and then gave a tortured sniff. "My *difficulty*. My *difficulty*." Her voice rose another half an octave, carrying over into the dining room, just as she probably intended.

"Is that what you call attempted rape?" She pounded her taffeta parasol against Mrs. Longwood's desk. Belvedere let out a squawk of alarm, but for once he had nothing to say.

By this time the few breakfast stragglers were crowded up to the dining room doors, and Rose, server Goldie Schweitzer, and two helpers from the kitchen were trying to listen but keep out of Mrs. Longwood's sight. Fortunately, the hotel lobby was empty of any paying guests at this hour. Only Caleb Barkham lethargically mopped the oiled floorboards, stopping to lean on his mop to listen whenever Mrs. Millett's voice rose.

"All I can say, Mrs. Millett, is that Mr. Jedediah Curtis has lived here at my hotel ever since I bought it one year and two months ago, and there have been no, I repeat, no complaints, ever, about his behavior towards women." Mrs. Longwood's manner was civil, but obviously she looked upon this woman as a hussy, bound to make trouble for the hotel and advance her own agenda, whatever it might be.

Her traveling companion, apparently a maid, a colorless waif with hair like bleached straw, stood off to the side with her pale, passive eyes fixed on Mrs. Millett.

"When that man asked me to dine with him last evening, I thought he was being hospitable and kind," Mrs. Millett dropped her voice confidentially. "I accepted, and we even shared a glass of wine together.

Then when I refused any further advances, as is my custom," she paused and smoothed the ruffles on the broad bertha that covered her shoulders, "he seemed totally understanding and gentlemanly."

"That's what I would expect from Mr. Curtis. He must have enjoyed your company as he's very lonely since his wife died," the hotel proprietor said in a placating manner.

"Well," Mrs. Millett pitched her voice toward the tin ceiling, causing Caleb to drop his mop and stare bug-eyed at this woman who would take on Mrs. Longwood, "gentlemanly he was not when we happened to meet later in the hallway near my room. I'm sure he was waiting there for me, and when I started down the hall, he grabbed me—and he—he pushed me into a clothes press. It was—ugh—full of dirty laundry." She tossed her bird-bedecked headful of auburn curls and wrinkled her nose in distaste. "It's only by God's own grace and a few tricks my brothers taught me when I was growing up that I was able to fight him off me. I was so exhausted and distraught that I didn't have strength enough to come to you last night and report this." Her voice began to quaver. "I retired to my room at once to recover from the shock. Millicent here," she indicated the motionless maid, "kept putting compresses on my poor head for hours."

"It's unfortunate," Mrs. Longwood said drily, "that you couldn't have spared Millicent for a few minutes to report this incident when it happened. Mr. Curtis left early this morning to go to his daughter's in Columbia to spend a few days. He won't be here today to speak in his behalf."

Mrs. Millett drew herself up, her ruffled bosom heaving, "If your sheriff is any kind of a lawman, he'll put out an immediate warrant for this scoundrel's arrest. He ought to — "

While Mrs. Millett raved on, the corners of Mrs. Longwood's generous mouth started twitching noticeably. She had seen Sheriff Maxson entering the hotel.

"Good morning, Mrs. Longwood. What can I help you with today?" The sheriff looked straight across the top of the bird of paradise, ignoring, for the moment, the person who must be the source of the trouble that had sent Caleb Barkham to fetch him. He'd sent Caleb back with the word that he would come to the hotel as soon as he finished sending some telegrams.

"I'm the one who needs help," Mrs. Millett screeched. "I was attacked in the hallway of this disreputable place — "

Bristling, Mrs. Longwood restrained herself.

Sheriff Maxson answered calmly, "Then we need to go over to my office, Miss–

"*Mrs.* Harriett Millett of Pittsburgh," the plaintiff answered haughtily. "Why should I suffer the indignity of going to an office of the law when I was the one who was attacked? Send out a posse for that man!"

"If we wished to do that, ma'am, we couldn't do it until a complaint is filed. So, come with me, and we'll get this over with as soon as we can." He took her elbow to steer her toward the door.

Mrs. Millett turned to the statue-like Millicent. "Go upstairs and pack my things so we can get out of this place. I knew we should have stayed in Cleveland at a *decent* hotel." She swept regally across the lobby, flouncing out the door that the sheriff held open for her.

Sheriff Maxson knew the hotel proprietor to be a no-nonsense sort of woman, but to assure her that he felt the charges were probably trumped up, he looked back over his shoulder and gave her a wink. She was looking stoically ahead, fanning herself, and didn't wink back — but Belvedere did.

Stephen spent part of the afternoon at the nearby McDermott Grindstone Factory, discussing with Michael McDermott how the quarries and the factory, which turned out thousands of grindstones yearly, could work together to increase production. The meeting with the no-nonsense factory owner, who was also a board member of the Cleveland Stone Company and had been in the stone business for three generations, had gone well. Stephen's only regret was the dense cloud of cigar smoke from which Mr. McDermott operated. Stephen himself liked an occasional good cigar, but this gentleman thrived on the constant presence of one, using it as a pointer or to gesture emphatically whenever it wasn't in his mouth. Sometimes, Stephen found himself distracted from their business at hand by wondering what Mr. McDermott would do next with his cigar. And, of course, the stench in his office was sickening. Pictures on the walls and framed citations for his civic goodness all bore a brownish-gray film, a union of years of cigar smoke and sandstone dust.

The meeting had at least taken Stephen's mind off the dreaded task facing him very shortly. He had sent Rufus out to notify George Wolinski and James Janek that he wished to see them before they left the quarries for the day. He knew that Rufus would do this quietly, but when George and James dropped out of the line of quarrymen as they left for the day, an undercurrent of speculation would rumble through the ranks.

The last Dinky engine for the day had rattled past, and Old Jumbo would sound the end of the workday in a few more minutes. Located at the McDermott factory from which Stephen had just come, Old Jumbo was the central timepiece for Berea. The town had no official clock and, essentially, the quarries dictated its ups and downs.

Stephen had always had straight-arrow powers of concentration. As a student, he had refused to let other things distract him. If he had a task at hand, whether a test, a speech to make, or a goal to accomplish, he could manage to dismiss anything else from his mind. Today, he had determined to put Rose out of his mind as he anticipated this meeting with her brother and his union-promoting partner. Every time he thought of her clear blue eyes, remembered her lilting laugh, or her graceful figure flashed across his mind, he forced himself to replace it with the stiff, authoritarian picture of Mr. G. H. Worthington, barking orders over his telephone. Occasionally, the image of earnest Sophie Wolinski tending the rosebushes outside the neat house on Pulaski Street that her father had built would crowd onto the stage of his consciousness. But he would quickly dismiss her image as well.

He could hear muffled voices as the quarrymen approached. Suddenly the air in the tiny office was stifling, and he once again had that feeling that the walls were closing in on him. It was a trapped feeling that he disliked, almost resented. But as superintendent, he had to shoulder this responsibility, regardless of how painful it was. Determined to handle this matter alone, he'd sent Rufus on an end-of-the-day errand.

Although the door was open, the two quarrymen knocked respectfully on the doorframe. "Mr. Ballard?" It was George who spoke.

Stephen unfolded his lanky frame, rising and moving toward the door. "Come in, George. James. Thank you for coming." George's face was pinkish-white with quarry dust, but his shoes had been wiped clean before coming into the office. He had removed his hat and clutched it fiercely in two hands, betraying his nervousness. His partner, James, still wore his bandana around his face and had kept his dust-coated hat on. He hadn't taken the trouble to wipe off his shoes, not that it really mattered in this bare-bones sort of office. For George, though, cleaning off his shoes must have been a token of respect.

Standing, facing the two quarrymen, both out-standing workers, Stephen again felt trapped, but he cleared his throat and began. "Gentlemen," his voice quavered for just an instant, then he plunged on. "I received an order this morning from Mr. G. H. Worthington, president of the Cleveland Stone Company. His order is that I am to fire the quarrymen who are organizers of the union." George's face went pale, and James' whole body stiffened. Stephen continued, "From the outset, you two have been the ones who have encouraged this union movement. Now, you were perfectly within your right to hold up your banner at the Summerfest. You did that with dignity. And what you do on your own time, away from the quarries, such as holding meetings at St. Adalbert's School—that's your business. But bringing an unauthorized person into the quarry on a working day for the purpose of recruiting union members, even on their lunch period, cannot be tolerated. This is trespassing, and I so informed Mr. Pritchett."

James looked as if he was trying to say something from under the bandana, but Stephen continued, a bit more gently. "I regret this action has become necessary. You are both excellent quarrymen, and I know that you have the interests of your fellow trades-men at heart. Your hours are long, the hazards are many, and you feel you deserve a more equitable wage. I cannot argue those facts, but neither can I ar-gue with Mr. Worthington, my superior."

James could be quiet no longer. "You tell us we're good workers, and yet you let that big shot tell you what to do."

"James, just as you take your orders from your foreman, so I take mine from the company president. I am an employee, not an owner of the Cleveland Stone Company."

"When will this happen?" George asked, a note of fear in his voice.

Stephen swallowed hard, looking from one to the other, then over the tops of their heads to the sun-shine outside. "It is effective today."

James pounded his foot, making dust fly. "Damn that bastard, Worthington. Plenty of other places have let their workers have unions. He's such a skinflint, afraid he'll have to pay some extra dollars for better wages and inspections." He kept clenching and unclenching his fists while he talked.

"What he doesn't realize," George said with a trace of sadness, "is that he'd increase production with bet-ter paid workers who work in safer conditions."

Stephen, eager to draw this meeting to a close with-out a debate on the position of the quarrymen, added,

"I know that your families depend upon your wages, and you'll need to find work somewhere. You won't find any kind of quarry work, since Cleveland Stone Company owns all the quarries around these parts. But there are good folks in Berea, who own businesses that hire workers. As I've said, I respect you as workers, and if I can put in a good word for you around town, I'll be glad to do that. Mr. Worthington can't stop me from doing that."

He shook hands with George, whose eyes appeared moist. "I wish you the best, George." Turning to James, who hesitated before shaking Stephen's outstretched hand, he said, "James, I'll have trouble finding another guyer as skilled as you. Good luck."

Sixteen

Mrs. Longwood swept through the hotel kitchen on her punctual eleven o'clock tour, checking readiness for the noon meal and eagle-eyeing everything in her path. Despite the overpowering heat, she wore her customary black ensemble. Her bombazine skirt just cleared the broom-clean wooden floor as she swished past bubbling stockpots and stacks of plates waiting to be loaded with chicken and dumplings, the noontime special. When she purchased the hotel, she had installed a new Garland range and oven, and daily she congratulated herself upon her wisdom. The lunch trade, in particular, had picked up thirty percent in recent months, and word of her varied and tasty menus and careful service was bringing more newcomers each week to her dining room.

She paused at the range, watching cook Frances Reinboldt flour and season Lake Erie perch, cautioning her, "Sauté them gently and don't overcrowd them in the pan."

On the pastry table stood four lattice-topped berry pies with crusts perfectly crimped. Rose sat on a nearby stool, her cheeks flushed, tiny sweat beads lined across her smooth forehead.

She stood as Mrs. Longwood approached. "I'm just waiting for the other four to come out of the oven, ma'am."

"Sit down, Rose. You should rest while you're waiting. The pies look excellent." Leaning her generous frame against the baking table, she lowered her voice. "I've been hearing many compliments on the pies we're now serving at noon. I want you to know that." Her words were clipped and matter-of-fact.

Before Rose could answer, her employer went on, "You made a very workable suggestion—that I should relieve you of serving breakfast so you can use your skill as a pastry cook. Almost anyone can be trained to serve breakfast, but few have the talent you have at the pastry table." She nodded approvingly, her jowls jiggling.

"Thank you, Mrs. Longwood. I'm glad people like the pies, and I truly enjoy baking."

"Rose," she arched an eyebrow, "it has been a very useful arrangement for us both, eh?" She swept up a handful of pastry pinwheels Rose had made from piecrust trimmings and put them on a small plate. These would likely find their way, along with a plate of lunch, to the tall man with the streaming hair who'd soon be stopping by, outside the kitchen door.

Continuing her tour through the kitchen, she spoke briefly to salad maker Alma Kretzhammer to make sure her slicing knife was sharp enough and stopped to check on cook's helper Molly Humphreys' forearm, burned in a small grease fire the day before. Then she marched on to inspect the dishwashing station for cleanliness.

'A useful arrangement for us both.' Mrs. Longwood surely understood part of Rose's reasoning for asking to move to the kitchen during the breakfast hour. Actually, the idea had come to Rose one night as she lay, saucer-eyed, until long after midnight. She could tell how late it was because No. 252 had gone through, the C.C.C. & St. L. train whose engineer apparently possessed a sadistic streak. He would pull on the whistle over and over while passing through Berea. Some people joked that he was saying hello to a long-ago girlfriend in town. Folks in Rose's north-end neighborhood ignored the noise, for the most part, although the trains made their windows shake and their dogs howl. Even the South Side folks could hear the hooting whistles, but everyone knew the trains were their lifelines, carrying Berea sandstone out of their quarries and into the world.

The trains usually didn't disturb Rose. She was young and worked hard all day, then walked the mile to Pulaski Street. But lately, she had turned and twisted in her narrow bed; she knew something had to change. Since Stephen had fired her brother and James Janek, she had avoided serving the quarry superintendent at breakfast. Goldie, sensing something wrong between the two of them, gladly seized upon the chance to serve his table while Rose waited on customers at the other side of the dining room.

But that couldn't last forever, and besides, Rose couldn't stand being that close to him. Her heart ached to be near him, but the strong bond to her family held her back like an invisible tether. Mentally, she could accept the fact that he had to do as his superior ordered, even though, as she hoped, he might feel differently in his heart. George had told her of his kind manner, almost as if he agreed with the quarrymen's demands. Rose's emotions cried out, longing for this man with whom she'd thrilled to a budding relationship that seemed to promise such joy as she'd only imagined. True, he was older—seven years older than she—and he treated her with such care and respect. But it was much more. "We're good together, you and I," he had said more than once. That summed it up. When their eyes met, when their hands touched, when they walked together, when they shared music, poetry, even simple pleasures like a game of dominoes—there was a feeling of oneness and a deep longing to be even closer.

With talk of a strike leaping up like a blazing fire, Rose concluded she could not possibly go on seeing

Stephen—just as she had told him that day on The Rocks. The memory of that always-to-be-treasured day often brought tears that she buried in her pillow at night. She had prayed for a way to keep her job at the hotel, yet not have to begin each day with seeing him. There was no question that her job was doubly important, now that George was without work.

This night, as she stared ahead into the humid darkness of her upstairs bedroom, she thought of suggesting to Mrs. Longwood that she make pies for the noon meal. Everyone always raved about her paper-thin pastries. This would maybe help Mrs. Longwood as well as keep Rose separated from Stephen. And besides, if people liked them, Mrs. Longwood might feel they were worth more than what she paid Rose for serving breakfast. This would help replenish the scrabbled-together family nest egg that Sophie was now dipping into.

There was no doubt that the discerning hotel owner knew Rose felt she should avoid Stephen. In fact, she secretly applauded the girl for her cleverness, and Rose's pies were truly delicious beyond belief.

As he watched the quarrymen assemble in the grassy area near his office, Stephen noted their mood was more constrained, more dubious than it had been last Saturday when John Seidler had read the proposals from the union. This was not surprising considering the presence of Mr. G. H. Worthington who stood beside Stephen.

Worthington, immaculate in gray worsted, carried a soft derby hat of lighter gray and sported his apparent trademark, a bright flower in his lapel. He was dressed much as the last time Stephen had seen him — at the Arcade. When he stepped off the train at Berea's Union Depot, he looked as if he could chew nine-penny nails in two. Clearly, he was not pleased with the urgent need to come out here as well as to other quarries to put down this union nonsense, once and for all. He had said scarcely a half dozen words as Pavel drove Stephen and him to the quarry in the two-seater that Pavel had wiped clean of quarry dust as a courtesy to the president.

Now, stepping forward, Stephen said simply, "Gentlemen, may I present Mr. G. H. Worthington, president of the Cleveland Stone Company." A spattering of applause riffed across the rows of quarrymen, almost like the sputtering of a stubborn engine.

Worthington stood motionless for a moment, as if wanting to make the men fully aware that this was the company president, actually in the quarry. With no introductory remarks, he pressed into the matter at hand. "I am here today to speak in response to your so-called demands presented to Mr. Ballard, your superintendent, last week.

"Be it understood, henceforth and hereafter, that the Cleveland Stone Company is the unequivocal, I guess I should say to you people, the sole owner and operator of these quarries. This is a thriving business, shipping this valuable sandstone all over the United States, Canada, and even to Europe. Decisions must be made. Intelligent persons schooled and seasoned in the ways of business and industry will make the decisions here. You people are hired to provide the necessary labor to keep this business going. That, and that alone, is your role.

"You will not be recommending policies to the Cleveland Stone Company regarding wages, hours, hiring or firing, or any other procedures, either as individuals or as what you choose to call the Quarrymen's Union. As far as the Cleveland Stone Company is concerned, such an organization does not and will not exist.

"Now you may return to the jobs you are hired to do."

Without so much as a "good day," Worthington turned stiffly and headed for Stephen's office, brushing a film of quarry dust from the shoulders of his otherwise immaculate suit.

The walls of Pop Melanowski's tavern gave off a pungent whiff of stale beer, quarry dust and pipe smoke. A few scarred tables and chairs lined the walls, and the high windows, covered with a dusty film, afforded little of the fast-fading sunlight. Quarrymen had gathered here for decades — some on their way home after work but most in the after-supper hours—for a pint of brew and a kindly respite from their bone-wearying, often-perilous jobs.

On the back of the door, visible to everyone as they would leave Pop's, a hand-lettered sign asked, "Do you want a better life? Join the union NOW!" Pop Melanowski was definitely in the corner with the union faction.

Viktor Mikolak didn't often come to Pop's after supper. Time with his wife and children meant more to him than jawing with men he'd worked with all day. Tonight, though, he wanted to put his finger on the pulse of his fellow quarrymen—to find out how heated their determination might be to push forward against the Stone Company.

Worthington's speech had rankled Viktor although he was not at all pro-union. But the company president's pompous attitude and his references to "you people" had stirred up Viktor's normally calm nature. The president's statement that decisions at the Company had to be made by "intelligent people" shot out his meaning like a well-placed bullet: The quarrymen were the next thing to dumb oxen, fit only for grunt and groan work.

Lean and fiery-eyed Mike Janovick, husband of Gretchen and father of Jake, climbed onto the stool next to Viktor and signaled Pop for a beer. "So, what's it going to be do you think? I hear the membership's climbing." Mike paused to light his pipe, smoke puffing from the corners of his thin lips in a steady rhythm. He wrapped his gangly legs around the stool and hunched his shoulders over the bar.

Viktor tightened his hands around his beer mug. "After that speech from Worthington, it will probably double," he grunted. "He's a real bastard. The union guys have a lot in their favor."

Mike cut in, nodding, "Yeah, that president got them stirred up all right. And I hear George and James have called another meeting at the school tomorrow night. Looks like they're going to stick with this and hope they'll get their jobs back if the union gets its way." He blew a curl of smoke up toward the ceiling. "And, hey, I was glad to hear George got a job at the *Advertiser*, even cleaning floors and delivering papers. Anything to help out his family. James hasn't found anything yet, so they say."

"Do you think they'll likely be hired back?" Viktor asked skeptically.

Draining his mug and laying some coins on the bar, Mike shook his head. "Not from the sound of what we heard today," he said sadly. "Old Worthington'll hold this union stuff against them from now 'til kingdom come." He looked sharply at Viktor. "Ballard acts and talks pretty reasonable, I think, but still, he takes his orders from downtown Cleveland."

Viktor ignored the reference to Mr. Ballard. Everyone knew that Anna's cousin Rose had been seeing him, but Viktor wasn't going to appear to have any inside information, one way or another. "Bet old man Worthington draws a salary as big as half a bank—probably enough to support all of Pulaski Street and then some." Viktor said. "Did you get a load of that dandy suit? And a red flower on his coat—to come to the quarry. What a joke!" Viktor threw his head back and gave a rip-roaring laugh, his round belly jiggling against the bar.

"Tell me more about Edward Kennedy, Martha. I understand he's a true hero in these parts—in the whole state, I guess." Stephen was helping Martha Adams pick up clippings she'd pruned from her spirea bushes. He enjoyed her garden almost as much as he enjoyed her company. In spite of the warm weather, Martha went about watering, weeding, and trimming with zeal.

"Oh, Stephen, he is an admirable man. He was wounded twice, then captured by the Rebels after the Battle of Spring Hill. Then he spent fourteen months in Confederate prisons, some of it in that most horrible of southern prisons, Andersonville." She took the basket from Stephen and set in on a slatted bench. "After Appomattox, they shipped him to Vicksburg and put him on that paddleboat, the *Sultana*, to head up to Cairo, Illinois. There the soldiers could be put on trains to go home. There weren't any railroads in the South. You're too young to remember, but that boat blew up near Memphis. More than 2,000 died, mostly soldiers like Mr. Kennedy, who were going home—and that boat was only supposed to carry about 375 passengers." Martha's voice quavered as she turned away for a moment. "What a dreadful thing to happen to those poor men who had survived so much. It happened the same month President Lincoln was shot. Captain Kennedy, he was, got badly burned, but he held onto a piece of wood for five hours until he was rescued. Can you imagine? In the Mississippi River? It was very high that spring, and the current was strong. When he came home to Berea, Edward Kennedy became a successful businessman and dedicated civil servant. Governor McKinley appointed him to the State Board of Pardons. It's like he feels he owes a debt to the world because his life was spared."

Although they could hardly see each other's faces in the growing dusk, Stephen didn't want to break off this conversation. Martha was such a storehouse of information. He always learned from her, and he enjoyed each visit with her more than the last.

"I understand he was mayor of Berea before the voters sent him to Columbus to be legislator."

"That's right. He served two terms as mayor and was elected twice to the Statehouse—and a great legislator he was. He spoke out for women, too. In fact, he was a strong backer of the bill that gave us ladies the right to vote in school board elections." She chuckled. "I guess I owe him my job on the school board. But we miss seeing him around town as much as—

What was that? Behind the Koellers' Rose of Sharon bush? A flash of blue—" Martha inched closer to the low privet hedge that partly separated the two backyards.

Edward narrowed his eyes and looked toward where she was pointing. "I can't imagine—"

"Ps-st. Mr. Ballard." A hoarse whisper came from the Rose of Sharon bush. "Ps-st." More urgent this time.

"Come out, whoever you are, so I can see you," Stephen said quietly.

A bedraggled Sam Mikolak emerged and crept toward Stephen. His sweat-damp blue shirt had caught Martha's eye. His voice, on the verge of changing, cracked as he spoke. "S'cuse me, Mr. Ballard, for bothering you." Then, as if remembering his manners, "Hello, ma'am."

"Why, Sam, what's wrong? You surely haven't turned up another counterfeit ring, have you?"

Small talk always helped Sam feel at ease. He hesitated, then rushed on. "Mr. Ballard, I heard some of the quarrymen talking at Pop's—"

"Slow down, now, Sam. Let's hear it straight."

As Sam moved out of the shadows, closer to the hedge, Martha tactfully headed toward the back of her garden to get rid of her clippings.

"I was cutting through the field back of Pop's when I seen a bunch of those union-crazies standing outside in back. Even George and James was there." He halted his rapid-fire account and took a deep breath. "So I sneaked up and hid behind the privy house, and I could hear 'em saying things like, 'We're gonna strike,' and, pardon me, Mr. Ballard, 'To hell with that bastard Worthington,' and 'We want a better life for us and our families.'"

"Did you get any idea when they plan this?" Stephen's tone had more of an edge now.

"No. Because they went inside Pop's then and banged the door hard. They weren't talkin' no more, but they couldn't know I was listening. I sure was scared one of 'em would come to use the privy house, though."

"Sam, Sam," Stephen reached across the hedge and shook Sam's calloused, clammy hand, noticing how it trembled a little. "You are a help to a lot of people in this town."

Moving closer, Martha said, "Sam, the whole town thanks you for doing your part in flushing out those counterfeiters at Lake Abram. When will you get that award I read in the paper you've been promised?"

"I don't know, ma'am. But it sure is nice of Sheriff Maxson to promise that."

"I know your folks are proud." Martha's voice was warm and sincere in the almost-dark.

As he watched Sam's slim form disappear in the shadows, Stephen said wearily, "It's coming, Martha, sure as tomorrow's sunrise."

"It's been a long time in coming," she replied, "several generations, in fact. The first people who came here to work the quarries were so grateful to be in this country, to escape the starvation, the political unrest, or sometimes even oppression in their homelands that they simply accepted their lot. At least, they had work, albeit toilsome and dangerous work." Slapping at a mosquito with her gardening gloves, she then stuffed them in the pocket of her apron. It was one she'd made especially for gardening, with lots of different sized pockets. "They lived in their tight little neighborhoods and spoke mostly in their native tongues."

"Some still do," Stephen said. "I know many didn't understand Mr. Worthington's speech the other day. I watched their faces. Some were blank, just weary, almost resigned. They probably don't really understand what the union people want."

Martha nodded. "But the ones pushing for the union are mostly the American-born sons and grandsons of the original quarrymen, and they are not going to stand by silently if they think they can improve their lot. Since they're better educated than their forbears and more comfortable with the language and what's happening, they are bound to know of the growing strength of unions in other industries and the progress some are making."

Martha turned to Stephen and took his long, firm hands in her own small ones, saying with conviction,

"And you, my friend Stephen, will see it through to whatever the outcome is. Pray for guidance and know that Bereans respect and support you. Together, we will all ride out this storm, however it may subside."

As the two friends parted, fireflies began to pinprick the now-inky surroundings, and crickets tuned up their nightly symphony. The calmness of the night was settling over Berea like a light summer blanket. From the north side of town came a rumble, shaking the ground on which they stood, then came the shrill hoots of an approaching train.

Seventeen

The trim grounds around St. Adalbert's Church sparkled. A welcome, soft rain had fallen during most of the night, but an uneasy Father Suplicki paced back and forth across the lawn after his morning prayers. His was an awkward position. He was the undisputed head of the Polish community, and rumor had it that he would be asked to speak for the quarrymen if an arbitrator was called in. This seemed likely since the Stone Company refused to acknowledge any of the strikers. He felt he should pray for and support the efforts of those in his parish, yet he did not wish to appear to be condoning any violence or destruction of property that could likely occur. He could only pray for God's will to be done and for the safety of everyone involved. Yet, the diligent parish priest longed to do what he could to help bring the strike to a peaceable end and, if possible, to improve the lives of his neighbors. He had begun a special Mass at four o'clock each afternoon, and now that thinning the plants in the onion fields was over, many of the women and children of the parish were joining him.

The strike, if it continued for long, would have far-reaching effects on his parish. Members could not tithe if they had no income, but already he was seeing people attempting to serve their church in other ways. Yesterday Vincent Morinski had begun washing the outside windows of the rectory, and Anna Mikolak had hung a new curtain she had made for the confessional.

St. Adalbert's was at the heart and soul of the Polish neighborhood. When the Polish people first began coming to work in the quarries after the War between the States, they had worshiped at St. Mary's, the Irish church. By 1873, Berea's Polish colony numbered around one hundred families who longed for their own church where they could pray and hear the gospel in their own language. They petitioned for and obtained needed funding to build their church, and a glorious celebration took place in Berea for the laying of the cornerstone of what would be the first Polish church in the state of Ohio. Visiting clergy arrived by train for the ceremony, and bands from neighboring communities, along with the children of the parish, led the procession from Union Station.

The following year, when the church was completed, God's heavenly light shone through imported stained glass windows, gifts of parishioners, which depicted patron saints — Saint Anne, Saint Joan of Arc, Saint John Cantius. The magnificent altars were hand carved in Poland and shipped to Berea piece by piece.

On this morning, Father Suplicki's prayers had beseeched the blessings of all of these saints. As St. Adalbert himself had struggled to evangelize the pagan Prussians, perhaps these honest workingmen could drive home their message of need to the formidable Cleveland Stone Company.

"Can you believe this, James? We only had fifty or so signed on last week." George's eyes swept the orderly lines of about 150 of his fellow Berea quarrymen. They filled the dirt street in front of St. Adalbert's School and stretched past the church and the parish house. But there was no shouting, no air of celebration. Although the strike was about to begin, even those who were most adamantly in favor of it were fearful. No one could know how the Cleveland Stone Company would react to a work stoppage.

James snorted. "That fancy pants from Cleveland done himself and the Stone Company in." He hiked up his pants and slapped his battered felt hat against his knee, causing a plume of beige-white dust to rise. "I'd like to see his frozen face when he hears about this."

George frowned. "Don't let's count our chickens before we hatch 'em, James. We're headed over to West View to start going into the quarries and shops to see if we can convince the others to quit work. We don't know if that'll happen, but we're not planning to make any trouble."

The strikers had met at their now-official head-quarters, St. Adalbert's School, at seven o'clock on this June morning. They were eager to begin their mission of shutting down the quarries. Then the strike would be officially on.

A murmur of voices from the ranks of quarrymen rose, fell, and died suddenly as the men sighted Father Suplicki making his way across the lawn that stretched between the church and the school. Even at this early hour, the priest was fully robed, his clerical collar pristine.

Following him in sedate pairs marched the four parish nuns, Sisters of Felicity — Sister Agnes, the eldest, moving slowly as if her arches throbbed, moonfaced Sister Christina, youthful Sister Mary Martha, and the ever-prim Sister Beatrice — their rosaries swinging in rhythm to the measured steps of their high-topped shoes.

Hands clasped before him, Father Suplicki faced the hushed, expectant crowd of soon-to-be strikers. "Good morning, my brothers in Christ." He paused. Other than the twittering of birds and the distant whining from the grindstone mill a half-mile away, there was a reverent silence. From high in one of the lordly beech trees, a lone cardinal flung down a message of "Good cheer, Good cheer."

The priest continued. "You are about to undertake a mission that you deem is within your right. We are here to ask God's guidance upon your actions. Let us pray." Heads bowed as the body of quarrymen, as one with the priest, crossed themselves. "In the name of the Father, and of the Son, and of the Holy Ghost. We are mindful of our many blessings granted by you. Today, we ask for that you grant wisdom and courage to these men here assembled...that they will demonstrate their concerns in a peaceful and respectful manner, always mindful of your commandment to treat others as we would have them treat us. Amen."

From Adalbert Street on down to Bagley Road they marched. As they filed by Grindstone Mill No. 3, workers there stopped to look open-mouthed at the sight of ranks of men—men they knew—marching past, daring to defy the Cleveland Stone Company.

"We will do this, James," George declared. He and James were at the front of the lines of quarrymen. "Even God is blessing us with this perfect day." Only a few cottony strands of clouds stretched across a sky as blue as a field of cornflowers. James grunted in assent and kept his flashing eyes straight ahead.

Along the route to West View, curious onlookers watched quietly. Mostly they were people who were half-fearful, half-angry that the quarrymen were so bold as to take this action. The quarrymen's wives watching the spectacle held their collective breath and prayed for the safety and success of their men.

Wriggling children looked on wide-eyed at a parade they couldn't understand.

The union men were persuasive that day and in the following week. Other groups visited quarries in Columbia and Olmsted Falls, and soon fourteen of the company's quarries were idled, including ten in Berea. The Stone Company transported the quarrymen who wished to work to its Amherst operation; the work force there was made up primarily of German immigrants who refused to strike.

There was no violence in Berea, although one striker, Thomas Kaslowski, had threatened to kill a deputy on duty at a grindstone factory. When he was tracked down at Pop's saloon, he resisted arrest and was hauled off to jail.

George regretted that incident in what thus far was a non-violent strike. "Tom was dumb to go to Pop's and brag about what he did," he remarked to James. They were headed home after a long dusty walk to the quarry at West View that had convinced more workers at that quarry to walk off the job.

James howled. "What was really a joke was when the deputy didn't find nothin' in Tom's pockets but rocks. He was so sure he seen a gun on Tom. Stupid — that's what all them deputies are. And they're probably paid a bunch of money for standing around trying to look tough."

George shrugged. "Six dollars a day, I heard. That's a 24-hour day, mind you. Old Worthington's got the town scared they'll have to pay for any damage to the Stone Company's property."

"That old goat makes me want to damage everything in sight that he has anything to do with." James picked up a stone from the side of the road and heaved it at a tree. "Take that, old man Worthington! That's what I'd like to do to you."

"But you won't," George said firmly.

For the most part, the Polish women knew little about what was happening with the strike. They knew their men marched out every day, after meeting at St. Adalbert's school, and went to the quarries and mills to get more and more quarrymen to stop work. In the evenings at supper they'd hear bits and snippets of what happened before the men would bolt from their tables and head to the school to plan the next day's strategy; afterwards many would stop at Pop's for what was left of the evening. They would nurse one beer, all they could afford.

One episode, however, thoroughly riled the women. Gretchen Janovick heard about it first; she always seemed to have her ear to the ground. Actually, her brother, Vincent, who'd lost an arm as a quarryman, often helped out at Pop's and was Gretchen's source of information about goings-on there.

Her cheeks flaming, her voice trembling, Gretchen was the center of a knot of women outside

St. Adalbert's church, following the afternoon Mass.

"He hit her! He hit Mary Kaslowski on the head with a billy, and she fell on the ground."

"No!"

"With a billy?"

"That bully!"

"She was only trying to help her husband."

"It sounds like they didn't even have a warrant to arrest Tom."

Gretchen said. "They never did show it to him. Those two deputies just swept into Pop's and charged him with assault and battery on that watchman at the mill. They roughed him up good, too. He was lying on the floor, holding his shoulder, when Mary came in." Her eyes filled with tears. "The minute she asked to see the warrant, that deputy turned on her and hit her. Then they took Tom off to jail. It's a good thing my brother Vincent was there. He helped Mary home."

Lucy Zielinski spoke up in quiet voice. "We've been inside praying that this strike won't lead to violence, but—"

Gretchen interrupted. "But does that mean we shouldn't protest against the kind of roughing up Tom and Mary got?"

The group of stirred-up women scattered, going to their separate homes to prepare supper for the men who would soon be returning.

Gretchen lay awake much of the night, trying to

think of ways to protest the treatment of Mary Kaslowski. Agitated over what had happened to Mary, the women should surely rally to some kind of action.

The next morning, an hour or so after the men had departed for West View, Gretchen Janovick picked up a hoe outside her kitchen door and headed for her nearest neighbor's house. That neighbor, armed with a stout rake, went to yet another's house. Before long, nearly fifty women stood in the middle of Pulaski Street, clutching every conceivable kind of makeshift weapon. It had taken just a little over an hour, running door to door, for the women to spread the word of the planned protest.

Only a half-mile from the Polish neighborhood, Grindstone Mill #3 was the chosen target. "Let's charge into the mill and tell the workers to go home, just like the men are doing at West View," Gretchen shouted.

"We'll show those deputies what Polish women are made of," yelled a beefy woman, rolling up her sleeves. Her only weapon was a wooden potato masher.

"Let's fill buckets at the pumps before we go," Gretchen shouted, "so we can put out the fires in the boilers. That will stop work for certain."

"Let's get moving."

"We want to get there before their dinner time."

"Let's do this for Mary!"

The holiday mood of the group waned as the women approached the grindstone mill. They were dead serious about their mission. As they crossed Bagley Road and stopped in front of the mill, Gretchen stepped out of the ranks of the outraged, formidable-looking group.

"You men need to go home to your families. Lay down your tools and go home—NOW. The union is going to shut down this mill."

For a few moments, nothing but silence filled the cavernous building. Then, singly and in twos, workers filed out and fanned into the streets leading to their homes. It's not certain whether they did so because they would not resist the women, or whether they actually needed an impetus to join the strikers.

Gretchen gave a shrill whistle, and the women charged into the mill. Brandishing their makeshift weapons, they yelled like drunken savages and cursed the deputies on guard there. Scarcely noticing when her skirt caught and ripped on a lathe, Gretchen led her screaming cohorts through the mill, claiming victory for the strikers. Timid Lucy joined the bucket brigade that poured water and sand on the boilers to dampen the fires. Deputies watching the foray sent word uptown for every able-bodied man to come to their assistance. But by the time reinforcements finally arrived, the situation was calm.

The women left quietly. They had accomplished their mission. Old Jumbo sounded for the noontime break, but there were no workers left at Mill No. 3.

"Rose, you should'a saw those fellows at West View just lay down their tools and walk out. Not a word. They just walked out." James slapped his knees. "By heaven, we'll show the Cleveland Stone Company. The Berea Quarrymen's Union ain't nothin' to trifle with."

"I heard the mayor went down there," Rose said.

"That he did. And that old goat Worthington came out, too. He told us we oughta go home and not destroy property or bother people that wanted to work." He threw back his head and gave a short laugh. "That's a joke. The people that wanted to work was us strikers. Like I said, all them lily-livered workers had put down their tools and went home already. At the mill they let a bunch of women run them off with rakes and hoes. They didn't want to work very bad either."

Flushed with success, James had persuaded Rose to come to the Carpathian Village with him tonight, so he was celebrating that success also.

This was their first time together since that ugly evening in St. Mary's cemetery. Of course, James had apologized the next night in his clumsy way. Standing in front of her house at dusk, he had said, "Rose, I shouldna' shook you. I shouldna' even touched you. But you oughta' know, I care about you." His coarse voice had softened as he lifted her troubled face. "I don't want to see you hurt by that—that patsy of the Cleveland Stone Company."

Rose had felt some kindness for him until he touched her and said that. Then as she looked at his face in the gathering darkness, his broad Polish features had dissolved into Stephen's finely chiseled ones. His glittering dark eyes became Stephen's kinder, softer ones.

She had turned away and said in a muffled voice, "I accept your apology, James. But right now—you must realize this strike business has made things difficult for me. I've told Stephen Ballard I can't see him while this is going on. He respects that." Her voice was tense and strained.

"Then come with me, Rose, tomorrow night, to the Village. There'll be celebrating—because we're going to succeed. There'll be dancing, too. You know you love to dance with me, Rose. We're good together—you and I."

Stamping her foot, Rose had let out a faint cry. Those very words. Those words Stephen had said more than once—"We're good together—"

As James took her hands, she had flinched. She could feel their roughness from less than a decade of quarry work. "He'd marry you one day," her brother George had said. But what would James be like in twenty, thirty years? Would he be like Pavel, his hands crippled and blistered, his breath coming in rattling wheezes? Perhaps he'd be only a shell of a man if he kept working in the quarries.

On the other hand, it is honorable work even if it's dangerous and toilsome. And if the union makes progress — better working conditions, shorter hours, more money — would life be better for everyone? Or would the Stone Company fire all the strikers and force everyone into sheer poverty? A torrent of thoughts whipped through Rose's mind.

She weakened. For a fleeting moment, precious times with Stephen took flight like a swarm of frightened hummingbirds.

"James," she had pressed his hands gently, "I'll be ready at eight o'clock. Please come by for me. I'll be pleased to go to the Village with you." Because dusk was turning to dark, he couldn't possibly have seen the tears that glistened in her eyes — tears of compassion for this earnest, hardworking man, mingled with tears of longing for the touch of that fine, gentle man for whom she knew she truly cared.

Sheriff Walter Maxson pulled off his hat and scratched his grizzled head. He hated to admit that he and his 115 deputies couldn't handle this uprising among the quarrymen, but recent events convinced him that he needed more force to preserve the peace in Berea.

He sighed and reached for the telegraph key to request help from the governor's office. "Send two companies of Ohio National Guard. Need to put down disturbances here in Berea before they get much worse." His message was as urgent as he could make it.

Hearing the office door open, the sheriff turned to find himself eyeball to eyeball with Editor Peebles. "Good evening, Elijah," the sheriff said. "What's on your law-abiding mind?"

"It's good that some of us are law abiding, now, isn't it?" Peebles grinned. "I'm not here to talk about the strike. I've got all of that I need to print. The less attention we give to these ruffians, the sooner they'll quit playing games, don't you know?"

"Could be," the sheriff shrugged. "On the other hand, they're dead serious, but they've been orderly and decent. They meet at the Polish school, and so far nobody has complained about them doing any damages when they march to and from the quarries and the mills." He grinned. "Those women, though, are the rowdy ones—"

Peebles leaned closer to the sheriff. "Speaking of women, what I really came about," he lowered his voice confidentially, "is what's become of the charges that Pittsburgh hussy filed against poor old Jedediah Curtis? If there's anything new on this, I can still get it into this week's paper. There's a passel of rumors flyin' around about this, and I'd like to report whatever the true account is."

The sheriff leaned back in his chair and hooked his thumbs through his suspenders. "And the truth I'll give you, Elijah. Jed Curtis can sleep easy in his bed at the City Hotel or in his rocking chair in the lobby. That woman, that Mrs. Millett, or whatever her real name was, must have guessed we were on to her. She wired in from Toledo the next day and said she wanted to drop the charges. Listen to this." He picked up a yellow paper from a pile that teetered on his desk. 'That doesn't mean I think he's innocent,' she said. 'Oh, no, not on your sweet patootie. That old lecher accosted me. But I don't have the time or the energy to pursue a trial.' "Then," here Sheriff Maxson grinned, "she says, 'Mrs. Longwood was good enough to give me a complimentary room for the night. That was extremely kind of her. Perhaps someone with more time to navigate the legal channels will have an occasion to file a similar charge, and you can then put this culprit behind bars.'"

The sheriff and the editor joined in hearty guffaws. "Do you s'pose she travels around, making complaints, and getting free rooms?" Peebles asked.

"That I can't say," the sheriff answered, rolling his eyes. "But she was one fine-looking specimen of womanhood."

"H-m. A bit racy-looking for my taste, Walter." The editor chuckled and headed toward the door.

Outside, a faint sliver of a new moon hung expectantly in the darkening sky that shrouded the Triangle. Stores were buttoned up for the night, and the area was curiously quiet. Even the air was calm and clear since there had been no blasting in the quarries for three days. But the calmness belied the turbulent mood of the town. Across town quarrymen planned for another march to West View to make certain no one reported for work. At Mill No. 3 the sheriff and a crowd of deputies encircled the building, ready to protect the quarrymen they hoped would report the next day and would work, under martial protection, all day.

Eighteen

Only thick, humid air rolled in through the open windows of the Carpathian Village where boisterous young quarrymen, flushed with success, crowded around the bar, lifting glasses and slapping shoulders.

"By God, we showed 'em." James Janek's booming voice leaped above the rest. "They gotta listen to us now."

"Hear, hear," cried the others. These were the quarrymen who had walked miles today, persuading men in quarries and mills to join the union cause and walk off the job. For a few brief hours they had brought their wives and girlfriends to this gathering spot for a bit of celebrating.

From a table in a corner of the dining room, a babble of female chatter arose from a bevy of posy-colored shirtwaists.

"Rose, it's good to have you with us. We haven't seen you in a while."

Rose refused to react to the biting tinge of sarcasm in Rebecca Morabovich's shrill voice. "Thank you. It's good to be with all of you."

"Well, Rose, we all want to know what it's like to be courted by the handsome quarry superintendent," Mary Stawicki cut in.

"Tell us, Rose."

Rose looked at her friends, these familiar faces she'd known since grammar school. "He's a very kind, interesting man, but I'm not seeing him anymore." She looked away from her friends' eager faces. Her tone was final, not inviting questions. At that moment, she was actually glad to see James coming toward their table.

"Come on, Rose. The dancing's starting." Ignoring the rest of the group, he threw a possessive arm around Rose's shoulders and steered her toward the next room where Stan Stawicki, Mary's grandfather, was thrumping out a polka on a tin-sounding piano. Pavel and his button-box accordion and a brassy-hot trumpet player had joined in.

At the girls' table, a twittering like a flock of sparrows arose as soon as Rose and James were out of earshot. "Wonder whose idea that was—not seeing each other any more," Rebecca whispered as Rose and James cut their way through the crowd. "I can't imagine the snobby South Siders thought much of their quarry superintendent going around with the likes of us."

Mary Stawicki's childlike face wore a dreamy expression. "He's so fine and prominent looking. At least Rose has some good memories."

"So now she'll just settle for James, I guess," Rebecca bent her head toward the group and lowered her shrill voice.

"He really cares for her," someone said.

"Humph. Next to caring about the union, maybe," said another.

Mary spoke out bravely. "Rose is different, you know. She always liked all that poetry Sister Agnes made us read in school. And she goes to the church and listens to Mr. Porubovich practice that holy music." She looked around at her friends and spoke out with force that was unusual for her. "I'm not sure she'll settle for James, as you put it. He's a good person, but he's hotheaded. He thrives on this union business and being a guyer, and it's one of the most dangerous jobs in the quarry."

"Well, at least he likes to dance. That's more than we can say for some others we know." Rebecca nodded toward the quarrymen clustered around the bar. "Why'd they ask us to come is what I wonder." She sipped at her root beer, then set the glass down with a snap. Catching George Wolinski's eye from across the room, she tossed her head with displeasure. He flashed her a smile and moved away from the men, inching his way toward the girls.

James and Rose, moving as one to the familiar beat of "The Sunshine Polka," whirled past the archway to the next room. Over her shoulder, Rose beamed an enigmatic smile toward her friends and tightened her hold on James' arm.

On the South Side of town another social gathering was in full sway. "Do keep the punch bowl filled, Clara. It's much more inviting that way."

Clara Trautman, the cleaning woman-turned-serving maid, adjusted her unfamiliar headband and headed toward the kitchen for pitchers of Mrs. Koeller's famous Hospitality Punch to refill the crystal punch bowl. Actually it was supposed to be Whiskey Sour Punch but the hostess never admitted to that; she always managed to be out of the room when Dr. Koeller laced the punch bowl with a few jiggers of bourbon.

Leila Koeller pushed her spectacles up on her perspiring pug nose and looked over the amply spread table on her back lawn. The table stretched over to Martha Adams' lawn as well, since Koellers and Martha were hosting their yearly midsummer lawn party for their friends and South Side neighbors.

"I do hope we've made enough cucumber sandwiches," Leila fretted to her daughter Jane, who was arranging punch cups on a tray. "They're always gobbled up so quickly."

"Surely we did," Jane reassured her mother. "I thought we'd never finish making them," she added. Jane's focus really lay beyond the refreshment table. She was scheming for a chance to talk with Stephen Ballard. He'd surely be here. And as she'd said to her friend Sarah Carman yesterday when they'd met at Mrs. Meacham's millinery shop, "He wouldn't dare bring that kitchen maid or whatever she is to my parents' party,"

Outside, as they left the shop, she had remarked, "That Polander woman that works for Mrs. Meacham overheard what I said and flushed as rosy as a peony in full bloom. Not that I care a fig." Jane secretly burned that so far she had failed to attract Stephen's attention in spite of her advantage over her friends since he lived at her parents' home.

"Hello, Jane. You're looking especially fetching this evening." Grace Christian, the mayor's wife, sidled up, her considerable girth blocking Jane's view of the forty or so South Siders — a to-be-expected mingling of business owners and college professors and their wives standing in clusters about the immaculate lawns. Their voices rose and fell in polite conversation like a well-orchestrated concerto.

"Aren't Martha's roses exquisite?" burbled bird-like Eliza Sterling.

"It's a wonder," Letitia Marks sniffed, "that she has any time to garden with all the other business she's in to."

"Hush," Eliza whispered. "She'll hear—and after all, you're her guest."

Martha, standing nearby with three men—Elijah Peebles, Thomas Mattison, the druggist, and a professor of German from the college—was in a serious discussion about the strike.

"But so far, the strikers have been very orderly, have they not?" Martha asked.

"Except for that dullard that wanted to kill a deputy," editor Peebles commented.

"We can only hope it doesn't go on much longer," said Mattison. "All downtown is hurting. It's not only that the quarrymen don't have money. But folks are afraid of what might happen, and they just stay at home."

Martha remarked evenly, "It must be very difficult for the quarrymen's families." She nodded graciously to the group and moved on.

"Good evening, Eliza, Letitia. I hope you're enjoying the party."

Letitia beamed. "Certainly. Your roses are exquisite, Martha."

Jane Koeller had pasted a duty-made smile across her face when the mayor's wife had interfered with her plan to approach Stephen. She'd made polite conversation with this woman as long as she could stand it, hearing about her darling son Percy who would be in Jane's class in the fall. She touched Mrs. Christian's plump, slightly moist arm. "Now if you'll excuse me,

I'll see if my mother needs any help."

Circling the crowd, Jane didn't go near her mother or the kitchen. Instead, smiling benignly to guests and enjoying how well she looked in her yellow dimity, she forged a path to where Stephen Ballard towered above gnome-like Professor Steiner and Professor Zirkle, two of her father's colleagues at German Wallace College. As a hostess, she could interrupt without seeming bold.

"Good evening, gentlemen. Are you enjoying plenty of refreshment? Remember, the punch bowl at the Koellers' never runs dry." The professors, like Tweedledum and Tweedledee, bowed their greetings and headed for the punch bowl, leaving Jane and Stephen alone. A playwright could not have scripted a scene more to Jane's liking.

Flashing a smile at Stephen, she didn't notice the tiny smile playing about the corners of his mouth. Taking her elbow, he said, "Let's step over here out of the crowd, why don't we? It might be cooler on the edge." He steered her toward a weeping willow tree that stood limp and motionless in the early evening heat.

"So, Miss Koeller, are you enjoying your summer respite from the schoolroom?"

"I suppose." Jane tried sounding careless, but his unexpected touch on her arm had sent a shock through her whole body. "Berea's a rather boring place to be though. I wish I could get to the city more often." No one had invited Jane to the Arcade outing, and the thought of this desirable man being there with Rose still rankled.

Stephen drained his punch cup, then looked thoughtfully at this young woman he hardly knew, even though he'd lived under her parents' roof for nearly four months. Her pale blonde hair was pulled back from her smooth brow, and her eyes, a deep indigo, shone, no, they glittered expectantly. Certainly her form was graceful and trim.

"Well," he began tentatively, then rushed ahead, "the fair is coming up soon. It's not big-city, but it should be a diversion, don't you think?"

Jane stepped closer to him, letting Billy Simpson and his wife pass. "Perhaps," she tossed her head with what she knew was a becoming gesture. She'd been practicing it for days before her mirror.

Plunging ahead almost as if he couldn't wait to get the words out, Stephen said, "You'd do me an honor, Miss Koeller—"

"Please—call me Jane. After all, we do live in the same house." She stifled a giggle so as not to sound foolish.

"All right...Jane, then." Stephen leaned down and spoke quietly. "You'd honor me by going to the fair with me one evening. When we find out what the programs are, we'll choose a night. How does that sound?"

Like just how I wanted this evening to end, Jane wanted to shout. Instead she said primly, "Very nice, thank you. I'll look forward to that evening." She reached for his empty punch glass. "Now if you'll excuse me, I should greet some other guests."

Stephen watched Jane Koeller move easily through the crowd, nodding, smiling graciously, comfortable among these South Side folks she'd known all of her life. Perhaps he'd overlooked this attractive young woman so nearby. He'd been so smitten with Rose— He hadn't planned to invite Jane Koeller to the fair; the words had burst from his lips almost before he realized what he was saying. When that sort of thing happens, his mother had always said, those are one's innermost thoughts surfacing. Perhaps.

"They look so good together," Muriel Simpson whispered into Leila Koeller's ear as she helped herself to her fifth cucumber sandwich. Leila couldn't help counting.

"Who looks good?" Leila was keeping watch, ready to replenish her abundant table. She couldn't expect her cohostess to be much help now that the guests were here although Martha had made dozens of her trademark Ladylocks. Now, though, she'd be caught up talking politics with the men— or worse yet, asking questions about that awful strike. Since Martha'd been elected to the school board, men seemed to listen to what she had to say about a lot of things. Leila had often seen young Stephen Ballard talking to her out in the garden in the evenings.

Mrs. Simpson swallowed the last bite of her

sandwich. Dabbing her lips with a tiny linen square, she hissed, "Why, your very own daughter, of course, and Stephen Ballard. They were having quite a cozy chat over there by the willow tree." She sighed. "It would be nice to see him keep company with someone on OUR side of town."

Nodding, Leila Koeller searched the crowd trying without success to spot her daughter. But she couldn't miss Stephen Ballard's rangy form as he stood alone, near the willow tree, gazing off into the crowd as if he'd lost something.

While parties were transpiring on two different sides of town, Sam Mikolak and Jake Zielinski sat on the grassy slope bordering the empty playground at Union School. Cross-legged, Jake flipped his pocket-knife first from his wrist, then his elbow, then his knee. Although the knife couldn't stick upright in the sun-baked ground, Jake kept practicing. He was the un-disputed champion of mumblepeg on the north side of town, and he never went anywhere without his knife.

"Can't you stop messing with that confounded knife and listen to me? This is serious stuff, and I can't tell if you even know what I'm saying." Sometimes Sam lost all patience with his younger friends. Because Jake was the most grown-up of the lot, he'd asked him to meet tonight at the schoolyard to share this latest piece of news.

Jake stashed his knife in the sheaf he carried on his belt. "I am listening — go on." He began chewing on a long blade of rye grass.

Sam leaned forward and lowered his voice as if he thought the silent oak trees surrounding the playground had ears.

"Well, this afternoon, just before Old Jumbo blew, Mr. Ballard sent me up to the *Advertiser* office with a notice for the paper. It said that the Stone Company had got a — in-gestion — injunction against the striking quarrymen that says they can't go on the property or try to run the business." Sam drew himself up importantly. "Mr. Ballard explained it to me. The strikers could get arrested, fined — maybe put in prison if they don't obey." He shot a what-do-you-think-of-that look at his friend.

Jake kept chewing his blade of grass and took his time in answering. "So, what do you think you're going to do about it?" He shrugged. "Change the strikers' minds? You'd better start with your cousin George. He and James are the ringleaders of that strike."

"Wait. You haven't heard everything yet. When I went to the *Advertiser*, Mr. Peebles had his back to the door and didn't hear me come in." Sam's unpredictable voice rose a half-octave. "He was talking to Mr. Webster, him what works there. He was sayin' 'Our sheriff's showing some sense, wouldn't you say, call-

ing out two more companies of the Ohio National
Guard to maintain law and order in this town? By
dern, we're not going to have our town torn to bits by
a bunch of ruffians.'

"Then he turned and seen me standing there with
my paper in my hand. I just handed it to him and left,
and he didn't say a word to me. He's usually pretty
friendly with me, though."

"So, you gonna tell somebody what you heard?"
Jake always liked to cut to the chase.

Sam shrugged his bony shoulders. "The strikers'll
find it out soon anyway, but it might help them to
know how outnumbered they're going to be."

Raring back, Jake hooted. "Maybe they'll just re-
cruit some more women with their brooms and rakes
and stuff. My mother was down there at the grindstone factory the other day. She said all those workers just up and left, and the women had a high old
time takin' over the place. They did a number over at
West View yesterday, too. The sheriff and his men
wouldn't touch 'em. Then they run the sheriff clean
off the place."

Of course, the boys knew the strikers and their
friends were celebrating tonight at the Carpathian
Village. They'd seen the men, hair slicked down and
dressed in clothes without a trace of quarry dust,
walking arm and arm with their wives or calling for
their girlfriends. Even George, who seldom paid attention to girls, had walked past with Mary Stawicki,

and to everyone's surprise, James was seen heading for the Wolinski house where he fetched Rose.

The Polish neighborhood was much like a large extended family. Everyone just about knew where anyone else was at any given time. This was not because of nosiness or malice. It was because they cared for one another. When Sam was younger, whenever he walked past his Aunt Sophie's house as the purplish evening shadows were growing longer and the crickets beginning to chirrup, if she was outside on her step or in her yard, she'd say, "Sam Mikolak, you're getting home mighty late, you hear? Get along now." And even though she wasn't a relative of whoever might be with Sam, she'd scold them just the same. And they'd all hightail it for their own houses, leaping over flowerbeds and scaring roosting chickens.

Sam stood up and stretched his long arms, saying, "We'd better be getting along afore it gets all the way dark. But let's just walk by the Carpathian Village to see if we can talk to anyone." Sam didn't want anyone to tell his father that he was having anything to do with the strikers, yet he badly wanted to let them know about the sheriff's call for new troops. Viktor was one of those non-striking quarrymen who feared the loss of his job above all else. He was content to trace and re-trace the timeworn patterns of his father and grandfather, walking to the quarry each day, eking out a scant existence, and yet finding simple pleasures in his family and the life of the Polish community.

Always the schemer, Jake didn't want to leave things to happenstance. He announced as they trudged up Front Street, "We could hide behind the privy house like you done the other day. Someone'll be sure to come out that we can tell and—

"Pooh-ee. Not tonight." Sam was adamant. "There'll be no hiding by the privy house for me tonight. There'll be a steady line of men in and out of there. Besides, someone would be sure to tell my pa." He stopped in his tracks. "What's that up ahead?" He squinted in the half-darkness. "Why, it's a couple of Sheriff Maxson's hired-on deputies." He grabbed Jake by the elbow. "You let me do the talking, will you, if they ask any questions."

At the corner of Adalbert Street stood two burly deputies. Both wore rumpled, ill-fitting uniforms. Their rifles stood like sentinels at their sides. As the boys came near, the taller one spat a long arc of tobacco juice into the dusty street, and the other one, a portly man of at least fifty with a beard that hadn't seen a trimmer in months, glared stonily at them.

"And just where do you two ragamuffins think you're off to?" Stony-eyes shifted his rifle from one side to the other.

"Sir," Sam spoke up, "we was just over to the school playground for a while. It's—"

"Ain't you Polanders got a playground at your school? Or won't those troublemaking strikers let you use it?" Not waiting for an answer, he motioned with the butt of his rifle. "Git along with you now. Git to your houses where you belong."

The boys passed by silently, heading toward their homes, as if all thoughts of the Carpathian Village had flown their minds.

Spitting again, then wiping his chin with the back of his hand, the taller deputy declared loudly, "A great example them strikers are for teachin' their young'uns about respect and right and wrong. Here they are, runnin' loose in the streets at night, just itchin' for trouble."

Sam walked quickly, trying to put as much distance between themselves and the deputies as they could. Jake ran along beside, trying to keep up. "How come those deputies could tell us to go home?" he panted. "We wasn't hurtin' nobody. We always play outside after dark and nobody cares."

Sam stopped and looked squarely at Jake. "Figure it out. They gotta take their meanness out on somebody Polish. They won't stand up to the women, and they're probably afraid of the men. Plus they gotta do something to earn their pay. I heard they was gonna get $6 a day for being on duty 24 hours at a time."

The new moon, barely visible when they were at the playground, now was a fingernail-like sliver. "The evening star'll be out soon," Jake said. "I'm gonna make a wish—that all the deputies would suddenly get pew-monia."

"Jake, that ain't a good thing. Mostly people die of pneu-monia." He pronounced it carefully.

Jake considered that possibility for a moment. "Well, I'll wish for lumbago for 'em then. That'll take 'em all out of action, won't it?"

Nineteen

"I can tell the difference already. We think the Polanders don't have much money to spend, but when they don't have any — well, we're feeling it. Besides that, other folks don't feel safe, so they stay in their homes." Downtown at the Triangle, A. A. Carman, the grocer, and George Neubrand, owner of the dry goods store, were comparing morning notes on the effects of the strike. Quarrymen were regular customers at Neubrand's, for it was the only store in town that carried the sturdy five-dollar-a-pair boots quarrymen had to save for and buy each year.

Folding back his shirtsleeves, Carman cranked down the green-striped awning over an array of vegetables. "It's a good thing for them they all have gardens. And it's a good thing for all of us we finally got some rain." The lawns on the Triangle seemed perked up from the early morning rain though perhaps it was only wishful thinking on the part of Bereans. More rain would surely be welcome.

"Maybe it'll be enough to quash the spirits of these strikers a bit," Neubrand said. "They need something to take them down a peg."

"I hear the sheriff's called for two companies of the state militia," Carman said, his face darkening. "I hope they're not needed."

"Well, the Stone Company notified Mayor Christian the company would hold the town responsible for any and all damage that might result to the company's property during the strike. That was more than enough to cause the sheriff to call for more help, I'd say." He pulled on his derby and buttoned his coat. "Well, time to open up. Good day to you, Carman." Neubrand headed toward his own place of business that had been in his family for three generations. He'd always felt secure here on the Triangle. Now, though, with idle strikers about, the militia called out, and the streets nearly empty of shoppers, he felt his very existence somehow threatened.

Disaster had visited A. A. Carman before; his Akron area grocery store had burned to the ground a few years before. He had come to Berea and purchased a thriving grocery business here on the Triangle and started a new life with his family in this placid town with two colleges. But a cold dread clutched at his insides; he feared what violence could erupt during a strike. His comfortable white frame, two-story home sat on East Bridge Street, within shouting distance of the Stone Company's office. If the strikers should decide to attack or vandalize the office, his family could be in danger. The town had never seen its immigrant population stirred up before; always they'd accepted their lot and kept mostly to themselves.

Over at the City Hotel, Stephen Ballard was finishing his usual breakfast of eggs and flapjacks. A lower-than-usual hum of voices rose from the tables around the dining room as if the townspeople knew they shouldn't approach him about the strike, so they purposely didn't involve him in their conversation. Usually, one or two shopkeepers would stop by his table to chat, but not today. Stephen, seated alone at a small table, suddenly experienced a sense of being adrift, as if he didn't really belong here. This nagging sensation had gripped him several times lately, one that he was doing his best to stifle.

He'd given up looking for Rose at breakfast. She'd either changed jobs or was working different hours. He knew she had to be working somewhere, but he dared not ask Mrs. Longwood. He didn't need that lady pronouncing judgment on him.

As he left the dining room, Stephen passed the half-dozen shopkeepers who regularly breakfasted at a round table near the door. Mattison, the druggist, was the only one who spoke. His tone was hearty. "Hopefully, it will be over soon, Ballard." The others, looking up from their flapjacks, nodded Buddha-like in agreement.

"Thank you, gentlemen. We are hopeful," was all Stephen could manage. He knew what the others did not—that the Stone Company planned to obtain an injunction, the most powerful method of breaking up strikes. This would restrain the quarrymen from entering the premises or interfering with its property or running its business. If the strikers disobeyed, they would be liable for arrest for contempt and could be fined and imprisoned.

About the time Stephen Ballard swallowed his last mouthful of the City Hotel's lighter-than-air flapjacks, George Wolinski and James Janek were leading their fellow strikers on toward West View by way of the railroad tracks. They hoped to induce more of the quarry workers there to join them. Sheriff Maxson and six of his deputies had learned of the intended march, and they rushed to reach the West View quarry ahead of the strikers by traveling a back road.

As the strikers came into view, Maxson ordered, "Go back." "Return to Berea." But his voice was swallowed up by shouts of the strikers who by this time were fired with determination to accomplish their goal.

The six deputies lined themselves opposite the angry strikers. Curses flew. A melee erupted. Strikers in the front lines fought hand-to-hand with the sheriff and his deputies, using clubs, gun butts, bare fists.

No one ever knew who fired the shot, but suddenly James Janek lay bleeding and writhing in the dust, shot in the chest and forearm. "That stupid deputy—Denby Whitlock—clubbed me, then shot me," he gasped.

The shock that a bullet had found its mark put a halt to the clash, and Sheriff Maxson again ordered the strikers to return to Berea. This time he made his voice heard, and for the moment he thought he and his forces had been victorious. But he underestimated the stamina and spunk of the astonishing sight of about fifty Polish women, charging into view, brandishing sticks, clubs rakes, hoes, brooms, even heavy wooden potato mashers. Their voices rose to a feverish pitch as they began marching toward the quarry.

"I feel like I'm doing something at last to help the men," Gretchen Janovick said to Lucy Zielinski. Gretchen carried a hoe with a handle as thick as a man's wrist.

Lucy's broom seemed far less threatening and she, herself, was not as confident as her friend. "I-I don't know if I can-if I can do this…"

"C'mon, Lucy. It's our turn to help the men." Gretchen Janovick shouldered her hoe and led her stalwart legion of followers into the quarry at West View.

Tightening her grip on her broom, Lucy Zielinski prayed silently for courage. "We can do it." Her voice shook, her lips clamped in a taut line, and her knuckles were white. Then her false courage failed her. "I'm afraid those d-deputies will turn on us and sh-shoot us."

"Nonsense," Gretchen scoffed. "Some of those deputies are way too old and paunchy — we can out-run the passel of 'em."

The women sailed into the line of the sheriff's men, flailing their weapons but not purposely striking anyone.

"Now, ladies — "Sheriff Maxson tried to speak, but his attempt at politeness was lost in a crash of rakes and hoes and pitchforks. A broom handle knocked his hat off into a ditch.

The sheriff and his deputies backed down, abashed, not prepared for or conditioned to doing battle with a horde of furious females, even if they bore only makeshift arms. Gretchen and Lucy and a half-dozen others chased the lawmen as they retreated toward Berea, leaving the other women to patch up James Janek, load him onto a quarry wagon, and haul him to Berea.

The story flew around town that James Janek was dead, but that proved to be an unfounded rumor when he was seen limping toward Pop's a few days later. The bullet had only grazed his chest, then imbedded itself in his forearm. The women had taken him to Doc McKelvey, who reportedly spent several hours digging the bullet out while allowing James to consume some of his best Scotch whiskey to deaden the pain. Now, displaying his wounded arm in a sling, James regularly held court at Pop's every evening where he fanned the fires of resentment toward the Cleveland Stone Company, recounting the saga of the victory at West View to eager strike sympathizers. He skipped lightly over the arrival of the Polish women with their rough and ready weapons.

His ears still ringing from G. H. Worthington's blistering telephone conversation, Stephen Ballard hopped in the quarry's runabout and called Rufus to drive him over to McDermott's Quarry.

A company in Wooster had placed a huge order for curbing, and Worthington was adamant. "Ballard, I don't care how you get that stone out." Worthington had thundered. "It's up to you to see that this order is filled. You're in charge there. That's all I have to say. Goodbye." The Stone Company president had slammed the receiver down mercilessly.

"Go uptown to the sheriff's office, Rufus. I need to pick up an officer of the law before I go into the quarry that's closed because of the strike." Rufus asked no questions but headed the runabout toward the sheriff's office near the Triangle.

Once at the quarry, Stephen jumped down and headed toward a derrick, with Sheriff Maxson several paces behind him. Rufus was already manning the cables and chains that would lift the heavy blocks.

Piles of stones lay everywhere, just where the men had left them when they walked off the job. Stephen would need to get them to the railroad tracks. Sheriff Maxson followed several paces behind him. Stephen, at this point, was wrestling each day with where his allegiance lay. Broken bodies, broken tombstones, broken promises—all of these injustices he weighed against his own comfortable, regular paycheck every two weeks. But for the time being, he was an employee of the Cleveland Stone Company and bound to do its bidding.

Stephen took a long look up at the 80-foot high derrick pole, then climbed the pole and prepared to attach the guy wires to various anchors to stabilize the system. His jaw was set. He'd lost his hat and the unruly lock of dark hair fell over his forehead.

After four and a half hours of intense derrick work, a job that he hadn't done since leaving Stone City, Stephen had piled up enough stone beside the railroad track to fill the Wooster company's order. A Dinky-led gondola of cars would pick it up later in the day and haul it to Union Station.

As Rufus pulled the runabout away from the quarry, Stephen massaged his aching shoulders and wished that some of the quarrymen could have seen him man the derrick.

Twenty

Despite several attempts by a representative of the State Board of Arbitration, the strike lasted six tense, non-productive weeks. Gloom hung over the town as dense as the usual scrim of beige-white quarry dust. With the drilling and blasting silenced, townspeople glided in and out of stores on the Triangle in the unaccustomed quiet like characters in one of Edison's Kinetoscopes. Some were fearful of moving about in their customary routine; the town resembled an armed camp.

Militiamen strutted importantly through the streets, and newly deputized citizens strained to look official. Quarrymen's families stretched their meager resources to the breaking point, depending upon their gardens and whatever odd jobs they could muster. Some people—Mrs. Longwood, Elijah Peebles, Mrs. Avis Meacham, the Koellers, to name a few—although not openly sympathetic to the union cause, helped fill the larders of the families of those they employed and gave them extra work whenever they could. Martha Adams found Sam Mikolak to be a dependable helper in her garden, and she recommended his father to help clean and paint the school buildings.

Upon Stephen Ballard, the strike weighed like a ponderous, immovable burden. The eerie silence of the quarry walls taunted him. Idle derricks stood like threatening behemoths. Sounds of trains roaring past Berea constantly reminded him that there were no carloads of sandstone to ship out. Realistically, he could not have averted the strike, yet he shouldered responsibility both to his employer and to the men he supervised. Guilt frayed his emotions and flawed his reasoning. Nightly in his dreams, an irate G. H. Worthington barked orders against a backdrop of Pulaski Street and the dire hardships of the quarrymen's families. And always there was Rose— her clear blue eyes searching his and her soft, firm voice saying, "...there may be circumstances when your idealism won't work." Now he found himself floundering in those very circumstances.

He began skipping breakfast at the hotel, picking at his dinner, and eating less and less of Mrs. Koeller's palate-pleasing evening meals. His record keeping at the quarry office now caught up, he spent his days there acting as a watchman to make certain strikers caused no damage to the office. Actually, so many deputies and militiamen guarded and patrolled near the quarries, Stephen's presence was not really needed.

His friendly neighbor, Martha Adams, waylaid him one evening as he arrived home from the quarry office. "Why, Stephen, you're becoming a recluse and, I might add, almost a shadow of yourself! Look how your coat just hangs from your shoulders. And your cheeks are growing hollow." Martha touched his face gently, her gray-green eyes searching his with genuine concern. Before he could protest, she said, "You didn't cause this strike, Stephen, and nothing you could have done would have prevented it. The quarrying business is no different from many others that have had or are going to have their labor problems," she said firmly. "There'll be a settlement of some sort before long, and maybe the quarrymen will have made some baby steps toward getting recognized by the owners."

Stephen looked away from Martha's questioning gaze. "It's just that I feel so helpless, Martha—and I really find myself sympathizing with the men—and that means that, in my heart, I'm disloyal to my employer." His eyes wandered over the carefully tended flower gardens in both back yards. The order and beauty of the gardens mocked his jumbled, guilt-ridden feelings.

"You take too much upon yourself, Stephen, and I suspect the more so because of your feelings for Rose."

She picked up the hoe that she'd leaned against the hedge. "My suggestion to you, young man, is that you take on some tasks to keep you occupied, tire you out, and whet your appetite. A wise person once said to me, 'When you don't know what to do, do something.'" She paused to let him ponder that simple bit of advice that had shepherded her through dark days of her own in past years. "Now I must get ready to go to the school board meeting. Good night, Stephen, and think about what I've said, won't you?"

Stephen watched his good friend disappear into her house and stood a long while at the hedge, watching shadows gather and cover the brightness of the gardens until the fireflies began poking holes in the darkness.

The next day he went to the hardware store and bought four gallons of whitewash, lumber, and some hand tools. Without asking for Worthington's blessing, he signed the ticket for the Cleveland Stone Company. After he'd freshened up the walls of his office, he began building a decent desk and shelving for the office. He worked slowly but carefully. Measuring, sawing, fitting, mitering—he took pleasure in what he accomplished each day. Woodworking was not one of his best-honed skills, but he discovered the taxing physical demands of the work began to relieve the mental anguish that had knotted his stomach since the strike began. As the week went by and his projects took shape, he ate Mrs. Koeller's suppers with a relish once again and slept more soundly than he had in months.

The strikers went back to work with a promise that their pay rate would be restored to the 1893 level of 17 cents an hour. The men who were fired were to be re-employed as fast as business picked up. This took some time because the long-awaited rains finally fell during the last week of the strike, and the quarries had to be pumped out before work could resume. Once they returned to work, the quarrymen felt insecure. The Stone Company could easily find fault with their work and fire them whenever they wished. This happened in a few cases, although Stephen interceded for some who were especially valuable workers. Among these was James Janek.

George Wolinski chose to continue working at the *Advertiser* where he had become familiar with the mechanics of the printing press and was working as an apprentice press operator to aging Wilbert Eckersly. When George completed his year-long apprenticeship, his wages would be twice what he'd made in the quarries.

Actually, the quarrymen had gained nothing much but a few cents an hour.

The Cleveland Stone Company still did not recognize the Quarrymen's Union as a bargaining agent, but their employer now had to be aware of the potential strength of the Union.

There had been little damage to the town because of the presence of the militia companies and the 115 deputies that Sheriff Maxson had hired. They had been expecting to earn six dollars a day for their 24-hour shifts, but the county commissioners ruled an allowance of only three dollars a day for the 24-hour duty, which was less than the wages the strikers were battling over.

"I'm so glad it's over," Rose said to James. On a quiet evening, they were sitting on the same stone bench in St. Mary's Cemetery where James had behaved so badly toward Rose only a couple of months before. "Everyone was hurting. I think if I had to face dandelion greens for supper one more time, I'd throw up. Mrs. Longwood helped us, though. She let me take home all the bread and eggs I could carry every day. We had enough to share with Anna and her family." She touched James' bandaged arm gently. "Does it still hurt much?"

James took her hand and brought it to his lips, a surprisingly gentle gesture for him. "It'll be all right. I'm tough, you know...but I'm soft where you're concerned." He searched her face as if looking for some sign of approval. "You must know I love you, Rose." Awkwardly, he put his good arm around her. "Say you care for me, too, that you might marry me one day. We'd be—"

Not wanting to hear those words, if he said, "We'd be good together," Rose turned her head away. She couldn't bear to face those questioning eyes, that earnest, worshipful expression.

"James, I can't...it's too soon—"

"Too soon! We've known each other nearly all our lives, Rose. Our families are like one. What can you mean, too soon?" Not waiting for her answer, he rushed on, his face darkening with hurt and anger. "It's him, isn't it? Even after he stood against us in the strike, went out there and showed off and ran a derrick himself to cozy up to that Worthington and make money for the Stone Company. You still care something for him...for that puppet of a man?" James was standing now, scowling down at Rose, much as he had that other unhappy time here at St. Mary's Cemetery.

Rose looked up at him, her expression calm and determined. "It would not be fair to you, James, to let you think I'd consider marrying you one day when I don't know my own mind." Now she was fighting back tears but was bound she'd keep her composure. "I still care for Stephen Ballard and cherish the times we shared together. It may be that this strike has destroyed all that, but until I'm sure, I'll never stop thinking of him. That's God's truth as I know it in my heart, James." She buried her face in her hands, her shoulders shaking. All the sounds of the woods around them seemed to cease. Their two figures could have been suspended in a frozen moment of time, like people on an artist's canvas.

Conscious of movement, she looked up to see James' broad back as he retreated through the rows of chiseled gravestones. His step was measured, determined, like a man who was vowing never to let himself be vulnerable again.

How long she sat there, Rose had no idea. She vaguely heard the mild cooing of mourning doves, usually a comforting sound, but now they tore at her heart like cries of an ailing child. A squirrel chattered crossly on a branch above her, and the far-off wail of an approaching train raised prickles on the back of her neck. As she smoothed out her green and white striped skirt, the stripes swam into a mass of green through her tears. Suddenly she shouted aloud, looking up through the trees at the patches of china-blue sky, "I know I did right. T'would not be right…to let James keep thinking I might want to marry him." She pounded her fists on the seat of the stone bench without caring she might bruise them. "He'll thank me one day," she said more quietly. "No man, especially a proud Polish man like James, would want a wife who has a yearning for another man deep inside her. Especially a man who is part of another world."

She'd finally admitted to herself the very feelings she'd stifled all during the strike. It was like shedding a heavy burden. As hard as she tried, as many times as she'd told herself Stephen and she were too different, she had not succeeded in putting him out of her mind. All of those mornings she'd stood in the hotel kitchen, rolling out and crimping piecrusts, she'd known he was out there, alone, in the dining room. He would be struggling, as he ate his breakfast, with how to deal with whatever new hindrance the strikers would engage in that day. More than once she had put down her rolling pin and prayed silently for courage to keep from rushing to him, taking his dear, gentle hands in her own, and reassuring him he must do, without guilt, whatever his employer charged him to do. The answer to her prayer always seemed to come in the parade of vivid images that would flash restraints across her consciousness—her family, her friends, her church—her life as she had always known it in her Polish neighborhood. But Stephen Ballard would be there as well, a blurred, nebulous presence in that sea of faces, one she could never blot out entirely.

"Put the loveseat there, like so," Mrs. Longwood gestured with a plump, jeweled finger. "No, I'd rather have it at a right angle with the sofa." She stood back, crossing her arms on her generous bosom, to survey the effect of the new furniture being uncrated in the City Hotel lobby. "Be careful that you don't tear that upholstery," she warned.

The two deliverymen, clearly intimidated by this

imperious woman, trotted around the lobby, placing and replacing the loveseats, sofas, platform rockers and ottomans, until the hotel proprietor was satisfied.

"I had this furniture especially made in Chicago and shipped here by rail," she announced to a bug-eyed Jedediah Curtis, who'd been rousted from his ancient rocking chair, and to two curious traveling salesmen watching the transformation of the shabby lobby. "The upholstery is a crushed velvet but guaranteed to wear extremely well. All of the wood is hard walnut. You won't find any finer furniture—even in the Forest City House in Cleveland." She threw this last in for the salesmen's benefit. "See how much better this place looks! It's worth every penny I've spent."

Mrs. Longwood's attention swung to the front door where she saw Amelia Pierce arriving. With her was an imposing looking woman wearing an ostrich feather trimmed hat and a dress of purple moiré with a wide lace bertha. Even Mrs. Pierce, in bottle green silk, appeared slightly overdressed for a weekday lunch at the hotel, indicating that this must be a very special visitor.

"Good day, Mrs. Pierce." Mrs. Longwood swooped toward the door to greet the pair. Not waiting for an introduction, she rushed on, "And this must be—"

Amelia drew herself up importantly. "Mrs. Longwood, may I present Miss Eleanor Peabody, president of the Cleveland chapter of the WCTU. " She emphasized the word *Cleveland*.

"Delighted, I'm sure," Mrs. Longwood said, her bulky frame almost managing a half-curtsey.

Miss Peabody's ostrich feathers curled within a fraction of an inch of her chin and jiggled as she spoke. "The Berea chapter of the WCTU has done such fine work. I'm here today to notify Mrs. Pierce of her appointment as a board member of our settlement house in downtown Cleveland — The Friendly Inn. I'm hopeful she'll accept."

Mrs. Longwood nodded thoughtfully. "Mrs. Pierce would be an asset to your organization, I am sure." She smiled benevolently at Amelia whose sharp, aquiline features seemed to soften as her thin lips managed a half-smile. "Now, why don't you ladies have a table in the dining room by the window and enjoy a nice lunch? The Lake Erie perch is especially fine today."

She turned back to the deliverymen who were edging toward the door, as if they hoped their duties were finished. Mrs. Longwood stood, hands on her bulging hips, surveying the room with obvious pride. "That will do, gentlemen. However, I have one more request." The men looked at each other helplessly. "Take the old furniture around to the back of the building. It'll do some folks some good. People will come along and pick it up before long. When you finish, you'll have the finest lunch the City Hotel has to offer, free of charge." She beamed broadly as the two men rushed to rid the room of its cast-off furniture.

Twenty-One

J ump up here, boys. Hop to it," said Mayor E. Christian, who held out a stubby arm, first to Sam, then to Jake, pulling them up onto the platform in front of a grandstand packed with fairgoers from all over the county. With three railroads and an interurban line and keen community support, Berea and neighboring Middleburg had finally, several years before, bested other locations as the site for the county fairgrounds. The first few years had been successful, but vicious storms, even a tornado, had wreaked havoc on the fairgrounds the past two years.

Today, good fortune seemed to be smiling on the county fair once again. Townspeople had pulled together, the county had granted some funds, and the racetrack, grandstand, and exhibit buildings stood repaired and ready in time for an early fall event. A tinge of autumn crispness laced the air. Trees that ringed the grounds wore splatterings of autumn color. The unmistakable once-a-year mingling of fair aromas crammed the air: popcorn, motor oil, yeasty baked goods, sawdust, sizzling frankfurters — and horse manure.

Mayor Christian, who was scarcely as tall as Sam, put an arm around each boy's shoulders and bellowed through a megaphone. "Good afternoon to all you fairgoers. We hope you enjoy yourselves today at our County Fair. Before the events begin, I have a long-awaited-for presentation to make on behalf of the town of Berea." He beamed at Sam and then at Jake. The boys looked as if they wished the platform would open and swallow them. They had never seen so many people — and all looking at them! Sam tried to pick out his parents in the crowd around the St. Adalbert food tent.

"During the summer these boys were fishing and hiking out at Lake Abram. Like all boys, they wanted to explore a bit and see what they could find. Well, folks, they found something all right. What they found was a nest of counterfeiters, operating a forge right out there in Podunk Swamp." The mayor paused to mop his rosy face with a handkerchief twice its size. "These boys put themselves in harm's way by watching to learn what those ne'er do-wells were up to. Then they did the right thing by telling Sheriff Maxson, who took a posse out there the next day. But the scoundrels must have known they were being watched because they'd cleared out during the night. Probably hopped a train and set up shop in some other town far away from here.

"Folks in town had already spotted some of these counterfeit dollars," he continued, rasping through his megaphone, "and before long they'd have been all over the place.

"Sam Mikolak and Jacob Zielinski (he pronounced their names Mike-lak and Zel-nicki) here are fine young men who did a service for the town. I want to present each of them with a Certificate of Community Service, which I, as mayor, have personally signed, as well as a *real* silver dollar for each of them. They are proof that a good citizen can be a person of any age. Thank you, Sam." He shook Sam's hand and handed him the rolled-up certificate and the silver dollar, then turned to Jake and did likewise. Lifting his arms to the crowd, he intoned, "Now let's hear a rousing cheer for these good young citizens."

The crowd erupted, especially in the area around St. Adalbert's tent where the Polish community was gathered. Sam and Jake clutched their awards and, at last, smiled and enjoyed their moment of praise.

While people in the grandstand began craning their necks for the start of the horse pulling contests, others milled toward the exhibits of farm products and equipment. Another building nearly overflowed with ladies' culinary and needlework exhibits. Curiously, the fair seemed to break down some of the social barriers among people in Berea. Here amid Leila Koeller's kuchen, Amelia Pierce's watermelon pickles, and Martha Adams' embroidery were Sophie's poppy seed rolls, three elegant hats by Anna Mikolak, and a beaded gown fashioned by Christina Seidel.

The ladies flitted back and forth among the displays like moths around a flame, admiring one another's talents. Sophie had been shy about entering her baking, but Rose and Anna had convinced her. Today, she fairly glowed and bobbed her head with pleasure as others complimented her on her blue ribbon. Still, she said little and stayed close to her niece Anna. As always, when she felt out of place, Sophie became nervous. Then her limited English would fail her, and strings of guttural Polish words would escape her lips.

Over at the St. Adalbert food tent, the crowd that gathered to cheer Sam and Jake had spread out in all directions, but soon more people pressed close to the tent, eager to sample the offerings of the Polish cooks.

Looking up from what seemed the hundredth pie she had cut into six even pieces, Rose remarked to Rebecca Morabovich, "At least, we can be thankful for a fairly cool day." Rose was comfortable in a simple printed challis dress with a pretty gathered handkerchief bertha that Anna had made for her. Its gathered belt and short lace-edged puffs made it easy to work in today. On another day, she could add coat-shaped linings to cover her forearms.

"At this rate, we'll be out of chrusckis by the middle of the afternoon," Rebecca complained as she arranged rows of the fried cakes on large, flat pans. "People think they're the greatest thing they've ever eaten."

"Well, they are—" Rose began, then stopped short and ducked her head. Picking up her knife, she concentrated on cutting a raisin pie.

Rebecca chattered on. "I hope Mary comes soon, so I can leave. I want to meet some friends and ride the Ferris wheel. It looks so thrilling. Imagine being able to see all over the fairgrounds..."

But Rose didn't hear her. She felt a tremor go through her whole body. Her hands began to tremble. She had spotted Stephen's familiar figure as he walked along the gravel path that separated the St. Adalbert tent from the WCTU ladies' root beer stand. Fairly skipping alongside him was spritely Jane Koeller, stylishly turned out in yellow polka-dotted Swiss. Her straw hat had a polka-dotted ribbon to match, and she carried a yellow parasol. With a pang of longing, Rose saw Stephen smile and lean down to say something to Jane, who barely came to his shoulder. Before Rose could make her heart stop pounding, the two of them were standing in front of her.

"Oo-ooh, I'd love to try one of those," Jane pointed to the tray of chrusckis. "I haven't the foggiest notion of what they are, but I'd like one." She motioned with a small, delicate hand. "I'll have that one." Rebecca handed her the chruscki while Stephen fumbled in his pocket for money.

Gathering every ounce of composure she could, Rose looked up from her task. "Good afternoon, Stephen," she said coolly, nodding and half-smiling to Jane Koeller, who had popped the whole chruscki in her mouth.

"Good afternoon, Rose," he said, handing Rebecca the money. Then he looked squarely at Rose. "Those are called chrusckis, I believe. Is that correct?"

Rose's eyes met and held his, unwavering. "Yes, they are very special," she said slowly. Neither of them could look away from the other. Between them stretched precious memories of not-to-be-forgotten afternoons—at the Arcade, at the Triangle, the German Wallace campus, The Rocks. For that moment the entire county fairground and all the people in it could have evaporated, so hungrily did Stephen and Rose search each other's faces.

Busy wiping her fingers on a dainty handkerchief, Jane Koeller failed to see the look that passed between Stephen and Rose. "I'm game to ride that new-fangled Ferris wheel, Stephen, if you'll make sure I don't fall out," she giggled, tucking her hand through his arm.

Rose picked up her knife and reached for another pie to cut.

As the pair moved away from the tent, she heard Stephen remark to Jane, "There's to be a McKinley for President rally at six o'clock at the grandstand. It's exciting to think we may have an Ohio president. I hope we can manage to go to that." While Jane fussed with trying to open her parasol, he looked back toward the crowd around the St. Adalbert tent, as if he hoped to get another glimpse of Rose.

"Oh, I suppose," Jane said, not looking at Stephen, "if you're set on going. But politics is really quite a dull subject, I think." She raised her parasol with a snap.

Red, white, and blue bunting swaddled the platform before the grandstand, and huge baskets of gladiolus and daylilies graced either end. Stretched between two trees nearby, a boldly lettered banner shouted OHIO FOR MCKINLEY. Band members, sweltering in capes and caps, flanked either side of the platform, tuning their instruments, waiting for the signal to begin. One was Peter Eliot's Berea band; the other was an all-cornet band, imported from nearby Strongsville. Small boys squatted near the platform playing mumble peg and shooting marbles, oblivious to the mounting excitement of the crowd.

The bleachers were filling up quickly. Mr. and Mrs. William Simpson cautiously made their way through the crowd and settled themselves near the end of the sixth row. Dr. Koeller and his wife Leila were sitting in the row just in front of them. They both smiled and nodded approvingly as their daughter Jane and Stephen appeared at the rally.

On the platform, master of ceremonies A. A. Carman positioned a podium so that speakers could avoid looking into the late-day sun. Amelia Pierce bustled to the platform and handed up a pitcher of water and two glasses.

Stephen and Jane found seats midway in the bleachers. "We should be able to see and hear quite well from here, don't you think?" Stephen turned to speak with Elijah Peebles and his wife who were sitting directly behind them.

"Good thing we came early," Elijah said. "I had to convince Nettie to leave the women's building and all that frippery and food." As he patted his wife's hand good-naturedly, she rewarded him with a tight smile.

Leaning forward, Jane chatted gaily with her good friend, Sarah Carman. Stephen recognized her escort as the same young man from the bank he'd seen with her at The Rocks that memorable Sunday with Rose; the way they had snubbed Rose and him still rankled.

"Ooh, look," Sarah cried. "There's that new teacher, what's his name? The one that's teaching history at the high school?" A string-bean like man sporting a green-patterned foulard vest, he carried a broad-brimmed sailor in one hand and a molasses-coated popcorn ball in the other. Swiveling his head back and forth, he seemed to be scanning the bleachers for anyone he might know.

"He's all by himself. Doesn't he know anybody?"

Jane glanced sideways at the unwitting bank clerk next to her friend and remarked, "Well, Sarah, maybe you can fix that."

Both young women exploded in a fit of not-too-polite giggles cut short by the Strongsville cornet band bursting forth with "There'll Be a Hot Time in the Old Town Tonight." Jane and Sarah clapped their hands and nodded their heads in time with the spirited music.

A. A. Carman was speaking from the platform. The crowd quieted except for a few fretful babies, the frankfurter vendor's cries echoing across the sawdust-strewn fields, and the distant whirring of the Ferris wheel. The sun was dropping behind the trees, and a hint of a breeze ruffled through the crowd. Mr. Carman stopped, as almost from nowhere a perfect V of Canadian geese yammered past overhead.

"And now, folks," Mr. Carman resumed, leaning his tall frame on the podium, "before the speechifying, we'll be awarding the prize for the barbershop quartet contest that took place yesterday afternoon. Our honorable judges, Mr. Rudolph Graham, organist at the Congregational Church and Miss Ruby Prince, piano teacher, have declared..." he hesitated and unfurled a red-ribboned scroll and read, "first prize in the 1896 Berea Fair barbershop quartet contest goes to The True-Tones, the best barber shoppers around these parts. So come up here, True-Tones, and get your prize."

Stephen recognized Carl Geiger from the hardware store and Louis Webster, pressman at *The Advertiser*, in the striped blazers that bounded up to the platform. He didn't know the others — a squatty, red-faced chap and a pole-slim fellow whose enormous curled mustache seemed to overwhelm his face.

"Before I hand you this award," Mr. Carman beamed, clutching the scroll and an envelope, "how about a chorus of "Sidewalks of New York"? Carl promptly hummed a note and the others seized their cue. Their tight-knit, perfectly pitched harmony floated out over the crowd as if to prove they were worthy of the award.

"Beats me why that song's so popular out here in Ohio. Most of us folks have never seen the sidewalks of New York," Elijah Peebles remarked, turning to Stephen and Jane.

"It's a lilting tune — and they do it justice." Stephen joined the crowd in a hearty round of applause for the group as they took their bows. He turned to say something to Jane, but she was leaning down, whispering to Sarah.

Mayor Christian was now taking the podium. He wiped his face and harrumphed loudly before announcing, "Immediately after our next speaker concludes his remarks, the Hook and Ladder Tournament will take place right here in front of the grandstand. The Berea Grit Company will take on the The Grindstone Company. And now, our speaker tonight is from Canton, the hometown of our next president, Governor William McKinley." A robust cheer and enthusiastic applause erupted from the crowd. "Now, now, folks, let's give this man a chance to tell us about Mr. McKinley— someone he knows well—as a neighbor and a friend. I bring you Mr. Alistair Fitch."

A portly gentleman in a striped morning coat that sported a red carnation stepped up, pumped the mayor's stubby hand, and waved to silence the roaring crowd. With his high, intelligent-looking forehead and flowing, collar-length white locks, Mr. Fitch looked as if he could have been a senator or a judge. Actually he owned a foundry.

Most Bereans had probably never heard of Alistair Fitch, but if he knew Governor McKinley, that was enough for many to register their overwhelming approval. Folks on the South Side favored Republican McKinley, while the immigrants more often voted for Democrats, if they voted at all. The issue in this election would be sound money. The Democrat, a young Nebraskan named William Jennings Bryan, advocated free silver, minting more silver money to keep the economy thriving. The Republicans, championed by McKinley, favored their version of sound money, keeping the nation on the gold standard.

Mr. Fitch took a long swig of water and launched

into his remarks. His made-for-politics voice carried over the crowd, easily overwhelming cries of the unhappy babies and the frankfurter vendors. "Before I tell you about my friend, William McKinley, let me say that Governor McKinley is greeting throngs of visitors every day, except the Sabbath, on his front porch on Market Avenue in Canton. Why, as many as twenty railroad carloads of people from Pennsylvania and Michigan came to his door at nine o'clock one morning, and he greeted and spoke with them warmly and graciously. In a single day, forty special trains brought forty separate organizations from twelve different states who sought to honor our candidate—the representative of sound money, sound financial principles and sound government." With each "sound" Alistair Fitch's voice boomed up a half-octave, setting the crowd cheering again.

"Governor McKinley would welcome all you Bereans to his home, but if you can't go there, why not plan an election night rally here?" Cheering began again, but Fitch motioned for quiet. He launched into a recital of McKinley's qualifications, his views on the importance of a protective tariff as a boon to industries, the danger of the great silver trust that he called a conspiracy among the millionaire mine owners to rob the public, and for an honest dollar worth 100 cents. He wished his excited listeners a return to what he called the splendid prosperity of four years ago, asserting that the Republican Party made it all right, and Grover Cleveland's administration kept it good. "This country has plenty of labor to make us prosperous, and if labor is paid in good, sound money, we will always have a good labor force."

Perspiring copiously in his overstated costume while consuming the entire pitcher of water, Mr. Fitch spoke for forty minutes. The carnation, worn in imitation of McKinley's trademark boutonnière, wilted visibly as he spoke.

To underscore the speaker's message, Peter Eliot concluded the rally by teaching the steamed-up crowd to sing "We Want an Honest Dollar".

"A judge up in Wisconsin wrote these words," Peter called out. "Now it's sweeping the country. You'll know the tune. I'll sing it through once. Then you sing each line after me." In his reedy tenor voice, he began,

We want an honest dollar, so we do,
We want an honest dollar, so we do,
We want an honest dollar and for it we will
    holler
If we have to burst our collar—
Now will you?
Free silver'll never do, don't you see,
Free silver'll never do, don't you see,
Free silver'll never do, only for a shabby few,
A repudiating crew—

* * *

"That was quite a crowd turned out for the rally, I'd say, wouldn't you, Jane? Must have been folks there from all over the county."

Not wanting her outing with Stephen to end, Jane had invited Stephen to have a glass of cider on the Koellers' porch when they returned from the fair. As they'd walked the length of Bridge Street just before sunset, there were few people about. "There'll be fireworks later. I guess that must be where everyone is," she remarked in a slightly peevish tone. Her right hand clutched her folded parasol, and she started to take Stephen's arm with her left. But he had not offered it. Instead, he appeared lost in thought. He continued to act this way when they reached the Koellers' porch. Shadows were lengthening now, and crickets were chirping their evening serenade.

"I'd think he could be fairly certain of carrying this county, wouldn't you?" Stephen's mind was still on the election.

Jane tossed her head slightly while settling herself in the cushioned porch swing. "I suppose so. What I liked best was the Strongsville Cornet Band. They really showed up our Berea band. That Peter Eliot could take some lessons from their bandmaster." She poured another glass of cider for him from Leila's heavy cut glass pitcher, her small hand shaking a bit.

Stephen took the glass absently, ignoring, perhaps only half-hearing her comment. "William Jennings Bryan from Nebraska will carry the farm vote, that's certain," he went on. "He's for cheaper money, coining free silver, and ending the gold standard. And that speech he made at the Democrats' convention where he said 'You shall not crucify mankind upon a cross of gold' went right to the rich businessmen." Stephen rambled on, apparently unmindful whether Jane was listening or not.

"They say he's made over 500 speeches and traveled thousands of miles already, and there's still six more weeks to campaign. Bryan's 36, just seven years older than I am. I don't believe I could keep up a pace like that." He settled back in his wicker chair locking his hands behind his head. "On the other hand, McKinley's hardly stirred off his front porch, so they say. His wife isn't well, and he doesn't want to leave her. But he's got Marcus Hanna, that rich Cleveland man, raising money for him. You watch. McKinley's going to carry the cities—where the workers are—if they'll turn out to vote. There ought to be a way—" Stephen stopped, his eyes fixed on a pot of geraniums at the end of the porch.

"A way to do what?" Jane asked. Again her voice was edgy.

Stephen leaned forward and looked intently at her, his second glass of cider untouched on the table beside him. "There ought to be a way to interest more workers, especially the immigrants, in voting in elections. So many have difficulties with the language, they are fearful of going to the polls."

"Then that's their problem, isn't it?" Jane fanned herself restlessly with a paper fan from Mattison's Drugs. "They've come to this country to live. Then they should learn the language."

Stephen leaned forward and looked at her squarely. "Working sixty hours a week as the quarrymen do, for example, doesn't leave much time for learning, Jane. Many of these men had to quit school in their early teens when their fathers were injured or killed in the quarries."

Jane persisted. "Their children go to school. They speak the language. The parents could learn from them if they tried — if they'd quit speaking Polish or German or whatever it is they talk in their homes."

Stephen sighed. "I suppose. But old customs die hard. Living as they do, clustered together by nationalities — and I'm talking cities now — Cleveland, Chicago, Buffalo, not just Berea — they all have their Polish Towns and Little Italys and so on. It makes it easy to cling to the old customs, the language — " He stopped. Jane was yawning discreetly behind her fan.

Stephen fairly leaped to his feet. He bumped the wicker table, causing the untouched cider to teeter dangerously. "Thank you for your company, Jane. I'll say goodnight now." He stepped inside the cool hallway and bounded up the stairs, two at a time.

Jane pushed herself out of the porch swing, grabbed Stephen's cider glass, and threw the contents over the porch railing.

Twenty-Two

In northeast Ohio, in the counties that hug Lake
Erie's shore, winter can attack in early November
and keep pummeling the flatlands, the sleepy villages,
the teeming cities until after Easter. In 1896, sluggish
winter months ushered in a measure of silence to the
streets of Berea. Old Jumbo still sounded its whistle,
morning and evening, but few laborers trudged to the
quarries. German Wallace College had managed to
dedicate its newest building, Memorial Hall, in late
November, just before winter hit in earnest.

Now piled-up snow covered muddy tracks in
streets, and the muffled clop-clop of horses' hooves
pulling cutters and sleighs over streets replaced the
sounds of clomping boots over the swinging bridge
to the quarry. Pristine, swirling snowflakes canceled
out the weariness and threat of quarry dust. Shopkeepers struggled to keep paths clear to their door-

ways; inside they stoked the fires in their stoves, inviting customers to linger and take respite from the bone-brittle cold.

From the frozen-over quarries rose the shouts of ruddy-faced skaters, schoolboys racing hell-bent on their swooshing blades, while local swains and their coquettish partners glided sedately beneath silent cranes and derricks that looked down like giant frigid chaperones. Other young couples huddled together under buffalo robes for long sleigh rides out the Hogsback, the grade that rose past the fine homes on Elm Street, then out to Fowles Road and through Middleburg Township and back Bagley Road. Through heaped-up snow banks, students at the two colleges trudged between buildings as slowly as Shakespeare's slothful schoolboys. Tapestries of snow and icicles graced stately South Side Victorian homes with splendor while drifts shrouded the gabled roofs of Polish town with weighty white parkas.

Just as the town marked time until winter's exit, so the nation was waiting to inaugurate a new president. Despite the populist appeal of the "Silver Knight of the West" — William Jennings Bryan — he did not muster the votes to defeat the conservative, sound money views of Ohio's McKinley, who chalked up a margin of more than a half-million popular votes. Berea was a stronghold of McKinley voters. In fact, an estimated five thousand people had crowded into the village for an uproarious Election Eve rally.

Although the candidate seldom left his home in Canton, McKinley's campaign, as orchestrated by the political acumen of Cleveland's wealthy Mark Hanna and a never-before-seen flood of political propaganda, proved too much for the youthful Bryan to overcome.

President-elect McKinley was spending the winter assembling a Cabinet and preparing for his March inauguration while President Grover Cleveland labored through his final months in office. As for Mark Hanna, whom one cartoonist depicted as delivering McKinley to the White House safely stashed in his bicycle basket, he opted for a seat in the United States Senate rather than a cabinet post. All things pointed to a shoo-in for Hanna's appointment by the Republican-controlled Ohio legislature that elected senators.

In Berea, winter worked changes upon many lives. Sam Mikolak, after his recognition as a town hero at the county fair, managed to get work shoveling paths at the German Wallace campus after school. He welcomed the change of wielding a shovel in the pure, snow-filled air instead of laboring under heavy water buckets. The vest Anna made him of scraps of fur she had saved at work helped stave off the cold. With Sam's help, Anna and Viktor were able to stretch their resources during the vicious winter. At Mrs. Meacham's millinery shop, orders poured in for winter hats as fashion dictated floppier brims and more elaborate trimmings such as longer ostrich plumes and delicate ruchings of lace, ribbon, and tulle. The South

Side ladies delighted in Anna's creations, and she often had more work than she could possibly do in a day's time. She took work home with her and sat at night, bending near the oil lamp, making tiny stitches until Viktor would insist she stop and sleep. Because Anna's wages were crucial to the family's survival, Viktor helped all he could, seeing that Sam and his two sisters did their lessons and got to bed on time. Although the Union School had called Viktor several times to substitute for an ailing custodian, and he had worked a few days painting at one of the mills, he had no regular work.

James Janek had fallen into a habit of spending nearly every evening at Pop's. He'd sit at the bar, spinning ideas about how to rebel against the Cleveland Stone Company. But his plans were just cobwebs, never well-formed, just talk. He was drinking more than he could afford, helping Pop clean up at night to pay his bar tab. Since he no longer was seeing Rose, or anyone else for that matter, people thought she had refused him and had broken his spirit.

Continuing his apprenticeship at the *Advertiser,* George Wolinski pleased editor Elijah Peebles with his progress. By next summer a substantial raise would help his mother. Sophie kept her stove going, making nourishing dishes from the yield of their summer garden. Sophie, George, and Rose had worked together to store beets, carrots, potatoes, and apples in the tiny root cellar. Sophie's special dishes were her savory stews, potato dumplings, potato pancakes, and a hearty beet soup that George especially liked — he'd eat three bowls, at least. Apple fritters were her favorite treat for Rose. When Rose was a tiny girl, she used to help her mother make these by cutting the core and seeds out of the apple slices, using her mother's sewing thimble.

Mrs. Lockwood continued to run a brisk business at the City Hotel. Salesmen and visitors to the colleges found it a clean and hospitable stopping place with better-than-expected food. Mrs. Lockwood added one employee to her staff, for the winter at least. After many days' soul-searching with Willem as he sat on the wall behind the hotel wolfing down the hotel's "mistakes," Mrs. Lockwood offered him space in a basement room in return for carrying out ashes, chopping firewood, and shoveling snow. She marched him to Machovina's for decent clothes and, once it was clean, trimmed his streaming hair herself. When he brought firewood into the lobby, he concentrated on his task, looking neither right nor left as if he feared someone might try to make conversation. He seemed still to be living his solitary life, only under the hotel's benevolent shelter. At least, he was clean and clothed and warm. Perhaps he would break out of his tortoise-like shell of silence one day.

Rose made apple fritters for the hotel diners and if Mrs. Lockwood could get cheese from a farmer, she would make crepes with cheese. Mrs. Longwood directed Rose to add a jigger of rum to each batch of crepe batter. She liked to have whiskey or rum added when Rose made fried dough or chrusckis as well. Although Rose obeyed, she felt self-conscious about pouring spirits into her batters and didn't think the spirits added much to her family recipes. Each time she used one of the bottles of spirits, she would return it to a spot behind the tall tins of flour and sugar.

To have her baking done in time for the noon meal, Rose started her day at six o'clock. When snow was knee-deep and the temperature dropped into the 'teens, Mrs. Longwood urged Rose to spend the night in a small room at the top of the stairs that she kept for overflow visitors. To help drive away the loneliness she felt there, Rose brought a few things from her room at home. She hung her crucifix over the bed and placed a slim copy of some of Browning's poems on the washstand. Stephen had given her the book at one of their meetings on the campus.

"You keep it and enjoy it," he had said. "I have another book of his poetry."

She didn't need to read the lines from "Pippa Passes". She knew them by heart. But she marked the place with a sepia-toned postcard of the Arcade.

Rose had never been away from her family. She missed Sophie, bustling about their tiny kitchen, singing Polish tunes off-key, and George's solid presence at the supper table. Each night, she would pray for her mother and her brother and thank God for her job and her warm place to stay. Then looking out the small window by her narrow bed at the snow-sculpted roof-tops of the Triangle, Rose could not help imagining what Stephen might be doing. She hadn't seen him with Jane Koeller again. In fact, she had met him only a few times in passing on the Triangle since the fair. They had spoken politely, but he did not stop to talk. Rose, too, would hurry past, not wanting him to see the pain she knew must be reflected in her face. The strike had underscored the differences between their two worlds, and probably Stephen's dark eyes would never again look at her with fondness and respect that could have swelled to what Rose was sure must be passion. Only now, in this tiny, box-like room with the water-stained wallpaper, alone in the darkness of winter, would she admit to herself how she longed once again to hold her head high when she and Stephen walked together, just knowing that he'd cho-sen to be with her for that afternoon or evening. Or how she ached for that overwhelming pulse of emo-tions that swept over her when he'd put his strong arms around her or even when he'd just take her hand to help her into a buggy or onto the train. Stephen Ballard was no ordinary man, of that Rose was sure. Times spent with him were buried deep in the cor-ners of her memory, like fragile treasures perhaps never to be unwrapped again, no matter how much she longed to hold them close to her heart.

As for Stephen, his duties for the quarries were

minimal during the winter since there were few workers to supervise. He focused on visiting the mills
and planning with the supervisors how to increase
production in the coming year. Since grindstones were
vital to all industries for sharpening tools, the mills
were operating with the backlog of stone that had been
quarried during the summer months after the strike
ended. Railroad cars loaded with grindstones continued to chug out of Berea, bound for destinations across
the nation. Occasionally, townspeople would stop to
watch a single grindstone as large as six feet in diam-
eter passing by, anchored to the flat bed of a railroad
car.

Some of the unskilled quarry workers were put
to work in the mills doing menial tasks such as cleaning equipment and painting walls and floors. Often
their pay would be as little as ten cents an hour for a
maximum of nine hours. Working indoors in the winter still did not give the laborers respite from dust.
The fine dust in the mills accumulated in the lungs
and made breathing labored. There was no remedy
for this. In order to feed their families, men were
forced to work under conditions that would threaten
a suffocating death.

Stephen's private life was just that: very private,
almost solitary. In spite of drafty floors and chairs that
cramped his lanky frame, he spent late afternoons in
the German Wallace College library, poring over
newer writers and dramatists. Some portrayals of

women especially captured his interest. He fairly grieved over Thomas Hardy's ill-fated *Tess of the D'Ubervilles*, while being amazed at Ibsen's spunky Nora in *A Doll's House*. Evenings would find him pulling up his platform rocker to the pair of long narrow windows in his room at the Koellers' that looked down on Bridge Street. He'd watch the foot traffic and the sleighs that passed by until darkness blotted out the street. Then he'd turn up the lamp and read until the words danced across the pages and he knew he could fall instantly to sleep.

After reading *In His Steps*, the book Dr. Koeller gave him last summer, Stephen and the professor had long talks about what life in Berea would be like if a mysterious stranger would come to town and convince a minister and five other influential citizens to walk in Jesus' steps every day, as the book described. It must be challenging Americans, at least conservative, churchgoing folks, for it was reported to be selling thousands of copies.

Stephen began examining his own life and comparing it with the characters in *In His Steps*. He'd once told Rose that he felt being true to one's deepest-held beliefs was the most important thing in life. Now he was questioning his own motivation. Was he standing on the rock of his true beliefs? Was this how he really wished to spend his life, crawling into a pile of books? Or was he simply escaping from his own dreary, lonely existence? All through the glorious days of autumn, he'd scarcely noticed the world around him. Mr. Worthington's demands to recoup the losses suffered during the strike goaded him to put an extra measure of energy into his job as quarry superintendent. In burying himself in books in his off hours, he tried to escape the desolation he felt, but when he read the poet John Donne's words, "No man is an island, Entire unto himself", he realized he was beginning to feel like an island. He admitted to himself that he missed Rose terribly. The few times they'd passed on the Triangle, he could hardly look at her for fear he'd shout out, "Rose, I miss you. I care for you..."

Since the fair, he'd gone to a box supper once with Jane Koeller, and holiday open houses at the Peebles' and several other families. Otherwise, he had no social contacts. He attended Sunday services regularly at the Congregational Church but didn't take part in Christian Endeavor or any other activities there. When his mother wrote to him, she now sounded an overtone of concern since his letters to her had become brief and less frequent.

The one pure pleasure he allowed himself was skating on the frozen surface of the quarry. One evening he'd been pacing in his room, full of Mrs. Koeller's fine cooking and feeling he needed exercise. He started down the stairs, intending to take a walk. Then he turned back and dug his ice skates out from under the bed. Growing up in Michigan, he had always enjoyed skating. Now he found it a splendid release from tedious office work and the burden of the quarries. The cold air stinging his cheeks, the steady, rhythmic motion that loosened and stretched his muscles, the hushed peacefulness of the idle quarry — all helped to clear his mind of anxieties.

"Hal-lo, Mr. Ballard." As he neared the quarry late one afternoon, his skates slung over his shoulder, Stephen recognized Sam Mikolak's reedy voice coming from the midst of a lively hockey game. "Would you like to play hockey with us? You can take my place as goalie." Sam, along with Jake Zielinski and several other water boys he recognized, skated up to Stephen, who was already lacing up his skates.

With his long arms and agile movements, Stephen was wanted by both teams for a goalie. Since that day, he played often with them, alternating playing goalie for each team. Since it was winter and they were not working for him, the boys treated him like one of their group, and Stephen found he liked that. Sometimes, after dark, they would stay by the fire along the edge of the quarry and tell stories, true stories and tall tales. Other times the boys would ask Stephen's advice about everything from geometry to girlfriends. Their eager questions and their respectful attention were refreshing. Stephen felt a connection to their lives.

Tonight he turned the lamp down low and sat a long time staring out at the heavy, wet flakes plastering the windowpane. He could barely see the outline of the street below. A nagging feeling tugged at the strongest fiber of his being, a yearning to do something more with his life than supervising under-paid, exploited workers for the benefit of an uncar-ing, greedy employer. All through the strike he'd felt guilt because he had such empathy for the strikers.

And there was Rose. Her winsome spirit was al-ways with him as hard as he tried to suppress it. No other young women appealed to him, although there were several in town who were attractive and might be good company. Yet he feared he might find a shal-lowness in them as he'd found in Jane Koeller, and he yearned for Rose—her vivacious, charming ways, her sense of wonder that made ordinary things seem extraordinary. He knew he cared for her far more deeply than what he had thought was love for Sally Westin. Over and over he replayed the dream he'd had one stormy night. A whining wind had wakened him, banging a loose shutter outside his window. All he could remember was that he and Rose were stand-ing on opposite sides of a quarry. He could see her quite plainly in the late afternoon sunlight that fil-tered through the trees above the quarry. She was wearing the rose-sprigged dress he especially loved, her tawny hair loose from the braid and ruffled by a cool breeze. Somewhere high in a tree a cardinal sang. He and Rose were calling to each other. But neither one could make the other hear.

Twenty-Three

Thirteen-year-old Frederick Schultz bolted ram-rod-straight in his bed, roused from a dream of catching a walleye at Lake Abram. Instantly wide-awake, he rubbed his nose, battling a peculiar smell that filled the air.

He leaped from bed, padded to the front window of his third-floor room, not noticing the bare floor, cold and clammy from the damp April air pouring in. Leaning out, looking across his Elm Street neighbors' rooftops, Frederick felt panic grip his insides. In the pearly near-daylight, he could make out tongues of flame arching up, a column of smoke rising from someplace on the Triangle.

Forgetting he was wearing only a nightshirt, Frederick grabbed the trumpet that always stood on his dresser. Later he said he didn't remember running down the three flights of stairs to Elm Street. He raced toward the Triangle, blowing blary, random notes on his trumpet to alert his neighbors.

"That puny stream of water won't do a thing with this wind whipping up those flames," Fire chief Francis Beck shouted to volunteers who were trying to coax water from the Triangle well with the old squirt gun of a fire pump. By this time, twenty or more volunteer firemen hustled about the scene, hauling water in carts and dragging the sprinkling wagon up from the Rocky River to the Triangle. The fire appeared to have started in an empty tin shop and was spreading rampantly.

"Probably some of those vagrants started it. The sheriff runs them out, but they keep coming back," Dr. Koeller remarked to Stephen as they hurried toward the Triangle.

South Side residents, some with greatcoats thrown over their nightclothes, had flocked to the Triangle and were helping store owners cart merchandise, furniture, record books, anything of value to what they hoped was safe ground.

"Let me give you a hand with those," Dr. Koeller took a stack of hat boxes from clothier Paul Machovina. The professor turned to find Stephen Ballard behind him, lifting down piles of work clothes from the tall shelves. They made their way out to the street, tunneling through wet blankets Paul had draped over his storefront, trying to keep out the onslaught of flames.

"That wind is wicked," Dr. Koeller remarked as he and Stephen pushed their way back into the eerie semi-darkness of the store for another load.

"Surely help will come soon," Stephen said with more confidence than he really felt.

Mayor Christian had telegraphed Cleveland for additional fire equipment, but by now the fire had been blazing for an hour. Still there was no sign of help. The fierce wind was whipping up the fire with a frantic force. It swept down several small sheds, then leaped across Bridge Street where it torched Smedley's photograph gallery and a restaurant that went up like tinderboxes. The Council Hall and the City Hotel stood directly in the path of the encroaching flames.

Mayor E. Christian, the rotund little tailor-elected-mayor, must have thought his term of office was doomed. First, the strike had turned the town into an armed camp for six weeks. Now this dreadful fire. He'd sent off two more frantic telegrams to the Cleveland Fire Department for help. Rounding up Sheriff Maxson and a few other men, he shouted, "We need to get into the Council Hall and get out what records and valuable papers we can. He looked up at the anxious, soot-streaked faces that surrounded him. "The Council Hall is a goner if help don't arrive soon." The sheriff and the others fell in behind Mayor Christian and headed for the Council Hall.

Several residences also stood in the path of the blaze, including the Beck residence where Mrs. Beck's mother, Alice Hall, lay deathly ill. A knot of folks gathered in front of the house, consoling Mrs. Beck and trying to decide how to get her mother to safety.

Billy Simpson rushed up to the group. "Doc Mc Bride says to bring Alice to his house." He stopped to catch his breath. "Says to pick her up easy, mattress and all, and bring her to his house. It's only a block." Gentle hands of concerned neighbors carried the bundled-up, ailing woman one block to the home of Dr. O. C. Mc Bride. Billy Simpson, his own jewelry store and workshop a safe distance from the fire, then joined fellow members of his Knights of Pythias lodge to save their robes and paraphernalia from the second floor rooms of a block of buildings that looked to be the fire's next target.

His eyes watering, partly from smoke, partly from emotion, A. A. Carman stood beside cases of food rescued from his grocery certain to fall victim to the blaze. Fire was no stranger to Mr. Carman. He had been through this once before in another town. To start over a third time at his age would be daunting.

A roar suddenly went up from the crowd, then a hush, as a Cleveland fire engine arrived on the scene lashed to a flatbed car on the quarry railroad.

"It's about time," Mayor Christian muttered from beneath the kerchief he'd tied around his nose and mouth.

Stephen Ballard, standing next to the mayor, set down the load of work clothes he was carrying and put his arm across the little man's shoulders. "You did your best, sir. It's not your fault they took so long. And the fire's not your fault either," he added.

Nodding his thanks, the mayor looked kindly at Stephen and dabbed at his red-rimmed eyes.

The Cleveland fire chief ordered the firemen to put the engine at the Berea Milling Plant to pump water out of the river. Just then, a Roman candle-like spray of sparks erupted and threatened yet another block of buildings on Front Street.

On a grassy knoll, apart from the swarming, shouting crowd, stood Mrs. Longwood. Clad in a full-length black cape, she was as still and as silent as if carved from marble. Clutching her record books to her bosom, she watched flames licking closer to her hotel every minute. At her feet, his willow cage shrouded with a blanket, sat a silent Belvedere.

At least, she had alerted everyone to get out of the building. Or so she thought. Suddenly the double doors of the hotel swung open. Out came Willem de Huis, his long coattails flapping, one of the platform rockers from the lobby hoisted over his head.

A cheer broke out among the crowd. George Wolinski, along with John Seidler, Fritz Lieberherr, and several other young quarrymen watching from the edge of the Triangle rushed to help Willem empty the hotel lobby of Mrs. Longwood's prized furniture, piece by piece, and stack it safely away from the blaze.

"We're still not getting much water up from the river," one of the firemen yelled. But what they were getting was helping to save a block of buildings, the only one that was built of brick. Yet the spray of water was hesitant at times, sometimes dwindling to a thin stream.

"The pumper's probably clogging with mud from the river," the chief called. "Just keep on doing the best you can. We'll hope it doesn't quit altogether."

The acrid smell of wet, charred wood hung in the air. A dense curtain of smoke blotted out the morning sunlight. Telegraph poles lay burned and splintered, hazardous webs of tangled wires threatened firefighters. Knots of citizens huddled together at safe distances, looking on with disbelief and pity, as building after building fell to the flames.

When the first walls of the Council Hall fell, a heartrending moan arose from the crowd as if people had lost a family member. A few minutes later, the City Hotel collapsed like a child's dollhouse. Heads turned in sympathy toward the stoic figure of Mrs. Longwood, but only one person approached her.

Her usually well-coifed auburn hair flying about her shoulders, Martha Adams had pulled on a shapeless slicker of her late husband's that swallowed her slight frame. "Mrs. Longwood, I'm very sorry for your loss." She reached out to touch the hotel proprietor's arm, but it was buried under her cape. "The hotel was such an asset to our town."

Mrs. Longwood turned her bleary eyes toward Martha Adams. "Thank you," she nodded absently, then turned back to the flaming mass that had been her hotel.

Martha spoke again, gently, for she could see the poor woman was nearly in shock. "Why don't you come with me over to the church? Some of the women are making coffee and soup for the firemen. A good cup of hot coffee or tea would help you, too." Feeling Mrs. Longwood's elbow beneath the cape, Martha nudged her forward. The two of them turned away from the devastated scene and moved toward the Brick Church. Although it faced the still-blazing remains of the Council Hall and two ruined homes, the church had stood unscathed throughout the inferno.

Most residents of the north end of town were unaware how serious the fire was. George Wolinski didn't usually go to the *Advertiser* office until seven o'clock, but he had headed downtown early when he heard the fire alarm.

Rose stood up from the kitchen table, pulled her wrapper around her, and poured her mother a steaming cup of tea. Sophie chattered nervously in Polish. "Do you think George will come back and tell us what's happening?" She stirred her tea. *Tink-tink-tink* went the spoon, over and over, against the earthenware mug.

Stepping into the parlor, Rose peered around the lace curtain. The Regulator clock had just struck eight, but the sky overhead was an ominous inky-dark.

"Do you see him yet?" Sophie's anxious voice called from the kitchen, this time in English.

"Mama, it must be a huge fire. The sky is very dark downtown." She patted her mother's plump shoulder and poured her another cup of tea. "We'll have to wait awhile longer until someone comes by who knows something. I can't think George will come back very soon."

Rose toyed with her teaspoon and wondered where the fire had struck. She pictured the streets of Berea, the stately homes, the churches, the businesses, the hotel—her heart leaped up, then seemed to collapse in her chest. She had a sudden, not-to-be-denied urge to go to her employer, to assure herself that the hotel was safe from the blaze.

After leaving the frightened Sophie with her cousin Anna, Rose started down Front Street. The familiar route she took each day was jammed with people, retreating from the downtown area, their smudged faces frozen in shock. Rose rushed on, not wanting to hear from anyone else what had happened. She had to see for herself.

Nearing the Triangle, she stood in disbelief, looking from one smoking ruin to another. Beckwith's livery stable. Gould's corner drug store. The blacksmith's shop and the ice house. Nokes-

Wernicke Dry Goods and Clothing Store. Mr. Smedley's photography gallery and Mrs. Magley's restaurant. Over on Seminary Street, the Beck home and the Cosgrove home. The Council Hall. Lifting her skirts, she picked her way across the Triangle through piles of goods, stepping over wires and charred remains of poles, piles of broken glass, shredded awnings, broken barrels, splintered timbers.

Before what had been the City Hotel, she stood rooted, her whole body shaking with a mixture of grief for Mrs. Longwood and near-panic at losing her place of employment. The brick chimney and a partial back wall were all that remained of the building that until a few hours before had been such a vital part of the town—and of Rose's life. Tears blurred the scene, rolled down and scalded her cheeks.

At a light touch on her shoulder, Rose turned to see the weary, earnest face of Sheriff Maxson. He held his hat in a bandaged right hand. His usually natty clothes were scorched and ragged.

"Rose, would you like to see Mrs. Longwood?" Rose nodded, wiping her nose with the back of her hand, then sliding it down the side of her skirt. "She's over at Mrs. Adams' house. You know where Mrs. Adams lives, don't you? Next to Dr. Koeller's."

Next to Dr. Koeller's. Rose hurried up Bridge Street, glancing over at the office of the Cleveland Stone Company. The only damage appeared to be a few charred shingles on the roof where sparks must have hit. The shade was pulled. There was no activity around the office.

She found Mrs. Longwood seated on a plum-colored damask settee in Mrs. Adams' front parlor. A single lamp with an opaque rose shade cast a comforting glow around the amply furnished room. Huddled in her dark cape, Mrs. Longwood somehow looked smaller and vulnerable. Dark circles ringed her eyes, her usually rouged face pale and expressionless. But with unusual warmth she held out a hand to Rose.

"Rose, child, come and sit. It's good of you to come to see me. Did you know that kind Willem de Huis saved all of my furniture?"

Rose fought back the huge lump she felt forming in her throat. How could this brave woman talk about furniture when her building had been totally destroyed? She tried to speak but no words would come.

"I have some insurance, not enough I fear. We never think such a thing as this will happen." She paused to blow her nose and dab at her eyes with a large lace-trimmed handkerchief. "But I have other means to draw upon. And the City Hotel will be rebuilt," she declared.

"That's good to hear, Mrs. Longwood. The town will be glad of that," Rose managed to say.

"Now, Rose," Mrs. Longwood's tone took on its usual clipped, businesslike manner, "rebuilding will take time. And you need work. I must confess to you that I've selfishly kept you from an opportunity. It appears this is the time to explore it."

Rose frowned, puzzled. "An opportunity?"

"Mrs. Amelia Pierce, you know who she is, don't you?" Rose nodded, though seeming confused. Mrs. Longwood continued, more animated than she had seemed when Rose had arrived. "Mrs. Pierce was recently named to the board of the Friendly Inn. That is a settlement house in downtown Cleveland, a place to assist newcomers, immigrants especially, who come here to live. Mrs. Pierce was quite taken with you one day when you served lunch to her and Miss Peabody, president of the board of Friendly Inn. There is a place for you there to work—not to bake—my dear, but to help people find jobs, a place to live, get medical care, learn the language—assist them in any way possible to get settled in Cleveland.

"With your intelligence and your kind ways with people, you will be an asset to this place. Not to mention that you speak Polish." Her tone grew more businesslike. "I'm not sure what the wages are but they would include your room and board at Friendly Inn.." She peered at Rose's anxious face. "You would have regular free times when you could come back to Berea to be with your family if that's what's troubling you."

"You're very kind, Mrs. L—" Rose began.

"Nonsense. If I were really kind, I would have let you go before this. I've been afraid I couldn't find someone to replace you at the baking. Now I shan't have to worry—at least for awhile," she added ruefully. "Mrs. Pierce will have to write to the board president, Miss Peabody, to get full particulars since there'll be no telegraphing or telephoning for a while.

"Come back to see me in a few days when you've had time to get used to the idea. I'll be here." She smiled at Martha who'd been standing near the doorway that led to the spacious foyer. "Mrs. Adams is kindly letting me a room while I oversee rebuilding of the hotel." Even in such a crisis, Mrs. Longwood seemed calm and self-possessed. Rose regarded her with newfound admiration.

In the foyer of Mrs. Adams' house, Rose caught sight of herself in a tall mirror as she was leaving. Her face was pale beneath the smudges, her eyes widening with a mixture of puzzlement and wonder. Martha Adams must have sensed her apprehension at Mrs. Longwood's sudden proposal. She took Rose's hands in her own, saying, "My dear, Mrs. Longwood would not propose you for a task she does not feel you are capable of. She regards you, as so many of us do, as a very special person with many gifts." Rose felt her eyes filling with tears. She could hardly mumble her thanks as Mrs. Adams opened the heavy, leaded-glass door.

Rose walked slowly down Bridge Street toward the still-smoking ruins of the heart of Berea, confused and puzzled that this tragic fire was offering her an almost unbelievable opportunity.

Twenty-Four

"Stack any of those good bricks over there, Willem. We must salvage any that aren't broken."

"Yes, mum," Willem answered, straightening up and getting to his feet. He'd been sorting out bricks from the ruined hotel's foundation. "The mayor stopped by a while ago to see how things are going. Said he'd come back this afternoon."

Mrs. Longwood nodded, stepping carefully about the site of the City Hotel, now nearly cleared of charred rubble. She had just finished a testy meeting with W. G. Frazer, the fire insurance agent, but had come away feeling reasonably victorious. As she had stated boldly on the day of the fire, she planned to rebuild. Insurance would pay for more than half; for the rest she would draw upon funds left to her by her late father, Woodrow W. James, a steel company owner in Buffalo. She had never disclosed to anyone here that her father had been a millionaire. She had come to Berea to begin a new life, completely incognito. Her husband, Mr. M. B. Longwood, had deserted her after only a few months of marriage because she refused to sign over her assets into joint holdings. This betrayal did not leave her embittered or distrustful of people; she was just extremely cautious about revealing information concerning her financial affairs.

The scene at the Triangle bristled with activity and testified to the will and determination of Bereans. The disastrous fire that two months before had swept the district bounded by Front, Bridge, North Seminary Streets and the buildings on the south side of Bridge Street between the Miller block and the Cleveland Stone Company office had turned it into a "burning, seething mausoleum," in the words of the *Advertiser*. Considering that there was, fortunately, no loss of life, perhaps Editor Peebles let himself get carried away by his own prose in calling the disaster area a mausoleum.

Today the activity appeared more like that of getting ready for a circus. Sawdust mingled in the air with the ever-present quarry dust. Stacks of new lumber gave off a piney smell. Shouts of workers punctuated a cacophony of hammering that echoed across the Triangle. A. A. Carman was rebuilding his grocery after all, and it was almost ready for the roof. The Nokes-Wernicke dry goods company had thrown up a temporary building housing their ongoing fire sale. Rumor had it that the company planned to erect a new building as headquarters for a different sort of enterprise. Photographer F. S. Smedley's studio was finished and ready for new equipment. He had run an advertisement thanking all those who helped save negatives and films from destruction. William Beck would soon re-open his blacksmith shop, and work was progressing on rebuilding his home. The Lawrence & Brightman block was taking shape.

The only building saved in the burned district was the brick shoe store occupied by C. W. Heath & Co. The town council at once passed a resolution to enforce the law that had been on the books for years about the required use of brick or stone for building material. Heretofore the ordinance had been ignored. The Heath store, still standing, was proof of the foolishness of this negligence.

Most business owners had, like Mrs. Longwood, been satisfied with their insurance settlement. The exception was the village itself. The insurance adjuster was hedging on paying the full amount of replacement to the Council Hall. It had cost the village $25,000, and several of the bonds were still unpaid. The loss was only partially covered by insurance as the companies had refused to carry the total risk on several buildings owing to their crowded situation and Berea's poor fire protection. Mr. W. G. Frazer was spending many hours in meetings with Council members as they tried to work out an equitable settlement.

Stephen pulled down the window shade on the door to his office, turned the key in the lock, and hopped into the runabout with Pavel.

"Thanks, Pavel, for dusting off the rig. I guess you knew I'd have on my city clothes."

"Quite a nice—a nice day for a trip—into Cleveland," Pavel wheezed, turning the runabout onto Front Street.

"I don't mind leaving the quarry one bit today," Stephen answered with more meaning than Pavel could possibly guess. "It will be a pleasant train ride. Rufus can handle things without me just fine."

Watching the Cuyahoga River valley unroll from the window of the train, Stephen thought about Rose's delight at seeing these same sights on the day of the Arcade excursion, last year. He tried to put her out of his mind for now, knowing that he had important business to take care of at the Stone Company's Cleveland offices, but this train ride brought back photosharp memories of that day.

This would be a day to remember also. With Dr. Koeller's guidance, Stephen had made some decisions about his future. Many winter evenings he had spent in the professor's book-lined study, discussing books he'd been reading.

The professor often found himself amazed at Stephen's grasp of new ideas and his perception. "Stephen, you should be earning college credits for all of this reading you're doing," Dr. Koeller had remarked one evening, pulling on his pipe. He regarded Stephen sharply, as if looking for a reaction. "Not to mention all of the discussing we're doing."

"And what would that mean to a quarry superintendent?" Stephen's half-laugh carried a trace of irony.

Dr. Koeller let that question hang unanswered while he re-lit his pipe. Then he poured a small snifter of brandy for each of them.

Finally he asked in a flat, unemotional tone, "Do you really see yourself spending your life as a quarry superintendent?"

Stephen crossed and re-crossed his long legs and shifted awkwardly in the leather upholstered rocker. He stared down into the snifter of brandy as if he were searching tea leaves for an answer. Dr. Koeller looked out the window into the snow-covered street, not pressing his younger friend to answer.

"I have the skills needed." Stephen went on, almost as if talking to himself. "I know quarry work from more than twenty years of it. It's all I've ever thought of doing, but this past year has taught me a lot—"

"About quarrying or about yourself?" From behind his rimless spectacles, Dr. Koeller's eyes searched Stephen's earnest face.

"About people, mostly. Including myself." Stephen's voice was low but earnest. "Living here in this college town, I've learned to appreciate many things—like music, literature, for instance—that I never knew I had the capacity for." He hesitated, then spoke more sharply. "And I've learned about the people that are the lifeblood of the quarry—and something of the employer that exploits those lives for its own greedy ends." He pulled his chair closer to the professor's and continued to speak in a hushed, confidential tone. "All through the strike, I had respect and empathy for the quarrymen, though I had to do the Stone Company's bidding. Dr. Koeller, they weren't asking for anything more than a decent living and safer conditions to work in."

"You're a perceptive young man, Stephen. I sense that not only in the feelings you have for your employees, but also I recognize your potential in other areas as well. He looked directly at Stephen. "You have the makings of a scholar, Stephen. Perhaps your being sent here to Berea as you were was an act of Providence, to expose you the possibilities of a life other than quarrying..."

Stephen's head snapped up, the stray lock of hair falling over his forehead. "Such as—?"

The professor smiled. "Well, I'm not here to make predictions. But with some college courses behind you, teaching is a possibility, writing, even preaching..." Stephen shook his head at the last-mentioned possibility. "A preacher I could never be. I have enough trouble living my own life without trying to tell other people how to live theirs."

Dr. Koeller made no response, but Stephen seemed not to notice. His dark, expressive eyes were roving absently over the rows of books that lined the walls, his features distorted with doubt and confusion.

When he spoke, his words seemed more like a conversation with himself than with his friend, the professor. "I—I'd never thought...it was always assumed I'd go...this is all I've ever known...could it be...I'm meant to do something else with my life?" Before Dr. Koeller could reply, Stephen answered his own question. "But if you think such a thing is possible, sir," he rushed on, "I'd like to find out what it would take for me to become a high school teacher. I've found I get along well with the boys who work for me, and the idea of helping young people to learn and stretch their minds and imaginations appeals to me." Stephen recognized a note of excitement in his own voice as he gave words to his intentions that he'd never before voiced to anyone.

Dr. Koeller searched Stephen's face for a long moment without replying, then nodded approvingly. "Good. Good." He reached for the brandy decanter. "I shall begin exploring your options tomorrow. Now, let us have another sip to toast the possibilities that lie in your future."

* * *

Now Stephen was ready to take the first step toward that future. The double oak doors of the Hickox Building swung open on well-oiled brass hinges. Stephen stood stock still, drew a deep breath, and pressed the UP button to the eighth floor. Nodding a greeting to the attendant, he stiffened his spine and told himself for the hundredth time that the decision he'd made was the correct one—for his future. If Mr. G. H. Worthington didn't choose to agree, Stephen would stand his ground. This was not a decision that Worthington could control with one of his barking, Napoleon-like commands.

Behind the frosted glass labeled Cleveland Stone Company in Old English lettering, Miss Estellita Gibbs reigned supreme in the reception area. Hired by Mr. Worthington when the Stone Company took over the Berea Quarries eight years before, waspish Miss Gibbs was a paragon of efficiency. Hardly looking up as Stephen entered the office, she appeared not to miss a stroke on her clattering Underwood. From each side of her generous iron-gray pompadour a yellow pencil protruded like an exploring antenna. Stephen's secret desire had always been to grab one of those pencils to see if one-half of the artfully arranged pompadour would come tumbling down.

Hat in hand, Stephen stood before Miss Gibbs' desk like an attentive manservant until, at last, the clattering and her flying fingers ceased.

"Good afternoon, Mr. Ballard." She eyed him expectantly as if waiting for him to request an audience with the esteemed G. H. Worthington of whose presence she was sole guardian.

"Miss Gibbs. How do you do this morning?" Stephen's voice sounded even and controlled. Actually, he was practicing on Miss Gibbs for his confrontation with Worthington.

Resting her dimity-clad elbows on her desk, Miss Gibbs clasped her ringless hands as if trying to keep them from leaping back to the keyboard. "Very well, thank you, Mr. Ballard. I'll see if Mr. Worthington is free to see you now." She peered at a leather-bound appointment book.

Inside Worthington's mahogany paneled office, lined with his collection of original Currier and Ives lithographs, Stephen felt his resolve ebbing. A stony-faced G. H. Worthington swiveled around from the 8-foot high windows that faced Public Square and Euclid Avenue. "Well, Ballard." No greeting. No pleasantries. Strictly business. He selected a cigar from a polished humidor and sniffed it approvingly..

"Mr. Worthington—" Stephen began, willing his voice to remain calm.

"Did you get that order shipped out to Toronto yesterday?" The president demanded.

"Yes, sir. It all shipped. I really—"

"And as it should have. No reason to delay a big order like that. Next week we'll—"

"Excuse me, sir." Stephen risked Worthington's ire at being interrupted, but he could wait no longer to say what he'd come for. "My purpose in coming here today is to bring you this." He pulled an envelope from inside his coat and laid it on the immaculate, shining desk. "My letter of resignation as acting superintendent of the Berea Quarries."

Worthington's eyebrows shot up, putting his pince-nez in dire jeopardy. Silence smothered the room.

Finally, Mr. Worthington spoke. "Well, it's as they say, I suppose. Blood's thicker than water. Not surprising. Your father must be thinking of retirement soon. Wanting you back home, eh?"

Stephen leaned forward in the Jefferson chair Worthington had waved him to. "Sir, my decision has nothing to do with my father or with the quarries in Stone City or any other quarries. I have other plans." He pushed the stray lock of hair back from his forehead.

Worthington whipped around in his chair, his back to Stephen, stiff and unrelenting. Silence again. Stephen hesitated to speak further until he knew what Mr. Worthington's mood would be.

He didn't have to wait long. The president wheeled back around, his flinty-gray eyes seeming to drill holes into Stephen. "Other plans?" His voice rose an octave and at least several decibels. "Other plans? What could you possibly do at which you'd be more good than what you've done all of your life — since you were old enough to be a water boy? As for running the quarries, you've done a tolerable job for a year. Now you're going to leave, just when you've settled into the job. What idiotic scheme can you be thinking of?"

Stephen swallowed hard, shifting from one foot to the other. "I'm going to attend college, sir. I plan to become a teacher. I've—"

"What a lot of poppycock. A teacher! You know what they say in the business world, don't you? 'Those who can, do. Those who can't, teach.' What rot! What a waste of years of experience!" Snipping the end of the cigar with a silver clip, Worthington laid it in front of him as if to relish it later when this ridiculous interview ended.

He went on, lowering his voice. "Of course, you've a bit to learn about labor relations. All through the strike, I wasn't sure where your deep-down loyalties lay. Oh, yes, you followed my orders, laid off the instigators and sent the non-strikers out to the Amherst quarries to work with the Germans who wouldn't strike, and so on. But your fraternization with the Polish—do you still see the girl—what was her name?"

"Rose Wolinski no longer lives in Berea, Mr. Worthington." Stephen's dark eyes shot a sharp message, declaring *That's all I'm going to tell you*. He tried shifting back to the subject of his future plans. "As I state in my letter, I am willing to remain until the first of July, if necessary. I will be taking classes at German Wallace College beginning in the summer term." He

refused to try to explain to Worthington his ratio-
nale for such a decided shift in his career; the man
was so obtuse, he would never understand. So be it.
Stephen stood, hoping he could leave quickly and
gracefully.

"We will have to advertise around the quarries to
fill this position. With the divided feelings left over
from the strike, I wouldn't want to try to hire anyone
from here. Anyway, there's no superintendent material in Berea. That's why we went outside and brought
you here. Hopefully, this time," his tone was cutting,"
we'll get someone who'll stick with us more than a
year." He was lighting the cigar now, not looking
Stephen's direction. From behind spirals of heady
smoke came his staccato words, "That will be all,
Ballard. Good day."

Passing by Miss Gibbs' desk, Stephen realized he
felt almost lighthearted enough to grab one of those
pencils. Instead, he tipped his hat and wished the good
lady a pleasant day, though how anyone could have
a pleasant day working that near G. H. Worthington
was beyond imagination.

Outside the sun was beaming down on Public
Square. Newsboys hawked the late morning editions,
a flower peddler sang out her wares, messengers pedaled their bicycles between office buildings, streetcars
clanged, people darted in and out of shops —
everything, everyone seemed to have a purpose.

Twenty-Five

Two weeks before, Rose had traveled to Berea on Thursday, her one day off in the week. She wanted very much for her mother to see the settlement house and to understand her work. Maybe her leaving home would be less of a puzzle to Sophie.

Sophie had been difficult. "Rozmary, why do you leave Georgi and me. You not love us no more?" She dabbed at her eyes with the corner of her apron as she had stood watching Rose pack her belongings.

Try as she would, Rose couldn't convince Sophie of the opportunity she'd been offered. "After all, Mama, it'll take months to rebuild the hotel, and you know I need work. At The Friendly Inn, I can start sending money right away." She eyed her mother warily, hoping she'd understand about the money part, but Sophie just turned away, shaking her head and muttering in Polish.

Rose had finally convinced her mother to visit for a few days and had arranged with Miss Van Fleet to have a cot in her room so Sophie could sleep in the bed. Sophie had grown excited about the train ride to Public Square. Once on the train, she pulled a crumpled envelope from her flowered reticule. "Mr. Ballard, the quarry man, came to see me."

At the sound of Stephen's name, Rose felt her face flushing. Struggling to keep a steady voice, she asked, "What on earth did he want?"

Sophie, who knew her daughter better than Rose could imagine, shoved the envelope in Rose's lap. "He want to see you, of course." She shook her head as if she could not believe her daughter's naiveté.

The long, white envelope lay untouched as the train rattled across the Central Viaduct. For nearly a year, Rose had put aside her feelings for Stephen Ballard, keeping to her own people, avoiding meeting him whenever possible. Now, just as she was devoting herself to a new life in the city, would she have to unlock that faraway place and deal with those memories of him once again?

Sophie pointed to the envelope. "Read?"

"Later, Mama. Look, we're coming into the station." As the train lurched to a stop, passengers began gathering their belongings, then stepping onto the platform and heading off in whatever directions their business in Cleveland carried them.

Yellow paint was the nearest thing to sunshine that found its way into this fourth floor room of the Friendly Inn. Located on the alley side of the building, it was blocked from natural light by the two-stories-taller neighboring bank building. But sometimes the brightly painted walls of her narrow room seemed to smile at Rose. She regarded the room as her own tiny piece of heaven and had delighted in giving it her own personality. When Anna had come with her on the train to bring her belongings, packed in a cardboard box and a carpetbag, her cousin had at once offered to make curtains to soften the two narrow windows that were covered only with green roll-up shades.

Now, after six weeks, the room looked lived in and feminine. Blue and yellow calico curtains picked up colors from Grandmother Rosciewicz's wedding ring quilt covering the narrow bed. On a small, white-painted table were books Rose's supervisor had suggested would be helpful to her during her training for her job. One was *The Housewife's Friend*. Another was *The Ladies' Etiquette Handbook: The Importance of Being Refined*. Resident aides at the Friendly Inn were expected to model exemplary behavior for the feminine clients of the settlement house. Other favorite books were stacked there—Emily Dickinson's poems, *Uncle Tom's Cabin*, as well as the slim volume of Browning's poems Stephen had given her—and her

Bible. When her mother had visited, she beamed when she saw the blue-and-white flowered dresser scarf with tatted edges she'd made. It covered the wash-stand that held an ironstone pitcher and basin, a gift from Mrs. Longwood. A glassful of tiny yellow roses from the flower vendor near the building brought a bit of outdoors into the room. This small luxury Rose allowed herself, their delicate fragrance reminding her of her mother's rosebushes and carrying her back to the openness and friendliness of Pulaski Street.

Since she'd come here to work as a resident aide at this WCTU settlement house, Rose had stepped into a new world. No longer did she begin her day at six o'clock in a gingham apron, rolling piecrusts. Rose now wore immaculate tailored blouses with full sleeves and graceful gored skirts that swept the tops of her spit-polished high-buttoned shoes. Each day she met with groups of women, many only recently arrived from Poland, to help them adjust to life in their new homeland. By chatting with the women in their native language, Rose could at once gain their trust. Her easy, natural friendliness and interest in others' well-being had buoyed her confidence as she eased into her duties and adjusted to life at the Friendly Inn. Her mother's visit had gone well. Sophie had enjoyed chattering in Polish to the newcomers under Rose's care. Often she had stood quietly by, watching her daughter in her new surroundings with pride and awe.

Though she owned only a few changes, Rose delighted in the new wardrobe she had assembled, again with Anna's help. She changed the looks of her blouses by wearing different collars and cuffs or sometimes adding a fresh flower from the bouquet. Gone was the everyday braid that hung past her shoulders; now her ripe-wheat blonde hair was coiled up every day with soft bangs across her forehead and wispy tendrils that framed her face. The china-blue eyes that looked back at her from the oval plaster-framed mirror danced with expectation each morning.

In her daily prayers, Rose gave thanks for this benevolent place, this opportunity that had come her way to work, helping meet the needs of so many. It helped her own family as well. Although her wages were only slightly more, to start at least, than Mrs. Longwood had paid her, they included her meals, which meant some savings to her family. Most important to her was this chance to live on her own, although under the ever-watchful eyes of Miss Van Fleet, director of the Friendly Inn, and to be so close to the pulse of the growing city of Cleveland thrilled Rose.

The Central Avenue Friendly Inn was the main branch of three social settlements the WCTU had operated in Cleveland for a number of years. It offered room and board, serving as temporary housing for recent immigrants of various nationalities. It also provided playgrounds and kindergartens and classes and clubs to teach basic housekeeping skills to mothers and daughters. Bathing facilities for men and vocational skills for boys were also offered.

The Friendly Inn's policy of hiring persons who could speak the native languages spelled, in large measure, the success of the Friendly Inn's programs. Rose was one of these resident aides who offered advice and guidance on personal matters and classes on American customs, speech, and laws, yet at the same time, keeping the memory of the homeland alive.

Unflappable but soft-spoken Elizabeth Van Fleet had interviewed Rose upon the recommendation of board member Amelia Pierce of Berea. Rose's freshness and warmth had charmed Miss Van Fleet from the outset, and she recognized her as a compassionate, sensitive young woman, who, despite her lack of experience, could be trained to become a decided asset to the mission of the Friendly Inn.

"Your previous employer, Mrs. Longwood, speaks very highly of you, Rose. She feels you would do well in a position where you are dealing directly with people."

Rose's final comment had won over the director completely.

"Miss Van Fleet," Rose's blue eyes met the older woman's steadily, "Mrs. Longwood has always been extremely kind to me, and I enjoyed my work at the hotel. I do like being around people, though, and I'd welcome a chance to help women who are just coming to this country."

The day that she and Anna had stood in the main room of the Friendly Inn, clutching Rose's belongings, both of them looked about in amazement at what seemed like organized chaos.

Behind a long, polished table at the front of the spacious room sat four neatly dressed young ladies, each presiding over a queue of babushka-wearing women. Before each group was a neatly lettered sign. Irish. German. Slovak. Italian. As they moved closer, Rose and Anna could hear a babel of different languages. Each group of newcomers was being instructed in her native language.

In a far corner, partially surrounded by colorful screens, chubby-cheeked youngsters crowded next to the skirts of a prim-faced lady in a blue-striped pinafore. She was reading from an oversized book. After each sentence she smiled engagingly and turned the book for the children to see the drawings. One rough-and-tumble towhead lunged for the book, knocking it to the floor. The reader, without a word, picked up the book and continued, unfazed.

In a line that stretched along a side wall, work-weary men each held a numbered card and a towel. From a door with frosted glass, a parade of slicked-down, freshly scrubbed men emerged, each allowing the next in line to enter the bathing facilities.

Seated in a half-circle near a pair of tall windows, a group of wide-eyed young women listened intently to an angular, composed woman in a simple gray dress with a wide organdy collar. Probably the mothers of the children in the story circle, they were hearing Miss Elizabeth Van Fleet instruct them in simple English and with gestures as to the house rules. Anna and Rose drew near to listen.

"You are responsible for caring for your own room and doing your laundry at an assigned time each week.

"You are to participate in at least one class or club meeting each day. Some of these meet in the evenings for any of you who find work in the area.

"You are free to come and go here as you need to. However, the doors are locked after 9 P.M. No one will be admitted after that time."

In a no-nonsense yet friendly manner, Miss Van Fleet answered a few questions, then dismissed the group.

"Rose," she said, offering a firm handshake and a quick smile, "how good to have you join us at Friendly Inn. You will be an asset to our organization, I'm sure."

On this day, six weeks later, Miss Van Fleet allowed Rose an extra hour for lunch, and Rose was dressing with special care. Instead of her usual tailored white shirtwaist, she chose a softer, rose-printed one with fuller sleeves. Peering at her reflection in the small mirror, she noticed her cheeks seemed to match the print of her blouse, and she felt her heart racing. On her washstand lay a letter from Stephen Ballard, its contents memorized days ago. Still, she kept it there, marveling at her name written in his bold script. The brief message inside had sent shock waves over her. Her hands shook as she read the words. Could he call for her at the Friendly Inn on August tenth at whatever time she had her lunch hour? He would be in Cleveland on that day and looked forward to seeing her and taking her to lunch.

How do you answer a question you thought would never be asked? How do you sound not too eager yet not too formal? Over and over Rose had practiced writing her response. When she finally threw down her pen in disgust, then began one last time, she let the words come naturally. *Stephen, I'd like very much to see you on the tenth. My lunch is at twelve o'clock. I will try to arrange a little longer than the usual hour. Thank you for your invitation.* After toying with several closings, she signed her note simply, *Rose.* He had signed his *Yours truly, Stephen Ballard,* which she thought sounded odd, but she supposed that was a frequent closing used by persons in business.

Today at three minutes to twelve, Rose stopped on the landing before going to the main floor of the Friendly Inn. The main room was nearly deserted as the noon bell had rung and the residents had filed into the dining hall. Miss Van Fleet stood near her office door, talking with Mildred Barnhart, one of the clerical helpers. Rose's heart fairly stopped. A rush of what she now admitted to herself was desire swept over her as Stephen Ballard walked through the front door. She stood perfectly still, just feasting on the sight of him after so many months. He looked even taller, his features more finely chiseled than she remembered. She smiled to herself, noticing his familiar habit of brushing the unruly lock of hair from his forehead.

He started toward Miss Van Fleet, then caught sight of Rose on the landing. For a moment he hesitated almost as if he did not recognize her.

"Rose." Stephen said, taking her hand as she joined him at the bottom of the stairway. "Rose." He said her name again, tightening his grip on her hand. His dark eyes searched her smooth face, nodded approvingly at her new hairstyle, then stepped back and said simply, "You look splendid."

Just the sound of his voice nearly unnerved Rose, yet she was aware of Miss Van Fleet's eyes from across the room. Forcing her voice to sound natural, she said, "Thank you, Stephen. It's very nice of you to come here...Let me introduce you to Miss Van Fleet, our director. She was kind enough to give me an extra hour today for lunch since I told her a friend from Berea would be visiting me."

The introduction went well. Rose knew Elizabeth Van Fleet well enough already to recognize that she quite approved of Rose's luncheon companion. She was reminded how his polite, friendly manner had won over her mother when they had met.

"Thank you again, Miss Van Fleet. I'll be back in plenty of time for my 2:30 class."

The director extended her hand to Stephen. "You're welcome to visit Friendly Inn any time and become acquainted with our program here."

Twenty-Six

"Is it too warm for a walk up Euclid Avenue—toward the Arcade?" Stephen asked when they were outside. "There's a new restaurant near there I thought we might try."

"I'd like that. It's not too warm. You know, I'm used to walking in all kinds of weather. Cleveland streets are easier walking on than Berea's—" she stopped herself. Why was she babbling on about such foolish things?

"What kinds of classes do you teach at the Friendly Inn?" Stephen was curious about Rose's new life. He took her elbow as they crossed Public Square after a carriage passed.

"Today's class is on United States customs and history—for the women who've recently come from Poland," she said. "I really enjoy that class. Last week I brought them here to see the Soldiers and Sailors

Monument. They were amazed to see that the names of all the men from our county who served in the Civil War are actually inscribed in the tablet room. And the bronze sculptures of the battle scenes here on the outside impressed them, too. Did you know that this one, *The Color Guard*, is based on the actual defense of the flag of the 103^D Ohio Volunteer Infantry?"

They had stopped near the monument, completed only a few years before, to let a group of visitors pass into the entryway. Unconsciously, she tightened her hand on his arm and laughed. "But not all the classes are so interesting. I have another one on laundering."

"Laundering?" Stephen frowned, puzzled.

"Most of these women have never lived in a place with running water before. And they have no idea about starching, ironing, caring for different kinds of materials, and so on. But enough about my laundry classes." She laughed again, that lilting laugh that had so many times lifted Stephen's spirits in times past. "I will just say that I'm very grateful to Mrs. Pierce for recommending me to Miss Van Fleet. It's exciting to be living in downtown Cleveland, and these women really appreciate the opportunity the Friendly Inn gives them." She paused to catch her breath. "I enjoy walking with them to Mass on Sundays at St. John's over on Superior Avenue. It's a gorgeous church, but the women wish the Mass would be in Polish like ours is at St. Adalbert's. Now," she declared, "I want to hear during lunch about Berea and your life. George

347

said that you left the quarries."

Though Euclid Avenue bustled with shoppers and workers on their lunch hours, carriages and street-cars clattered by, vendors approached, hawking their wares—Stephen and Rose made their way to the Arcade, seemingly unaware of anyone else.

At a small table in a crowded restaurant, Stephen launched into details of his own life in recent months. Over beef stew and dumplings, he fairly dramatized his memorable visit to the Cleveland Stone Company's office to deliver his resignation. He even shared with her the lighthearted feeling he'd had afterwards. Rose giggled behind her napkin as he told of wanting to tug on one of Miss Gibbs' sprouting pencils.

"That took a great deal of courage, Stephen, to resign from such a responsible position." Rose buttered a biscuit and looked thoughtfully at this man she had not seen for many months. She wanted to pinch herself to be sure this lunch was really happening.

"Rose, it would take even more courage, no, audacity, I suppose would be a better word, for me to continue on as a quarry superintendent who really doesn't believe in the company's policies. I was torn nearly in two by the events of the strike. When that pompous Worthington came out and spoke to the quarrymen—your brother George was right there in the front row—I felt far more empathy with them than with Worthington's greedy, overbearing attitude." He reached across the table for her hand. "I told you once that being true to my own beliefs and standards was my most important goal — what I try to live by." She nodded, remembering. He went on, leaning forward and keeping his voice low as the waiter cleared their plates. "During the winter I realized I had strayed far off course from that goal. While the workload was light, I spent a lot of time reading and discussing books I'd read with Dr. Koeller."

Rose's shining eyes widened as Stephen continued his story.

"To make a long story short, Dr. Koeller arranged for me to begin taking courses during the summer term at the College, and in the fall term, I'll continue on a program that will lead to a teaching certificate a year from now." Embarrassed, he drew back, realizing how hard he was squeezing her hand in his excitement.

"Oh, Stephen, what splendid news! You will be a great teacher." She smiled mischievously, her eyes dancing. "How I'd like to go back to school with you for a teacher!" Then, more serious, she asked, "What about your parents? Was your father disappointed that you gave up the quarry?"

Stephen measured his words carefully. "I don't believe my father was disappointed as much as he was embarrassed at the position I put him in with the Stone Company. But Worthington didn't trust me completely anyway, in spite of my father's reputation in Stone City. He suspected my loyalty to the company was not what he would wish from a superintendent." His face brightened, "But my mother—well, she's ecstatic. She never really wanted her only offspring to spend his life in the quarry, yet she couldn't say so."

Rose nodded. "I know how often you've spoken of your mother's love of music and books and art. She's the one who interested you in all of those things."

"Well, eventually, she influenced my father—to come around and be reasonable. As it turns out, they are going to pay my tuition at the college. But I've saved quite a bit of my salary this year, and I thought I'd find a small house to rent near the campus."

For a few moments they were quiet, attacking the ice cream sundaes they had ordered for dessert.

"I've actually dreamed of telling you all this, Rose." His voice was low but with a note of urgency.

Rose said nothing for a moment or two, keeping her eyes on her sundae. "That would be fine for you, Stephen," she said finally, "to have a place of your own."

"I thought so, too, until something else came my way—completely out of the blue."

"Oh, tell me, what—"

"Someone I hardly know, Reverend Wiedeman, the superintendent of the orphanage—the German Methodist Orphanage—sent a note, asking me to come to his office. He stated a time. I racked my brain to think what he could want with me." He tapped his sundae dish with his spoon. "This ice cream is marvelous, isn't it?"

Rose nodded impatiently. "Yes, but do go on about Reverend Wiedeman."

"I'd never been in the orphanage before—didn't really know how many children live there or much of anything about it. When I stepped inside the front hallway, children burst from everywhere—from behind doors, beneath furniture, peering over banisters."

"How many do live there?" Rose asked.

"Right now there are 72. It was started right after the War to take care of children who'd lost parents."

"Anyway, the children all scattered when Reverend Wiedeman came out of his office and greeted me. We made small talk for a bit, then went into his office, and he got right to the point."

"Which was?" Rose couldn't contain her curiosity.

"He said, 'I know you are taking summer classes.' I don't know how he knew that, but I suspect Dr. Koeller is behind all of this. He went on to say, 'I understand you plan to matriculate as a fulltime student in the fall, working toward a teaching certificate.' Then he offered me a position at the orphanage. Can you imagine?"

Rose frowned. "But he knows you're going to school—"

"Yes, and the two fit together—just so." Stephen crossed his long index and middle fingers together tightly. "Seems the orphanage employs students to help oversee the children, help them with lessons, even teach some classes. Most of them go to school right there. Really promising ones may attend Berea High School when they are older. I'd get room and board there and a small salary. If I do this, I guess I'll still be living in one room." He shrugged. "So, it's a trade, don't you see—a chance to work with youngsters in return for giving up a year of my privacy."

Rose's face glowed with admiration. "I'm so pleased for you, Stephen. First of all, I admire your decision to enroll in college. It seems like a perfect move for you. But I'm sure it took courage."

"Does it strike you as coincidence, Rose, that each of us has had such a change in our lives these past months, while we've been apart?"

Rose spooned the last bit of her sundae from the tulip-shaped dish, wiping her lips after she'd finished. "What seems even more remarkable to me is that we're each now in the same sort of situation—helping other people make something of their lives instead of—"

"Instead of satisfying appetites," Stephen burst out, pushing away his empty dish.

"I don't see how you—" Rose began.

"Oh, yes, I was helping to satisfy appetites—more than appetites—the insatiable greed of the Cleveland Stone Company—at the expense of men like your father, like Pavel, at the expense of families like yours, like Sam Mikolak's, like all up and down Pulaski Street and the others in Polish Town—not to mention the other neighborhoods." He dropped his voice, realizing how tense he'd become.

"But, Stephen, the important thing is you faced up to your problem. You recognized that you wanted to do more with your life than take orders from a greedy employer, even though you would sacrifice money and position." She took his hand without seeming to realize it. "You stood firm on the rock of your own values—and look at the good things that are happening to you."

Stephen felt his eyes grow moist, hearing these words from this dear young woman whose presence had fairly haunted his room at the Koellers' all winter as he'd agonized over his decision. He had known in his heart all along that he hoped she might be in his future. He ducked his head and pulled out his watch.

"Is it time to leave already?" Rose asked. She looked around. They were the only diners left in the restaurant. "I didn't realize everyone else had left. How can time go by so fast?"

Stephen smiled down at Rose as he pulled back her chair and picked up the check. "Don't you think it says something about two people, who, when they're together, can lose all track of time and be unaware of everything and everyone around them?"

Rose's bright smile gave him his answer.

Twenty-Seven

"Good of you to take me to the cemetery, Rufus." Rose dabbed her cheeks with a handkerchief. "It would have been a hot walk, and I'd have probably missed the whole committal service."

"I'm honored, Rose. I know how close your family's always been to Pavel." Rufus turned the runabout onto Bagley Road and headed for St. Adalbert's Cemetery. "I couldn't get to the church in time for the Mass, but I'll go pay my respects at the buryin'." The quarry foreman had been at the Triangle to ship some parcels to the downtown office of the Stone Company when he'd seen Rose step off the interurban train. He knew without asking why she was in town. Since he was in charge until the new superintendent arrived, Rufus felt he could offer her his help.

"I feel like I've lost a link to the past, Rufus," Rose said, her voice breaking. "Pavel came over from

Poland on the ship with my grandfather. He worked with him in the quarry and with my father, too. In fact, Pavel was in the quarry the day my father was — had his accident." She twisted her handkerchief in her lap. "He called himself my godfather. I can remember so well sitting on his lap in our kitchen when he came to tell us about Papa." She hesitated, trying to keep her voice steady. "I've always remembered his words. 'Little lady,' he said, "he always called me that even when I was only four, 'your papa's gone away — to a place that's even better than America. And one day we'll all see him again.' Then he gave me a peppermint and went over and hugged my mother and tried to get her to stop crying. He always looked out for us. Sometimes he bought George and me shoes for school or took us to the fair. He probably did a lot of other kind things I never knew about." Rose looked ahead toward the gates of the cemetery. "Such a good man. And now he'll be with his dear Julia again."

"She's been gone many a year, hasn't she?" Rufus made a half salute to the driver of an empty flatbed wagon that was passing out of the cemetery. He'd ordered that the quarry would provide transportation for Pavel's coffin.

"At least ten — maybe more." Rose smoothed her black moiré skirt and stepped down from the runabout without waiting for Rufus to help her. "Thank you ever so much, Rufus."

Fairly running up the grassy bank, Rose could hear

the priest intoning the committal service. The mourners who gathered around the newly dug grave were mostly women, dressed in their dark Sunday-best on this Saturday morning; only a few men, closest to Pavel, were excused from the quarry to attend the Mass and the burial. On top of the simple pine coffin lay a wreath of daisies and daylilies, probably made by the children who loved Pavel and his music so much. Three men flanked Father Suplicki on each side, the ones who'd carried Pavel to his final resting place. One was George, another was Viktor—Rose realized with a start that the dark-haired, erect man on the left end squinting in the sunlight was Stephen. It didn't surprise her that he was among the group. She knew that Stephen had confided many things to Pavel as he drove him around from quarry to quarry, and that they'd grown close.

One day she had taken Pavel a crock of Sophie's sauerkraut soup, and as they sat on his front steps, she'd told him of her plan to go to work at the Friendly Inn in Cleveland.

"You'll not be the only one changing jobs before long, I'm here to tell you," Pavel had said, leaning against the top step and stretching his long spindly legs in front of him. "That fine Mr. Ballard's not cut out to be a flunky for the Cleveland Stone Company much longer." He'd hardly got the words out when a fit of coughing racked his body. "Guess I spoke out of turn maybe," he said when he'd recovered. "But since you're leavin' town, it won't matter none."

Rose was silent. She'd never imagined Stephen would leave his position at the quarry.

Now Rose stared at Stephen, not seeing anyone or anything else for a moment; then she scolded herself for not paying attention to the burial service. She pulled a crucifix from her reticule as she listened to the priest intoning the familiar passages:

I am the resurrection and the life; he that believeth in me, though he were dead, yet shall he live; and whosoever liveth and believeth in life shall never die.

And then,

Absolve, we beseech Thee, O Lord, the soul of Thy servant, Pavel, that being dead to this world he may live to Thee, and whatever sins he may have committed in this life through human frailty, do Thou of Thy most merciful goodness forgive, through our Lord Jesus Christ.

As Pavel's coffin was lowered, the women and children came forward and threw flowers they were holding into the open grave, bidding their last farewell to Pavel, who had been their friend for most of their lives.

The service concluded and his duties as pallbearer ended, Stephen lost no time in finding Rose. He had seen her arrive, almost like a vision, dressed respectfully in black and wearing a hat trimmed of gauzy material. He had watched as shafts of sunlight danced through the trees and highlighted her blonde hair that today tumbled about her shoulders. He saw her eyes cloud with tears as she watched the flower-decked coffin lowered.

When he found her afterwards, she was talking with Rebecca Morabovich and Mary Stawicki. "Stephen, I'm so pleased you were one of the pall-bearers. Pavel admired you so." Rose could hardly believe that her voice was steady and that she felt so at ease when Stephen appeared. "I'd like you to meet two of my friends." Stephen was polite and courtly, while Rebecca and Mary were virtually tongue-tied. After the introductions, they moved away tactfully, though slowly. Rose saw Rebecca take one last look at Stephen over her shoulder.

"Rose, I—" Stephen began.

"There's to be a collation at my cousin Anna and Viktor's house—on the lawn between their house and the Stawicki's. That's where Mama and Anna are— that's why they're not here—they're helping with the food. Will you come?" Rose was amazing herself with her newfound self-confidence. Was it because Stephen had come to see her at Friendly Inn? Or was it because he was no longer the superintendent of the quarry?

"I was told about it...asked to come." Stephen hesitated. "I'd feel comfortable going there with you, Rose." He smiled and offered her his arm. "I have a buggy here. Dr. Koeller insisted I take his for the day."

Rose, too, appeared at ease, taking his arm as they made their way through the cemetery, nodding and smiling, past the remaining knots of mourners and through the rows of silent gravestones.

Her face flushed from cooking and the early afternoon heat, Sophie stabbed long-handled spoons into oversized, flat pans of golabki, while Anna stirred tall kettles of lemonade, a very special treat. Mr. Carman, the grocer, had sent over a case of lemons for the occasion. Pavel, it seemed, had made many friends among the townspeople as he drove about on errands for the quarry. Carman, Martha Adams, Mrs. Longwood, and Willem de Huis, wearing neatly pressed work clothes, had all attended the funeral at the church. Though none were Catholic, they sat in their pews stiffly but with quiet respect during the unfamiliar Mass spoken in Polish.

"Thanks be, they're coming now," Sophie said, shooing away flies from the table that fairly groaned with food. The cooks had planned that there would be enough left for the quarrymen's dinners when they got home later. Aromas from platters of biala kielbasa, as well as placki or potato pancakes, and earthen bowls of tomato and pickled dill cucumber salad all mingled to tantalize the crowd that was beginning to gather.

"We'll keep everything covered till the last min—" Anna stopped, staring at a couple getting out of a buggy. She turned to Sophie. "You didn't tell me

Rose was going to be here. And just look who she's with!" Stephen had handed the reins to one of the boys who'd offered to mind the horses, and he and Rose were making their way across the lawn.

Sophie whispered nervously, "She didn't know if she could get her weekend leave changed, so I didn't say anything."

"My, aren't they a beautiful pair!" Anna whispered to herself.

Rose scarcely had time to hug her mother and to reacquaint Stephen and Anna before the crowd began lining up to fill their plates that had appeared from countless baskets dotting the lawn. Other women helped, but Sophie and Anna kept busy directing others to refill dishes and bring more pans of food from the kitchens of the two houses.

Rose watched her mother with admiration. "Mama has done this for so many years—taken charge of the dinners and collations, and she does it so well. Now she's training Anna to take her place—whether she knows it or not! But Mama will never want to quit."

Stephen was looking about, trying to spot familiar faces. All around, sounds of Polish voices thrummed in Stephen's ears, as friends and neighbors chatted while heaping their plates with savory Polish dishes.

When Stephen and Rose moved toward the back of the line, Stephen spotted Rufus Warner standing alone, looking warm and uncomfortable and as if he felt out of place.

Stephen leaned down and spoke quietly to Rose. "Would you mind if I asked Rufus to join us? He seems all alone over there."

"Of course, it's fine, Stephen—and very thoughtful of you." The three of them feasted on kielbasa and placki and finished off by introducing Stephen and Rufus to pickled watermelon rind and honey cake. Others, including Father Suplicki and Sister Agnes, stopped by their table. Everyone appeared genuinely pleased to see Stephen. "We know how much you thought of Pavel," was what they all wanted to convey. Some of the older men spoke in halting English, but Stephen would wrap their words in his memory and later reflect upon how the death of his good friend had seemed to begin building a bridge for him to the Polish community.

Now George Wolinski climbed up on an empty table and rippled his stubby fingers across the buttons of his accordion. "I can't play as good as Pavel, but I guess I'm going to have to practice up now. Before everybody leaves, let's all sing together—one song that will always remind all of us of Pavel." He swung hesitantly into a chorus of "Krakowiak."

"Now, everybody, sing." Leon Sobieski, a strong tenor in St. Adalbert's choir, leaped up to join George, waving his arms in time with the lively tune. Though more women's and children's voices than men's rang up through the trees, they were lusty and spirited nonetheless. Rose joined in the Polish words as

Stephen and Rufus listened and watched the smiling, swaying crowd with obvious pleasure.

Stephen glanced at Rose and noticed two fat tears rolling down her cheeks. Reaching into his breast pocket, he handed her a folded handkerchief and took her other hand in his. "I bet Pavel is smiling. He's surely hearing this," he said.

"This — this was the f-first song he ever taught me," Rose managed to say, blotting her tears.

"Everyone enjoys singing it so, and look, some are dancing. But what do the words mean?"

"They mean 'Darling maiden, Hark, I ask thee—'" As her eyes met Stephen's, Rose felt her cheeks flame. She hurried on. "The tune comes from a Chopin rondo, believe it or not. That's one reason it's so special."

"I'll take care of Daisy, Mr. Ballard." Sam Mikolak tossed aside his hoe and leaped over a low hedge when he saw Stephen pull the buggy up in front of the Koeller house. "Dr. Koeller lets me ...whenever I'm here next door working for Mrs. Adams." He took the reins as Stephen helped Rose step down from the buggy onto the mounting block.

"Hello, Sam." Rose gave her young cousin a quick hug. "You're working...even though you had the day off from the quarry?"

Looking down at his dusty boots next to Rose's skirt, Sam stammered, "M-Mrs. Adams wanted me to help her weed her flower beds. She's havin' a big meeting at her house tomorrow."

"Here, Sam," Stephen said, reaching in his pocket.

"No, Mr. Ballard," Sam shook his head. "You don't need to give me anything. Dr. Koeller always pays me when I look after Daisy."

At the rear of her yard next door, Martha Adams waved from beneath a battered straw hat. "Hello, Stephen. Nice to see you, Rose." She quickly turned back to her weeding as if to show the couple she didn't expect them to head in her direction.

"Mrs. Adams was so kind to me the day of the fire," Rose said as she and Stephen started walking toward the German Wallace campus. "Is Mrs. Longwood still living at her house, do you know?" She slipped her hand easily through Stephen's arm.

He laughed. "I guess that busy lady sleeps at Martha's but she spends most of her waking moments overseeing the rebuilding of her hotel, so everyone says down at the Triangle. She must know exactly how many bricks have been laid and how much mortar has been mixed every day."

"She's an amazing lady, for all her unusual ways," Rose said.

Stephen, turned and looked squarely at Rose.

"What?" she asked, puzzled.

"Rose, one of the things I love about you is that you always see the good in everyone. I'm sure Mrs. Longwood wasn't the easiest person to work for."

Rose colored slightly at Stephen's compliment. Did he really say "love"? She changed the subject as they approached the college chapel. "Look, there's a poster for a concert by the Schiller Quartet at four o'clock today. Who are they and what time is it now?"

Smiling at her eagerness, Stephen pulled out his watch. "It's twenty past three. And to answer your first question, the Schiller Quartet is a singing group from the club by that name that reads works by the German poet, Friedrich von Schiller. Many of them have been set to music."

"Oh, Stephen can we go? Or do you suppose we need a ticket ahead of time?"

"We can try. I'd forgotten this concert was today. Let's sit over there in the gazebo for a bit until the doors open. There doesn't seem to be anyone else around."

"I'd like that," Rose said simply, but her eyes held Stephen's as if to say, "That was always our special place..."

"Here, Rose, let me—" Stephen was brushing dry leaves off the stone bench with his handkerchief.

"Your handkerchief is busy today," Rose said. "Thank you. I'm afraid my clothes may look a bit wilted to go to a concert."

"No one will notice that. They'll be too busy looking at your lovely smile."

They sat quietly for a few moments, listening to the sounds of twittering birds, the hoot of a train coming in to the north end of town, rowdy shouts from the ball field at the Union School playground, and muffled blasts from a distant quarry. But both of them had to be remembering other times together in this place—shared confidences, caring, whispered words, tender embraces.

Rose cleared her throat. "Will you really finish your schooling by next summer?"

His words poured out in a torrent. "By next June, I should be able to sit for the examination for a teaching certificate...provided I do well in my classes, of course. Then I'll be ready to move out of the orphanage and take a position wherever I can find a suitable one. I'm looking forward to the year at the orphanage, but I saw the room I'll have." Smiling, he added, "It's a far cry from the Koeller's chintz-and-mahogany room where I've been living. Actually, it looks like a cell in a monastery—or what I think one would look like." He laughed. "But working with youngsters will be good, and it should help me get a teaching post ."

'You'll do well—in your classes and at the Orphanage. You're doing fine this summer, aren't you?"

Stephen didn't answer but shifted in his seat and slipped his arm around Rose's waist. Brushing his lips across her forehead, he delighted, as always, in the lemony-sunshine fragrance of her hair.

"And what do you see down the road for you, Miss Rose? Do you plan to dedicate your life to the Friendly Inn? Be another Elizabeth Van Fleet?"

For once, Rose had no quick reply. She swallowed hard, looking straight ahead. "I don't really know, Stephen. Things have happened so fast for me. A few months ago, I was walking through the mud every day to bake pies at a hotel. Now...well, you know where I live and something of what I do. I can't think...way down the road."

"A teaching career isn't all I hope for in the future," Stephen fairly whispered. Then abruptly he withdrew his arm and jumped up, turning his back to her and gripping the railing of the gazebo. "I probably have no right, Rose, to keep on asking to see you, much as I care for you." He rushed on as if he feared he couldn't continue if he stopped for breath. "I never want to put myself between you and your family, your people...your church—" He wheeled toward her, pain clouding his brown eyes.

Rose stood before him, putting two fingers across his lips.

"Why, Stephen, do you feel you have no right to speak your feelings to me? 'We're good together, you and I.' Haven't you told me that more than once?" Her voice, urgent now, echoed in the gazebo. She took his hands. "So...we have differences. Haven't they drawn us together?" More relaxed, she added, smiling, "Just think of the things we've shared. Why, you've come to like chrusckis, and I've learned to appreciate Browning."

"But there—"

Rose refused to let him interrupt. "Seriously," she went on, "think of the barriers that have already dropped away, Stephen. You saw how pleased folks were to see you today. No one seemed shocked to see us together...now that the Cleveland Stone Company doesn't stand between us—like a threatening giant," she added.

"I have Dr. Koeller to thank for that change in my life," Stephen said. "If he hadn't recognized I had other abilities..."

"And don't I have Mrs. Longwood and Mrs. Amelia Pierce to thank for what's happened to me? For giving me a chance to try out a different world?" Without realizing it, Rose was squeezing Stephen's hands tighter and tighter as she spoke.

"People like them are saints in our lives, I call them, Stephen. Oh, I don't mean churchy-like saints, but more like shepherds, maybe. They guide us along our journey and help things to happen in our lives, help to give us choices to make." She lowered her voice. "And as for church, well, I know we both believe in the same God. That's a good place to start, isn't it?"

Ignoring the few people strolling past toward the chapel, Stephen took Rose in his arms, burying his face in her hair. "Dearest Rose—" His words were muffled.

Ever since she was a young girl, Rose had always heard that when your one true love kisses you, you'll hear bells clanging—even crowds cheering. But she was unprepared for the wildly dizzying sensation that the whole world was falling away as Stephen's eager lips found hers, and his strong arms drew her body close to his. His insistence didn't frighten her. Instead, she felt a sense of peace surround her, a feeling of belonging, as if she'd finally arrived home from a long journey.

Suddenly, she was aware that some of the bells she was hearing were real, that the chapel bells were ringing, calling people to the concert. She drew back, then took Stephen's face between her hands and kissed him gently on the lips. She smiled shyly. "Now if we're going to that concert, we'd better move along."